A LITTLE BIT LIKE LOVE

South Haven Series

BROOKE BLAINE

D1520528

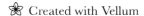 Created with Vellum

DEDICATION

To anyone who has ever been brave enough to fight for who they loved.

Jackson

WITH THE NOTE from Principal Stewart crumpled in my fist, I stalked away from his office, away from the words I knew would haunt me forever.

*"I'm sorry, Jackson. Your father is quite...*insistent *you return to Connecticut immediately."*

Immediately...immediately... With every echo of that word through my mind, my heart battered my chest, the ache to rip itself free of my body a plea I was helpless to honor.

There was only one reason he would've demanded I leave South Haven before the end of classes next week. My father had been adamant I receive the best education his money afforded, choosing to ship me down to south Georgia to attend the most prestigious all-boys academy in the country. I'd done him proud, rising to the top of my class, and I'd been practicing my salutatorian speech for days. Skipping out on graduation and the pomp and circumstance and recognition that came with it? Out of the question. Which could only mean one thing.

He knew. Somehow he knew.

That was the only explanation for the letter in my hand, for the abrupt dismissal this late in the evening and this close to the end of the school year. My father hadn't gotten to where he was by being stupid or blind, and I'd seriously underestimated how many eyes and ears had been watching me during my four years. Although it would've only been the whispers over the last few months that piqued his interest, only the last eight that he would've had any reason to give me a second thought.

And that reason wasn't a what—it was a who.

The halls of the St. John's dormitory were silent when I entered, all the students down at the mess hall for dinner, followed by the final bonfire of the year. So there wouldn't be anyone around to see me sneak down the hall to where I knew I shouldn't be going but couldn't help myself. My feet seemed to move of their own accord, the countdown to my utter devastation causing me to pick up the pace. The private plane would arrive in a handful of hours, giving me just enough time to pack my things, but there was no way I could leave without a goodbye. Not going to happen.

I wasn't ready. I was supposed to have more time. As a cold sweat of panic seized me, I balled the letter tighter in my fist and chucked it into one of the trash bins as I passed.

Screw my father. Screw the life he'd set out for me, the one I was destined to live and hate with every fiber of my being. I wanted to bottle up every one of his expectations and throw the blasted thing out at an angry sea to swallow up and tear apart instead.

I wished it could be as easy as that. I'd been able to fool myself into a sense of freedom, but the cell door was about to smash shut on every dream I'd let myself have these past few months.

His private dorm was at the end of the long hall, last one on the right, and I rapped on it twice fast, waited a moment, and then repeated the pattern that we used for each other. A few seconds later, the door swung open, and seeing the sole object of my daily and nightly thoughts standing there in front of me with a mixture of surprise and delight in his eyes made me think that coming here had been a mistake. It was only going to sink the dagger in further.

"Hey…I thought we were meeting la—" Lucas's words cut off and the smile curling his lips fell as he got a good look at my face. "What's wrong?"

You should tell him. Tell him what's going on and that it isn't your fault. Look him in the eye when you tell him you can never see him again.

A shooting pain tore through my chest as I realized what this goodbye actually meant. I wasn't saying I wouldn't be seeing him for the next couple of days or weeks. When I left South Haven's campus in the early hours of the morning, I wouldn't be seeing him again...ever.

God, can I do this? Break his heart as well as mine?

No...no, I couldn't tell him. He'd look for me, find me, and there was no telling what my father would do if that happened. The letter had been my old man's warning. Disobeying his orders would mean consequences neither of us were prepared for.

"Jackson?" Lucas's voice dropped low, and then he looked past me out into the deserted hall. When he didn't see anyone to blame for my current state, he frowned and waited for an answer.

The words didn't come, though, so I stood there staring at him, taking a mental snapshot that I'd store away in a place no one could find and destroy. His black hair was casually tousled, and I knew him well enough to know he'd worried his hands through it, maybe wondering if I wouldn't follow through on our plans tonight. He wore a simple grey t-shirt and low-slung jeans on his long and lean frame, and the swirl of black tattoos he'd recently inked on his tanned skin could be seen peeking around his right bicep before disappearing from view behind the thin material of his shirt. He was striking, both in looks and personality, and to say I hadn't been expecting the force that was Lucas Sullivan when he'd transferred to the academy eight months ago was an understatement.

Quite simply, I'd been lost to him the first time I laid eyes on him.

Forcing myself to shake off my dread, I said, "I'm okay," and tried to believe it for his sake.

"Well, you look like hell." He leaned against the doorway, one of those charming half-grins cocking up one side of his lips. "Hell on wheels, anyway. What'd you do, run all the way here?"

Not too far off there. I didn't even remember crossing campus to get to his dorm until I was in front of the building.

When I didn't laugh at his teasing, Lucas's expression fell again and his brows pulled down, a crease forming between them as his eyes, the color of a stormy sky, gave me a thorough once-over, looking for the source of my pain. He was silent for a long moment, but he must've seen something he didn't like, because he stiffened and his jaw clenched. Then he took a deep breath and let it out in a rush.

"Tell me."

"Tell you what?" I asked.

Lucas shook his head, his arms going over his chest. "I'm not helping you out here. If you came here for a reason, get out with it."

Did he know? He couldn't. I'd only just found out myself, and... No. There was no way. "It's...complicated."

"Complicated?"

"Yes."

Lucas gave a humorless chuckle. "Jackson Davenport, I knew you were scared, but I never took you for a coward.

If you don't want to do this, you can man the hell up and tell me to my face."

"What are you... I'm not..." I ran my hand over my face, struggling to understand the conclusion he'd come to for why I was standing at his door. My lack of a poker face had put him on the defensive. He thought I was here to reject him. An idea so completely unfathomable to me that it made my stomach turn thinking about it. "Lucas... you've got this all wrong."

"Do I?"

"Yes. I'm not here to—" I almost said *"end things with you,"* but I didn't want to lie to him. I never had and I never would. Instead, I said, "Fight with you. I don't want to fight."

"Then why are you here, Jackson?" he asked, and my gaze fell to his lips. I'd tasted those lips only a few times, not nearly enough to quench a starving man's hunger. All these months I'd wasted, warring with myself in my head, never letting myself have the thing I wanted most. And now I was down to a matter of hours. It wasn't enough, not nearly enough. But it was all I had, and I wasn't wasting another second.

If I couldn't tell Lucas how I felt about him, then I'd show him.

Finally.

Irrevocably.

And starting now.

CHAPTER 1
JACKSON

Present Day

"**O**LE LOUIE'S FAVORITE Omelet, hash browns scattered, smothered, and covered, and a side of bacon, extra crispy for my new friend, Jackson." The waitress at the Second Street Diner gave a friendly smile as she lifted the heaping plate of food from her tray and set it down in front of me. Everyone I'd come across in the twenty-four hours I'd been in Savannah had given me that same smile, the one that seemed to be ingrained in all Southerners from birth. That and the "mornin's" as I'd walked from my hotel to the corner diner for breakfast weren't the only distinguishing trademarks of this city, but they were a marked difference from the keep-to-yourself disregard in Connecticut, and I had to force myself to reply in kind.

"Thank you," I said, returning her smile, which only made hers grow.

"Can I get you anything else? More coffee?"

"Coffee would be great, and keep it coming." I held my half-empty mug toward her and she topped it off, then she took a handful of creamer packets out of her apron pocket and laid them on the table next to the others I'd left untouched. In the land of tea served with a quart of sugar, it was probably unheard of to leave any drink untouched by a sweetener, creamer, or slice of lemon, and her gesture seemed to be an automatic reflex.

"There you go, hon. Enjoy, and holler if you need anything."

"I appreciate it."

She pushed her oversized pink frames up her nose and winked, and as she walked off, I took a long draw of the bold coffee and lifted my cell back to my ear.

"You still there?" I asked.

"I'm here," Sydney replied. "So you think the acquisition will take longer than a few days? What's the holdup?"

I crunched down on my bacon, perfectly crisp and seasoned with a hint of maple, and thought back to the meeting I'd had the day before. "I think they're less willing to let go of AnaVoge than we'd anticipated. If I can get some face time with the CEO then I think I can work out a deal within the week, but so far they've given me a bit of a runaround."

"Have you told your dad that yet?"

"Just because they haven't signed the papers, doesn't mean they won't."

"So that's a no." She laughed, a light, tinkling sound that always reminded me of wind chimes. "Well, if anyone can convince them to sell, it's you."

Which was exactly why my father had sent me down here instead of one of his other associates. I'd only been working at Davenport Worldwide since I'd graduated from Yale four years ago, but I'd already built a reputation for being able to close a deal without the hard-handedness my father was known for. And where fear had propelled my father to the top of the tech stratosphere, my willingness to listen and negotiate had more doors opening in the ever-changing market.

"No need to offer up information until I have the contract in my hand." And I would. I downplayed my successes, but I knew when I held the upper hand, and figuring out a client's bottom line was my strength.

"I wish I had half your confidence." Sydney sighed. "Maybe when you come back you can show me how you do it."

"How I do what, exactly?"

"Make it look so easy. Win over all these CEOs with your charm." Her voice dropped to barely a whisper. "How you make everyone fall for you."

My hand froze where I had been cutting into my omelet. *Hell.* I knew where this was going, and it made my chest tighten.

"Jax?" she said when I didn't respond.

I cleared my throat. "Sorry. I'm here. Bad connection."

"Oh, okay." Sydney hesitated. "I miss you."

I closed my eyes and forced air into my lungs. I hated that those words from her mouth made me cringe. I hated that she said them to me when I didn't deserve or want them. And most of all, I hated that my reaction was to hate them.

"Me too," I finally said, the lie rolling off my tongue as easily as it always did. Maybe it made me a horrible person to give her words I didn't mean, but I'd long been backed into a corner with no alternative.

I could almost see the hopeful smile on her face when she said, "I guess I'll see you when you get back, then?"

"Yeah. Yeah, I'll see you then, Syd."

"Okay. Good luck with the AnaVoge account. Oh, and Jax? Don't forget to think about…you know. What we discussed before you left."

My jaw clenched of its own accord and my grip tightened on my fork. That had been exactly why I'd needed to get away in the first place. Run away from the responsibility and decisions that loomed over me like an ominous cloud. But even now, a thousand miles away, I still felt suffocated by the expectations I couldn't escape. No matter how far I ran, the time still sifted through the hourglass, reminding me that I was just putting off the inevitable. Sticking a Band-Aid over a gaping wound.

Fuck. I tossed the fork down and ran my hand through my hair, my appetite gone. Somehow, though, I managed to say, "I will."

"Good. See you soon, Jax. I lo—"

I hit end before she could say it. The same three words she'd told me before I'd left to come down here played on a loop in my mind already, and I couldn't bear hearing it again. I felt like a dick hanging up on her, but what could I possibly say? "Thank you?" "Back atcha?"

"How are we doin' over here?" The waitress returned to refill my coffee, and she frowned as she looked at my practically untouched plate. "Is your omelet okay? Bacon crispy enough?"

I waved her off. "They're fine. Just the check, please."

The woman's fair eyebrows practically hit her hairline, but she didn't say a word as she walked away. A few minutes later she came back with the check and a to-go box, and I handed her my card without looking at the bill.

"Oh my God! You didn't," came a loud male's shriek from the table behind me. "You dirty slut. That is the *same* Monico's shirt you wore out last night."

Another male's voice, slightly lower-pitched but just as loud: "It is not."

"It is *so*. Besides, I'd know that guilty look on your face anywhere." The guy began to clap and he singsonged, "Trip got la-id, Trip got la-id," as I inwardly groaned. His voice, so animated even at the early hour, echoed across the room, but no one else seemed to pay them any mind. The only noise complaint seemed to come from my head, which had begun to throb before I'd hung up the phone. I rubbed my temples, hoping like hell the waitress came back soon so I could go pop a few Advil before my next meeting.

"You could do with a sleepover yourself," the guy I assumed was Trip responded.

"Oh, I plan on it. I've got a full night planned: a new outfit for the Argos benefit in South Haven and *cock*tails with that hottie with a body, Lucas."

The response to that was a howl of laughter followed by a hand slapping the table repeatedly, while the one planning the hot night shouted, "What's so funny about that?"

My head couldn't take much more, and I turned around to face them, ready to tell the guys to keep it down, but the one in a fit of laughter managed to catch his breath and say, "If you think Lucas Sullivan is gonna pay your twink ass any mind tonight, you must be smokin' something stronger than Mary Jane."

My heart fucking stopped. Did he just say Lucas...*Sullivan*?

"I'll have you know that we had a *moment*," twink guy said, brushing off an imaginary piece of lint from his shirt as I stared.

Trip snorted. "Bullshit. His hot ass will walk right on by you tonight, just like every other night. Lucas Sullivan is a god. A sex god."

Sweet Christ...

I couldn't hear anything else they said over the roar of blood rushing to my face, the hum of it drowning out everything around me except for the heavy *thump, thump, thump* of my heart as it restarted. My body was on fire, my skin prickling with awareness like I hadn't felt in years... eight years, if I was counting.

No… I'd heard wrong. There was no way they could be talking about the same Lucas I'd known. It was a coincidence, that was all. There could be any number of people with the same name running around South Haven Island. Right? Right.

Then why did my intuition tell me they'd been discussing the very man I'd tried so hard to forget? Lucas. *My* Lucas.

He was never your Lucas…

A sick churning twisted my insides, and I rubbed my face, trying to scrub the memories away before they could make a full-fledged reemergence. It wasn't until I looked up that I realized the two guys had stopped talking and were staring at me.

The one in a neon-blue tank top and bike shorts spoke first. "Need somethin', handsome?"

My throat had gone dry, as parched as if I'd spent days in the desert inhaling nothing but dust. My mind raced, but the words I was dying to ask wouldn't come out.

"Maybe he's never seen someone wearing spandex at breakfast." Trip pulled on his friend's tight black shorts and let them go with a loud smack. "These are a mistake."

Spandex guy's mouth fell open. "I cycled ten miles before meeting your ass here—what the hell did you do today? Bitch." He rolled his eyes and turned back to me. "I'm sorry, you needed somethin'?"

"I, uh…" I wanted to ask if they were talking about who I thought they were. I wanted to ask what they knew about him, how he was, any scrap of information they could give me to feed my curiosity. But better judgment held me back. It wasn't any of my business anymore, and nothing good could come from knowing the answers I craved. "Could you...pass me the salt...please?"

"The salt?" Spandex guy didn't even bother to hide his disappointment at my request—and my lack of interest—but passed me the shaker anyway.

"Thanks," I said, and quickly turned back around before he could engage me further. My appetite still hadn't returned, so I went through the motion of sprinkling salt over the untouched hash browns and waited to see if the guys would drop any more crumbs. Sure enough, they resumed their conversation, and I found myself holding my breath.

"Anyway, you going to Argos tonight or not?"

"Not."

"Skipping out on a charity fundraiser. You cold-hearted bitch."

"Bitch, if you call me bitch one more time..."

As they continued to argue on their way out of the diner, my mind went into overdrive. I hadn't gotten much, but I had a venue, I knew the date, and most importantly, Lucas would be there.

Emotions that had long lain dormant rose to the surface, threatening the unsettled calm the last few years had afforded me. The urge to fuck it all and drop every-thing just to catch a glimpse of the man I'd left behind was so strong that I had to physically pry my fingers from the edge of the table when the waitress returned with my card.

I had a full workday ahead of me, with the possibility, if things went well, of dinner and drinks after, but that would give me enough time later if I wanted to head over the bridge. It was a charity fundraiser, after all, so it couldn't be that—

Wait, what was I thinking? That I'd walk into some club, track down a man I didn't know anymore, and...do what, exactly?

Get a fucking grip, Jackson. That kind of idea was too dangerous to actually consider. I'd come here for a job, and that was it. There would be no late-night excursions to South Haven Island, no wondering about anyone or anything other than the company I was here to buy out.

Lucas Sullivan would stay in my past—right where he belonged.

CHAPTER 2
LUCAS

ANOTHER NIGHT, ANOTHER splashy event at Argos. As I sauntered through the filled-to-capacity converted warehouse, I could feel their eyes on me, but I couldn't bring myself to care.

They stared—they always stared. And over the years it had changed from the lustful, eager gazes of men looking for a young, hot plaything to wide-eyed hope that they'd be the one to land in my bed tonight. Or me in theirs, rather. I never took anyone to my place.

"Yo, Lucas," the DJ called out, and he gave me a wink as he turned up my favorite song to throbbing, and as the lights pulsed around the darkened club, I made my way to the center of the dance floor and closed my eyes, losing myself to the rhythm. Here I didn't have to think about anything, not anyone's opinions of me, not the workload I had piling up, and not the fact that I was completely and utterly alone in the world.

Cue the sentimental fucking violins.

I wasn't always in such a mood, but this particular time of the year had given me a one-two punch in the past, and though I'd tried, I hadn't been able to shake the feeling that some other bad surprise waited around the corner. Everything always came in threes, after all, so why should Fuck with Lucas Month be any different?

Lost in my thoughts, I didn't put up a protest when a freckled hand snaked around my waist, pulling me back against an athletic body.

"Mmm, I've been thinking about you in my bed all week," came the voice from behind.

But as soon as the words hit my ears, my eyes flew open. This wasn't someone looking for a one-nighter. This was a been there, fucked that. And that went against every self-imposed rule I had.

"That's nice, but no thanks," I said, not bothering to turn around. The guy's hand traveled lower, and I grabbed his wrist to pry him away, letting it drop back down to his side—and away from my dick.

"Aw, don't be like that," he crooned in my ear, coming in close. "We had a good time the other night."

Without seeing who was behind me—and that probably wouldn't help either—all the men just melted together in a blur of limbs and cocks and cum. "Did we? Can't seem to remember."

His nose nuzzled behind my ear. "Sure you don't. You

had me against my front door. On the dining room table. Again in the shower."

"Exactly. *Had* you," I said, turning around so fast he stumbled forward, and I put my hand out to stop him from getting all up on me again. Putting a face with the voice didn't help to jog my memory much, though if I'd had him in all the places he'd mentioned, he probably had a bigger-than-average dick. *That* I might remember. "Which means I'm not interested in having you again. So you can run along now."

He blinked. "Excuse me?"

"You heard me. I'm not interested in repeats."

The shock on the redhead's face quickly turned to embarrassment, as his skin heated to match his fiery hair. "Fuck you."

"No, *I* fucked *you*. And you're welcome." Glancing over to the corner where a six-foot-six, 270-pound wall of muscle stood keeping an eye on the crowd, I lifted an eyebrow, and he nodded and began to make his way over to us.

"You're seriously gonna pretend like you don't remember?" Red shook his head in disbelief. "Unfuckingbelievable. You've got a helluva lot of nerve, you know that?"

As the head of security cast a shadow over us, I nodded at the slighter man in front of me. Gabe something? Gary? Oh, who gave a fuck. The guy was two seconds away from starting a scene, and I didn't have the energy for that tonight. "Paul, could you?"

Paul grabbed hold of Red's arm and began to haul him

off the dance floor like he was nothing more than a rag doll, and, as predicted, the guy thrashed about, struggling to break free.

"What makes you so goddamn high and mighty, Lucas?" Red shouted, and even over the booming bass his voice could be heard, causing the dozens standing between us to stop dancing and turn in my direction, their eyes wide.

"Poppers seem to work well most nights," I said with a lazy shrug.

An angry sneer crossed his face. "One day some guy is gonna get the best of you, asshole, and when that happens, you'll wish you were dead."

"That," I said, stepping in close to the man still struggling to get loose from Paul's hold, "will never fucking happen." Then I glanced at the revelers standing around me, meeting their eyes one by one. "Go on. Show's over."

"The fuck it is," Red shouted, but Paul had him through the crowd and out the exit before he could put up much more of a protest. But even after he was gone, everyone's gazes stayed on me, which only made me scowl.

"I said the show's over." *Jesus*, it was too early in the night for this. I needed another drink, and I needed it now.

The bar was two deep when I walked over, but that never mattered. I caught Shaw's eye behind the bar, and when he nodded, a couple of regulars glanced at me over their shoulders and quickly moved out of the way.

"Tequila too," I said when he pushed my usual draft beer my way.

Shaw lifted an eyebrow but quickly poured a couple of Patron Silvers. "Someone's in a mood tonight."

I didn't respond as I threw the shots back in quick succession before chasing them with my beer. I chugged the ice-cold brew down in several long gulps and then handed Shaw the empty glass.

"Feeling guilty? I saw the way you had Gavin dragged outta here," he said, mixing up a round of apple martinis for the pair next to me.

Ahh, Gavin. Close enough. And did I feel guilty? Fuck no. If a guy didn't know the meaning of the words "casual fucking" by now, then that was their own damn fault.

South Haven was a tourist island, and Club Row in particular had a reputation as the spot to hit for singles'— and not-so-singles'—pleasure, many staying at one of the resorts along the beaches or venturing in from Savannah off the mainland. And that meant there was always a steady supply of new faces and bodies for my consumption, so the thought of double-dipping was not only unnecessary, but cruel and unusual punishment.

"No, I don't," I said. "And I don't need a guilt trip from you either, Shaw, so fuck off."

"Maybe you could try getting laid *before* coming out next time. Work off some of this aggression."

As Shaw winked at me, I rolled my eyes. "Thanks for the advice, but what are you doing behind the bar? Cock trouble at work?"

"I don't fuck my staff, Sully boy." He scooped ice into a new glass, hit a button on the soda gun, and filled it to the top before handing it to me. "Kev's got the flu, so I said I'd hold things down tonight. Supposed to be busier than usual."

"Aren't you a saint." I sniffed the drink that looked way too clear for my tastes. "The fuck is this? Water?"

"Thought your liver could use a break."

Shooting him a glare, I said, "I'll pass. And tell your brother you make a shitty replacement. Stick to tattoo guns."

The side of Shaw's mouth lifted into a half-grin. "I'll do that. Now, you care to tell me what's on your mind, or do I have to guess?"

"Well, look who sounds like a bartender," I said, before getting jolted from behind. As I turned to see the clumsy offender, a hot stare greeted me, letting me know his casual bump hadn't been an accident at all. As the built blond walked by, his eyes dropped down my body, but when my cock barely stirred at his brazen appraisal, I turned back to face Shaw. "Same as any other night."

He snorted. "Running out of options already? Time for a move?"

"Hardly."

Something in my tone must've set off an alarm, because Shaw stopped what he was doing and narrowed his eyes slightly. With every inch of his skin tattooed, from his wrists to his neck, and with the jagged scar in his left eyebrow, Shaw was an intimidating figure even when he wasn't gazing intensely at you, trying to figure out your secrets. And he always did figure them out eventually, which was the scariest thing about the motherfucker. But that was also the reason he was one of my best friends— the guy locked that shit up, which was why I knew the second he saw the scars he'd been searching for, they'd be left untouched, zipped back up and left where they were like he'd never been there.

"Ah," was all he said once he'd finished his appraisal, and then he went back to work, and it was that small nod of acknowledgment at my pain that made it ease for the briefest of moments, a small flame lighting up the darkness. Then it flickered and faded, the emptiness slowly reemerging and the need for a bigger distraction intensifying.

"Time to hunt," Shaw said, noticing the change as quickly as it happened, and a sad smile played on his lips. "You seen Bash?"

"Not yet."

Shaw checked his watch and cursed. "Send him my way if you do. He's supposed to be the guest emcee tonight."

"Check," I said, pulling a couple of bills from my wallet and tossing them into the tip jar. He was right. It *was* hunting time, and my fingers itched with the need to feel the hard plane of a body beneath them, pushing them inside a tight, willing ass.

"You didn't finish your water," Shaw called out after me, sarcasm dripping from his words, and in response, I held up a choice middle finger and headed back to the dance floor, this time toward the far corner near the back room where the more…*sinful* deeds took place. And it was there that I laid eyes on the man I knew would be occupying my next few hours.

Tall. Brunette. Slightly built in the way most of the barely-legals were. He reminded me of someone I used to know.

And that, for tonight, was good enough for me.

CHAPTER 3
JACKSON

"THAT'LL BE TWENTY-THREE fifty."

I peered out of the back of the taxi cab window at the nondescript black building the driver had stopped in front of. Even though it was centered in the middle of Club Row, it looked like nothing more than a deserted warehouse. No sign, no visible entrance. No line of people waiting to get in, just a crowded sidewalk of people walking right past it.

Shit. I leaned back in the seat with a sigh, rubbing the bridge of my nose. This had been a mistake.

"Did you hear me, son?" the driver said. "That'll be twenty-three fifty."

What do you think you're doing, Jackson? It's not too late to turn around… "Look, are you sure you've got the right place?" I asked.

The driver met my eyes in the rearview mirror. "I

spend every night droppin' guys off here. Yeah, it's the right one."

Glancing out again at the building that should've been Argos, South Haven's most popular nightclub, at least according to the hotel clerk I'd spoken with earlier, I waited to see if anyone would sneak inside some hidden door or something, but there didn't even seem to be an entrance.

"It's in the back," the man said, pointing at a couple of guys who slipped out of the crowd and turned down a narrow side street. The more I watched, the more I noticed others doing the same.

The coil of nerves in my stomach tightened, but my resolve—and curiosity—was stronger. I hadn't come all this way to chicken out at the last minute, and there was no telling if he'd even be here anyway. I'd just go in, get a good look, enough to satiate my curiosity, and then leave.

With my mind made up, I pulled a couple of crisp twenties out of my wallet and handed it to the driver. "Thanks for your help," I said, cracking open the door, but his hand on my shoulder stopped me.

"Hey, wait, kid. I don't carry change."

"Keep it." Shrugging off his hand, I stepped out of the cab and onto the busy sidewalk, turned down the side street, and stopped in my tracks. There was, indeed, an entrance, and a thumping techno beat filtered out from the cracked door that was guarded by a burly man with a take-no-shit expression. Above him, in unilluminated grey cursive that almost blended into the paint, was the word

Argos, and outside the door was a line that stretched at least half the length of a football field.

As I scanned over the faces, half hoping I'd seen the one I'd come for, two things struck me. One, the line didn't seem to be moving. And two, they were all men.

What the hell kind of place was this? A redundant question, of course, because I knew the answer to that. Just as I should've realized where my search would ultimately lead.

Yeah, this was a mistake, all right, I thought, as several of the men in line nudged their friends to look in my direction, each of them sizing me up, and by the grins that crossed their faces, they liked what they saw.

Shit.

I'd never been on the receiving end of such blatant perusals by other men—well, not since Lucas, anyway—and the urge to get out of there was so strong I practically tripped over my feet as I backed away—and ran smack into a hard body.

"Well, hello there, sexy." The man chuckled as he helped me right myself. Well, I was pretty sure he was a man. In high-heeled boots and a face full of makeup, he stood tall in front of me, a match for my six-foot-two frame, though he was on the slim side. He wore tight leather pants and an off-the-shoulder black shirt, and with his pitch-black hair slicked back from his face, he was a striking figure—and one that would never be seen back home in Hawthorne, Connecticut. There was an amused tilt to his red-lined lips as he let me silently take him in, and he didn't seem bothered at all when I jerked out of his grasp. "Where you runnin' off to so fast?"

"I didn't… This isn't…" I shook my head. "It's not my thing."

"Nonsense," he said, a Southern twang to his words. "Dancing is everyone's thing."

I didn't have time to protest because he wrapped a lithe arm around my shoulder and, with a strength that belied his frame, pulled me toward the entrance, bypassing the line completely. Stopping just long enough to kiss his fingertips before pressing it to the cheek of the guard, he smiled and said, "He's with me."

No. No, I'm not with him, I wanted to say, but then we were inside, bypassing yet another line of people waiting to pay, but the man still holding on to me merely waved with the tips of his fingers as we passed. Was he the owner or something? Did he work here or was he just a VIP? But another question weighed more on my mind as the room opened up into a large space crammed full of bodies— what would he expect in return for getting me inside?

"I'm Sebastian, by the way, but my friends call me Bash," he said, as if reading my thoughts. As his arm left my shoulder, his hand trailed down to squeeze my bicep, and then he threw me a cheeky grin before pulling his hand away. "Mmm, you are quite the muscle man, aren't you. Got a name?"

To answer or not to answer. My plan to sneak in without notice had failed already, but Sebastian seemed harmless enough. "Jackson."

Sebastian's smile grew, his white teeth gleaming under the black lights. "Well, Jackson, I hope you enjoy yourself. Maybe grab a drink first to loosen up."

As he began to walk off, I found myself saying, "Wait… that's it?" Not that I was complaining about him ditching me already, but I'd expected to have to fight off an advance or something. God, that made me sound like an asshole, but why else would he go through the trouble of helping me out if he didn't want anything in return?

Sebastian pivoted on his heel to face me. "You seem like you're here for a reason," he said, giving me a playful wink. "But let me know if you don't find what you're lookin' for."

Yep. I was the asshole. But screw it—he seemed to be a man with connections, so maybe he knew who I'd come to get a glimpse of. *Come on, just spit it out.* "Actually, maybe you can help me. Do you know where I can find Lucas Sullivan?"

One of Sebastian's eyebrows arched. "What do you want with Lucas?"

Oh God, he knows him. I swallowed hard, the tension in my body back. I was close, so close I could practically feel him, but I struggled to remain casual. "So you know him?"

"Maybe."

Okaay. I looked out over the vast warehouse. Lucas could be anywhere, and it was so dark he could pass me and I probably wouldn't realize it. "Do you know where he usually, uh…hangs out? When he's here?"

"You didn't answer my question." Sebastian took a step

toward me, crossing into my personal space. "What do you want with Lucas, handsome?"

"He's, uh…" How to explain who Lucas was to me without going into over eight years of history? I didn't know this man, though, and I didn't owe him any explanation. "A friend of mine," I said, and by the way Sebastian's painted lips thinned into a straight line, I could tell that wasn't the right answer.

"Oh, honey." He sighed, and the look he gave me was sympathetic. "A sweet thing like you? Sorry, but I'm not gonna help you there." He patted my face and then backed away, letting the crowd swallow him into the dance floor and out of sight.

Great, what the hell was that about? And why was he so cagey about Lucas? It was obvious he knew him, and I was in the right place…it was just a matter of wading through the club-goers.

Yeah, this called for a drink first.

The bar was thick with customers by the time I made my way over there, but either luck or my size had the crowd parting, so I took the lone empty barstool and waited patiently for one of the bartenders to look my way. I'd never been one to wave cash or yell or whistle to get attention—I never had to where I was from, and though I'd never been to Argos before, it only took a few seconds for one of the guys behind the bar to glance my way.

He was an intimidating mountain of a man, tall and muscular, with dark hair at the roots that melted into blond spikes, diamond studs in his ears, and there were tattoos covering every inch of his body that could be seen. There were even tattoos covering his neck above his neatly knotted black tie, and as he came over to stand in front of me, I knew he'd caught me staring, but I couldn't seem to help myself. He was a contradiction: everything about him screamed bad boy, but his attire, down to the black vest he wore over his shirt and tie, said something else entirely. A quick glance down the bar told me there wasn't a dress code, since everyone seemed to have a different personal style on display, and it made me curious about the man behind the bar. The one staring at me with his eyebrow raised and his hands spread wide on the bar top. He gave me a long once-over, taking his time, and when his eyes met mine, he smirked.

I wasn't one to get embarrassed easily, but this guy had heat rushing to my face, and had I not been there for a reason, I probably would've hightailed it out of there.

Like a fucking pussy.

"You need somethin', or you just here for the view?" the bartender said, his voice deep and rough, sandpaper on a sunburn.

"No, I wasn't… I mean, I don't…" *Shit, Jackson, get a grip. It's not like you were checking him out because you're interested.* "I'll just have a Sam Adams."

"Right." The man whose nametag read "Shaw" grabbed a cold one out of the fridge and popped the top off. "Starting a tab?"

"Just the one for now," I said, sliding my card across the

bar and then taking a swig of the beer. It was ice cold, and a welcome relief for my dry throat.

"Where you from?"

I glanced up at the bartender, who was watching me as he capped a shaker and went about mixing the contents.

"How do you know I'm not from here?" I asked.

He poured the contents of the shaker across the line of shot glasses, filling them to the top, and then gave my khakis and white t-shirt a pointed look. "And that was before you opened your mouth."

I frowned and looked down at my clothes. "What's wrong with what I'm wearing?"

"Look around."

A quick glance at those lined up at the bar revealed just how horribly out of place I was. I looked like a preppy frat boy in a sea of jeans and leather.

"Well, thank you for the fashion advice"—I looked at the bartender's nametag again—"Shaw."

"Eh, don't worry, Yank. I'm sure it'll only help you get laid."

Yeah, if the looks I was on the receiving end of were any indication, there were plenty of guys around to help me out of my fashion faux pas. *Jesus, what am I doing here?* I'd lost my mind. That was the only explanation.

Shaw nodded at my almost-empty beer. "Want another, Jersey boy?"

"Jersey boy?"

"Isn't that where you're from?"

"Connecticut."

He shrugged and popped the top off a bottle of beer before passing it to the guy next to me. "Close enough."

Turning the bottle in my hands, I debated whether to grab another one and stay or whether to get out now before I called any more attention to myself. Before I could make up my mind, Shaw slid another full bottle in front of me.

"You look like you need it."

With a sigh, I downed the rest of the first beer and then lifted the second one in salute. "Thanks, but I think this was a bad idea."

"The beer or coming here?"

I opened my mouth, but didn't know what to say that wouldn't offend him. Had I known it was a gay club, I'd still be back at the hotel.

"Ah," he said, his perceptive eyes catching my drift. "First time?"

"Sort of." And what came out of my mouth next I had no explanation for, other than the beer had relaxed me and this guy seemed harmless enough. Besides, I didn't know anyone there, and I'd never see them again, so what did it matter? "I'm in town for a few days and thought I'd…see about someone I used to know."

"And now you're thinking that was a mistake."

Pointing my beer at him, I said, "Bingo."

"This guy have a name?"

I nodded.

Shaw waited for an answer, and when it was apparent I wasn't going to offer more, he laughed. "Well, if you need me to point you in his direction, let me know. Or if you just want to get it off your chest..." He shrugged. "I'm a vault."

A vault, huh? The thought was tempting. I'd never been able to talk to anyone about Lucas before. And maybe if I could just see him then I'd realize I'd exaggerated everything in my mind and that the feelings I'd had back then were nothing more than a crush. A simple infatuation caused by loneliness and lack of options.

Leaning over the bar, Shaw met me halfway, and I whispered the name of the person I still tasted on my tongue when I closed my eyes at night.

"Really?" Shaw said, his eyes widened slightly as he straightened. "Well, if that's who you have your eye on, you're gonna need something a lot stronger than that. Especially tonight," he said, nodding at the beer in my hand, and then he pulled two shot glasses from beneath the bar and filled them with tequila.

"Why does everyone keep saying that?"

"What?" he asked.

"Nothing." Instead of my card, I pulled out cash from my pocket and held it out to him. "Thanks."

"This one's on the house."

"Then keep it," I said, shoving the fifty in his tip jar, as Shaw raised a brow. Then I picked up one of the shot glasses and, before I could think too much about it, gulped it down. The burn left my throat raw, but I picked up the second glass anyway, drinking it in one gulp and letting the trail of fire it left in its wake spread to my chest and through my veins. I should've done this earlier. Liquid courage first, tracking down Lucas second. I hadn't even worked out what I would say to him if I saw him. Too many years had passed without a word. Would he even remember me now? High school was a long time ago, and maybe what had happened hadn't meant as much to him as it had to me.

This had been stupid. A stupid, spur-of-the-moment mistake.

I should go. Get out of here before I did something really dumb, like actually find the guy and…do what, exactly? *Way to think things through.*

When I pushed the empty shot glass away and stood up, Shaw eyed me curiously, and he seemed to be debating with himself about something. Then his gaze traveled around the club, searching for someone. "If it's Sully boy you want, he's over there in the corner."

It took me a minute to work out that he was talking about Lucas, and like he'd shocked me with a defibrillator, I jerked around, looking over at where Shaw had indicated. I couldn't see him at first, only a crowd of bodies, some of whom were half-naked already, grinding on each other or dancing on their own. But then…

But then for a brief, flickering moment, the crowd parted, and the boy I'd once known came into view, only he wasn't a boy anymore. He was a man—the most striking man I'd ever seen in my life, and the only one who'd ever had an effect on me. My body hummed, suddenly alive and aware as my focus zeroed in on Lucas and my cock stirred.

He'd shot up at least a couple of inches taller than I remembered, maybe about six one now, but he had the air of a man much larger, one who owned the room and everyone in it. With a cocky half-smile on his face, he eye-fucked the guy he was dancing with as those around him watched his every move, as though waiting for a chance to be the one who had his attention.

God, I couldn't blame them. He was magnetic, his lean, muscular body undulating to the beat, and his head falling back as he lost himself in the music. His hair was shorter now, but just as inky black from what I could tell under the colored lights that flashed across his body, and I had the ridiculous urge to run my fingers through it the way I'd done the last time I'd seen him.

As the song changed into a slow-building track, his partner pulled a tiny bottle out of his pocket and twisted off the cap. Then he passed it to Lucas, who inhaled deeply in each nostril before passing it back for the guy to do the same. A few seconds later, as the music began to throb, Lucas moved in close, way too close, and arched into the guy so that the man's hands fell to Lucas's chest. Then he trailed his fingers down Lucas's abdomen, dipping past the waist of his jeans—and I saw fucking red. Which was stupid, because he didn't belong to me, and I didn't even know him anymore.

So why do I care?

But when Lucas grabbed the guy's wrists and flipped

him around so his backside was against Lucas's front, I let out the breath I'd been holding—though my relief would prove to be short-lived. Because then Lucas's mouth moved to the man's ear, and he whispered something that had the other guy biting his lip, and God, I wished whatever those words were, they had been spoken to me instead. The scene before me had my heart beating faster and my dick twitching as Lucas licked a path up the guy's neck while his hand moved down to cup between his thighs.

Fuuuck. I knew exactly where this was heading, and what it was like to be the focus of that man's attention, and the hunger for something I hadn't even realized I'd been missing was like nothing I'd ever felt.

I had to get out of there. But I couldn't bring myself to stop watching. I needed to see this. Needed to see that he'd moved on. That I no longer knew the man only a few feet away from me. That he was no longer my Lucas.

As if he'd heard me say his name out loud, Lucas's eyes flicked up and met mine from across the room, and I caught fire.

My heart clenched.

Time stopped.

And Lucas's smile fell.

CHAPTER 4

OLY FUCKING SHIT. I had to be seeing things. Because there was no way the man I was looking at was Jackson Davenport. No way in hell.

This guy had to be at least six foot two or more, with an extra thirty pounds of muscle on his frame, evident by the way his white shirt stretched across his broad chest and massive arms. But it was the chiseled jaw that had always reminded me of Superman that stood out the most from my view across the room, and that hadn't changed in the long years since I'd seen him last. God, the man staring back at me wasn't just hot—no, he put hot to shame.

My pulse sped up as my body prepared to go after the one who now had my attention, but it was then that the guy gripping my cock in his palm moved into my eye line.

"Care to take this to the back? Or maybe somewhere a

bit more private?" he said, as the fingers massaging my dick became more insistent. But half-cocked or not, I'd lost my interest in what he had to offer the second my past had come into play.

"Not now," I said, removing his hand, but the guy must've thought playing hard to get was part of the foreplay, because his arms went around my waist, and then his hands snaked down to grab my ass.

"Seems like now's as good a time as any," he whispered in my ear, as I looked over his shoulder to where Jackson was standing—

Wait, shit. Where the fuck did he go?

There was no trace of him as I scanned over the crowd, a kind of panic seizing my chest as I struggled to figure out if what I'd just seen was the real thing or a hallucination. Because what would Jackson Davenport be doing at a gay club in South Haven? It made no sense. None at all. This was the last place he'd ever come back to, and I was the last person on earth he'd want to see.

At least that was what I told myself when the wanting flared up again, when the memory of him was too strong and I needed the tip of the knife to dig into the scarred wound, to make it hurt until I could forget.

But just as that thought crossed my mind, I caught a flash of white, a figure moving in and out of the crowd, and…*fuck*. Maybe all the nights I'd spent jacking off to the memory of him had finally done my head in, but I had to know for sure if my eyes were playing tricks on me.

"Gotta go," I said, shoving the guy away with enough

force that he got the picture this time, and then I was moving, my eyes focused again on the tall, muscled guy with chestnut-brown hair heading away from the bar. With his wide back to me, I couldn't tell if he was who I thought he was, but just as quickly as he had reappeared, he vanished again in the strobe lights.

"Goddammit." I stopped in my tracks, worrying my hand through my hair as I searched the club.

"Well, well, well, if it isn't South Haven's finest all alone in the middle of the dance floor." Bash strutted up alongside me. "I thought for sure that hand job would've led to an out-of-commission Sullivan, but I guess I was wrong. That's a first."

"Not now, Bash."

He frowned and followed my gaze. "Why do you look like you've seen a ghost?"

"'Cause I fucking have." My eyes flicked from the exit to the bar and back again. He was gone. If he'd even been there in the first place. "Shit."

"Maybe you should stick to the live ones tonight. There was even a sweet thing lookin' for you earlier, but—"

I blinked him back into focus. "What did you just say?"

"Don't worry; I let the poor guy down easy. Too pure, that one."

Taking hold of Bash's arm, I said, "Who the fuck was he?"

Bash tilted his head to the side, his eyes narrowed at my outburst, but a small smile played on his red lips. "I don't know. I've never seen him before. Quite a gorgeous specimen, but like I said, too innocent for the likes of you."

"His name, Bash."

"I believe he said it was Jackson."

"*Fuck.*" I dropped his arm like it was on fire and pushed past him and the rest of the dancers blocking my path.

He was here. And not only that, but he'd asked around for me. *Me,* specifically. After eight motherfucking years.

I couldn't even process that as I blindly made my way toward the exit in case he'd decided to make a run for it.

Punching open the door, I stalked out into the alley past the security guard, who did a double take.

"Hey, Lucas, everything okay?" he called out, but I ignored him as my eyes took a few seconds to adjust to the darkness.

I squinted, searching him out, and then…there. Top of the alley. *Fuck me.* It was him, definitely him. He was turning to face the three men who'd approached him as he'd been heading toward the street, and holy hell. Eight years hadn't done anything to change the way I sucked in my breath at the sight of him, or the way my legs faltered so that I had to reach out for the brick wall to hold me steady. If I'd thought he was beautiful back then, the man standing only a few feet away was somehow even more incredible, but I didn't have time to dwell on the fact that he was really there, because he began to shake his head at the men before him and that move alone was enough for me.

I recognized them immediately, of course—J.T. and his

constant companions had Jackson cornered where he didn't want to be, that much was obvious. That asshole was nothing but bad news, and his drug-addicted followers were no better. No doubt they were looking for a fourth to fill a hole for the night.

And it sure as fuck wouldn't be Jackson.

Jesus, it was no secret my dislike for those three ran deep, but the fact that Jackson had been here all of two seconds and they'd already set their sights all the fuck over him? I wanted to rip their cocks off and let 'em choke on them for dinner. Not that he'd need my help—Jackson looked like he could bench-press my weight without breaking a sweat—but seeing him with someone else had my long-dormant possessive streak out in full force.

"Evening, fellas. Can't blame you for trying, but I'd prefer my conquests *not* have a case of the clap before I get a chance to play. So you can move along now," I said, my tone brooking no argument as I walked up behind them. Out of the corner of my eye, Jackson visibly startled, but I didn't dare look directly at him. I couldn't.

J.T. craned his head around and, when he saw me, pinned me with an icy blue glare. "'Scuse me?"

"You heard me. He's with me."

With a rumbling laugh, J.T. straightened and faced me with his arms crossed. "Says who?"

"Says me. So you can back the fuck off now."

"And what if I don't want to? Seems to me he was on his way out—*without* you."

Stepping up toe to toe with the bastard, I squared my

shoulders and had to keep my hands from clenching. "He was just heading out to grab our cab. So I suggest you boys find someone else to screw."

J.T.'s piercing stare held mine for a long minute before he glanced over his shoulder at Jackson. "Is that right?"

Jackson was still looking at me with something like surprise on his face, but when he realized we were waiting for an answer, he nodded. "Yeah. That's right."

"Then I guess it's too bad Lucas saw you first." J.T. smirked. "But when he throws you out with the trash tomorrow, you can reconsider my offer."

"The only trash I'll be throwing out are your asses if you don't get the fuck out of here," I said, and inclined my head toward the avidly watching security by the door. But these guys were chicken shit and high on coke, and they'd be leaving in three…two…

"Chill your shit, Sullivan," J.T. said. "We're out."

I waited, teeth grinding together as they took their sweet-ass time heading down the sidewalk, and it wasn't until they'd turned the corner, out of sight, that I finally let myself look at the man I'd followed outside. *Followed*. I never followed anyone, and sure as hell not someone who'd left me like I was nothing and no one.

But there he was, all wide-eyed innocence even at the age of twenty-six, staring at me the way he had all those years ago.

And there was nothing I wanted more in that moment than to hate him.

FIRE BLAZED IN Lucas's eyes, his whole body taut as a live wire as he watched the guys who'd propositioned me head back out into the night. This close, I could feel the raw power he exuded coming off him in waves, and I shivered.

The night had taken an unexpected turn. I thought I'd be able to come here, sneak a peek, and no one would be the wiser. What I hadn't counted on was my reaction upon seeing Lucas again, and that in my moment of vacillation, he'd see me.

And I especially hadn't counted on him following me outside…

Because that was exactly what had happened. He'd come out here…for *me*.

"Lucas." I tested the word out on my tongue, tasted it, wanted more of it. "Lucas, look at me."

And then, finally, his eyes met mine, the fire I'd seen there cooling to embers as he schooled his face into a mask of indifference that stung a little more than it should've. He looked at me now without the heat of a few seconds earlier. It was like looking at a stranger, and I found myself struggling for words.

Say something...anything.

"Hi." That was all I could seem to manage, all the eloquent charm I'd been teased about in business meetings flying the fuck out the window. I couldn't find my tongue to save my life, but then it seemed like he couldn't—or didn't want to—either.

"Hi," he said, clipped and to the point.

Hi. One simple word from the voice so familiar it was like no time had passed at all. And yet, looking at him, I knew that wasn't true.

"It's really good to see you," I said, biting down on the inside of my lip, a nervous habit, and offered him a tentative smile, which he didn't return. But what had I expected? That he'd be happy to see me after the way things had ended?

Yeah. Yeah, I guess I had.

"Is it," he said. Not a question, more like he was bored with the conversation and humoring me.

"Well...yeah. It's been a long time."

"So this is a social visit?"

His sudden abrasiveness took me back for a second, and I frowned. "Uh... I was just in town and—"

"Thought you'd come to say hi?"

That hadn't been the plan, but… "Yes."

Lucas gave a curt nod. "Well, then. Mission accomplished," he said, and turned on his heel.

Wait…that was all he was going to say to me? After all this time?

"Lucas," I said before he could go anywhere, and he paused before facing me again. "Thank you. For blowing those guys off."

"I'm not sure what you saw, but I'd never blow *those* guys off," he said, so deadpan that it took me half a beat to find the joke, and then I chuckled.

"Well, that's good to know. Don't wanna catch the clap, as you said."

Lucas's lips twitched at the edges so briefly that if I'd blinked, I would've missed it. Then he caught himself, looked down, and shrugged, as if he couldn't care less. "I'd do it for anyone. J.T.'s a piece of shit."

Ah, so it wasn't just the fact that he'd been messing with me that had Lucas moving to action. I felt a flicker of disappointment, but quickly snuffed it out before he could sense it.

"Right," I said. "Well, thank you, anyway."

He still didn't meet my eyes, instead looking with interest as a small, rowdy group of guys filtered out of the club. "No problem."

We stood there in awkward silence, me watching him, him catching the attention of the guys and inclining his head at them as they passed by and invited Lucas to join them. Thirty seconds. One minute. With each moment that passed, I wondered if he'd say anything else at all.

His attention wasn't on me, but he hadn't left. Yet. Shit, I didn't know what to say now, or if I should bother saying anything at all, and as he glanced again toward the guys still chatting animatedly by the door, I shifted uncomfortably. "Do you have somewhere to be?"

"Actually, I do," he said, finally looking at me. The indifference I saw in his gaze cut deep, and that was when I knew my hunch had been right. Coming here *had* been a mistake.

Only…I couldn't bring myself to regret it. This close, I could see all the changes I hadn't been there for—the stubble that lined his cheeks and upper lip, the twisting black lines that trailed one of his upper arms. Lucas wasn't the boy I remembered anymore, and maybe that was what I'd needed to see. There was something hard in his expression now, like he'd put up a ten-foot wall brick by brick. Things had changed, and the fantasy was gone, disappearing like a puff of smoke in a windstorm.

There were a million questions I wanted to ask him, a million sorrys I wanted to say, but now that he was standing there in front of me, I couldn't seem to utter a thing. Instead I stared at him, watched as he shoved his hands into his jeans pockets, as he kicked a rock out of his path, as he kept his eyes anywhere and everywhere but on me.

And then the words tumbled out, so fast I didn't realize what I'd said until it was out of my mouth.

"I'm…" I ran my hand through my hair. "I'm here for a few days…"

With his gaze on the cars passing by, Lucas's eyes narrowed ever so slightly, like his mind was kicking around the reasons for why I had said that. God, why *had* I said that? Hadn't tonight been enough of a mistake?

"Lucas, you coming?" A blond about our age called out to get Lucas's attention, a devilish grin on his face as he brought a cigarette to his lips and took a deep inhale that he obviously meant to be indecent, because I had to look away.

You have got to be kidding me. You're not good enough for him. You're nowhere near good enough—

"Enjoy your time back," Lucas said to me coolly, like I'd been some random he'd happened to come across on the street. And then he was backing away, but his focus was on me now, daring me to try to stop him.

Do it, Jackson, his eyes challenged. *I fucking dare you.*

But I was no match for the one waiting behind him. I couldn't offer him what they could, and did I even want to? Hell, I wasn't gay, and Lucas had been my friend, someone I trusted who knew my secrets, and I knew his…and yeah, maybe things had gone a bit over the friendship line, but in the years since, I'd chalked it up to high school experimentation in an all-boys academy. It hadn't meant anything, not really…

Yeah, keep telling yourself that.

As the blond's arm went around Lucas's waist, they

disappeared back inside the club, and, swallowing hard, I made my way to the street, catching the first cab I saw.

Slamming the door shut, I slumped in the seat and rattled off the hotel address, and as the driver sped off, I rubbed a hand over my face. With my adrenaline crashing, it felt like I was waking up from a bad dream. Had that really happened? I'd gone to a club in search of a *man*? A man I sure as shit didn't seem to know anymore?

Stupid. Stupid, stupid, stupid.

Lucas had made it clear he didn't want anything to do with me—that much he'd all but said. But if that was true, then why had he been wearing my necklace?

CHAPTER 6
LUCAS

"MIMOSAAAS, BETCHES!" BASH singsonged as he slid into the seat beside me and set two bottles of champagne on the table. Wanda, our regular waitress at the Overlook, was right behind him with a couple of carafes of orange juice. When she went to set them down in the center, Bash took one from her.

"Oh no, honey. Today it's one for Lucas and Shaw, one aaaall for me." He shot us a smile full of sass and not the least bit apologetic. "Sorry, boys, I'm thirsty."

Shaw's lip curled up on one side as he sat back in his chair, the wicker groaning under his weight. "Looks like someone had a long night."

"You mean weekend," Bash said, as Wanda popped open the champagne and went about pouring our drinks into flutes.

"Was there an orgy I missed?"

Bash batted his lashes at Shaw and took a sip of his cocktail, pinkie out, always out. Even in the daylight, without full makeup, there was something ethereal, almost feminine about Sebastian. It was in the high cheekbones and alabaster skin, which served as a dramatic contrast to the jet-black hair he kept slicked back away from his face. It never failed that he'd get stopped by women while we were out, wondering what his secrets were, but that wasn't the most frustrating thing about him. After all, you couldn't help but be drawn to the guy. No, the most annoying thing was if you were the rare asshole who didn't pay him mind, he'd wear you down until you made him a part of your inner circle.

Not that I'd know from personal experience or anything.

"What?" Bash said. "You mean you didn't get the invite? Shame."

Shaw gave a put-out sigh. "Some friend you are."

As they continued to jab at each other, I mindlessly rubbed the smooth metal of the necklace I wore and looked out the floor-to-ceiling window that took up the entire south wall facing the Savannah Sound. Every Sunday we took up residence at this same table for brunch, usually hungover and armed with stories as we people-watched and geared up for a long workweek. Outside, it was one of those picturesque beach days that'd brought all the tourists in town for the weekend. Sunny and warm, but without the extreme heat the next couple of months would bring. What they didn't seem to notice were the choppier than normal waters, or that the wild wind coming in off the Atlantic to cool things down wasn't just an ocean breeze, but a storm on the horizon, courtesy of Tropical Storm Adelaide heading our way.

And speaking of storms… The weekend had brought in one hell of a wallop in the form of Jackson Davenport. His name had been volleying in my head since I'd walked back into the club Friday night. *Like an idiot.*

There couldn't have been anything that would've shocked me more than that man reappearing in my life. But what I couldn't understand was why. What was he doing here? *And why now?*

Fuck, I didn't want to care. I'd moved on a long time ago, same as he'd done. There was no need to dredge up the past again, and yet…he had. He'd breezed on in, caught my attention, and now I couldn't seem to think of anything else—something that had ruined my Friday night *after*-party plans as well as the rest of my weekend. And even sitting here now with Bash and Shaw, I couldn't focus, because all I could see was the hurt on Jackson's face when I left him standing in the alley alone.

Good. Maybe now he knows how it fucking feels.

That was what most of my brain said. The same side that wanted to know what Jackson had expected me to do —kiss his feet for coming back at all? Yeah, it was harsh. I knew it, and it told me exactly what kind of foul mood I was in, but the fact that he'd provoked this strong of a reaction from me at all was what pissed me off the most.

Scrubbing a hand over my face, I sighed quietly. I should've stayed home and gotten ahead on orders instead of inviting what would surely be an inquisition if Shaw took notice. And speak of the damn devil…

A wadded-up straw liner whizzed past my hand from Shaw's direction, and I reluctantly met his eyes. Damn that overly perceptive bastard.

"You're awfully quiet over there," Shaw said. "This have anything to do with that guy from Friday?"

Uh, no, I wasn't answering that loaded question with the truth. How to tell my friends I'd spent all weekend angrily jacking off to the surprise visitor I wanted nothing more than to forget? Not gonna happen.

"There were a lot of guys that night," I said with a shrug.

Shaw smirked. "Only one I can remember."

"Because who could forget? *Fuck me*, that boy was pretty," Bash said, and then turned to me. "He was even prettier than you."

I picked up my water and swirled it around before sucking a couple pieces of ice into my mouth. "Don't know what you're talkin' about."

"Sure, you don't," Shaw said, stroking the scruff on his chin. "You know, Bash, I don't remember seeing Sully boy the rest of the weekend, what about you?"

Bash gave a mock gasp. "Why, Shaw, you're absolutely right. I don't recall him sexin' up the tourists on Saturday, and there was a *delicious* bachelor party in town. The Lucas I know would never turn down a guaranteed good time."

"Hmm, so you think that Yank caught his eye?"

"I think he caught more than his eye... Jackson, was it?"

My head shot up, and both their mouths curved into sly grins.

"Ladies, I think we have a winner," Shaw said.

"You know shit," I replied.

"Oooh, look who's defensive..." Bash leaned forward on his elbows and bumped my shoulder. "If you don't want him, mind if I call dibs?"

I whirled around so fast that Bash stumbled back in his chair, and then, before I could stop myself, my finger was in his face. "You won't fucking touch him."

The smile left his lips, and his eyes widened, the shock from my outburst surprising us both.

"I mean it, Bash," I said. "He's off-limits, even for you."

Bash blinked, immediately sobering, and then nodded. "Yeah. Yeah, okay, I won't touch him."

"Good." Ignoring the curious look Shaw was aiming my way, I finished off my water, trying to calm myself the fuck down. My heart was pounding so hard that I could hear the rush of blood in my ears, and I'd broken out into a sweat.

Jesus, did I really just accost my friends over brunch because of a guy?

"Damn," Bash said, and then chuckled. "I didn't mean to hit a nerve."

"You didn't."

"The hell I didn't. You were ready to attack me. I saw you grow claws."

"Fuck off, Bash," I said, crunching down on my ice.

"Can I call you Wolverine?"

When I grunted, Bash's lips twisted into a grin.

"I think the name suits you," he said, reaching out to scratch just under my chin. "Look at what happens when you don't shave, you hairy beast."

Batting his hand away, I let out an exasperated sigh, but I knew it was Bash's way of breaking the sudden tension that'd cropped up. God forbid I be mad at the guy for more than five seconds—he'd grow a fucking hernia.

Still, the annoyance persisted, but it wasn't either of the guys who were the issue. No, the issue was thinking about *anyone* else with Jackson, and—

God. No. I wasn't gonna go there. This shit was getting ridiculous.

Pushing back from the table, I stood up and pulled my wallet out of my back pocket as Bash pouted.

"Where you going?" he asked, and held up the champagne. "We haven't even finished off a bottle yet."

"Gotta get some work done," I said, throwing a couple of bills on the table. Then I glanced out at the gathering clouds. "Make sure you get someone to board up if it gets bad. Or call me."

"It's not gonna get bad," Bash replied, and then inclined his head at Shaw. "Our mystic said so."

"You don't have to be a *psychic* to watch the Weather Channel," Shaw said.

Bash shrugged. "They're wrong all the time. You're not."

Waving a quick goodbye to Wanda, I turned to leave, but Shaw called out my name before I could go very far.

"You sure you're okay?" he asked when I glanced over my shoulder, his tone casual, but his eyes showed a concern that I hadn't been on the receiving end of in a long time.

I wasn't a liar. To myself, maybe, but not to my friends. So when I gave him a small nod, I tried not to feel any guilt, because I knew that he likely saw right through me.

Was I okay?

I didn't even fucking know.

CHAPTER 7

JACKSON

ANOTHER DAY IN Georgia, another brisk walk across the lobby of AnaVoge, and another denial coming. I could feel it before I stepped through the glass double doors first thing Monday morning, and I could see it on the receptionist's face as she glanced up at me and gave me a tight smile.

"Hello again, Mr. Davenport."

"Good morning, Astrid," I said. "I'd like to see Mr. Vogel." It was pretty damn pitiful that I was on a first-name basis with the receptionist at AnaVoge, but after getting nothing but the company's voicemail all weekend, I was ready for some face time with the enigmatic CEO. Anything to get my mind off the events of the weekend and a certain other man I didn't need to be thinking about.

"I'm afraid Mr. Vogel is unavailable—"

"Of course he is."

"But he did wish to set up a meeting with you for Thursday afternoon at two."

I raised my eyebrows. "Really? Four days from now?"

"Yes, sir."

This guy was playing hard to get, and he was good at making me sweat it out, I'd give him that. His delaying tactic wouldn't deter me, though, so if Thursday was what he wanted, then Thursday it'd be.

"Then I suppose two o'clock is fine," I said.

"I'll mark you down now."

Drumming my fingers on the counter, I glanced at the clock on the wall and inwardly sighed. It was only nine on Monday morning, which meant I had quite a bit of time to kill, and since it didn't make much sense to fly back to Connecticut only to come right back, it looked like I was stuck here. There had to be something to occupy my time, something other than dance clubs and men with black hair, angry eyes, and cocky smirks.

I pushed that thought back into the far recesses of my mind. For now.

"One more thing," I said, and Astrid glanced up. "Since it looks like I'll be here for a while longer, could you recommend any must-sees in town?"

"Oh, of course," she said, brightening, as though she'd expected a fight and was pleased I'd let it go. "Let's see… there's always the beach. Make sure you go to Dolphin Sands, because it's the best public beach on the island and there's a great bar on the pier. You can also find some shops along the boardwalk, but that's mostly tourist stuff, like t-shirts, keychains, beach souvenirs. The real shopping is over on Ocean Avenue. Lots of artsy stuff, like galleries and bookstores. Some good cafes and restaurants over there, too."

With a smile, I nodded. "Thanks, I appreciate it."

"You're welcome."

As I turned to leave, a huge metal sculpture on the wall to my right caught my eye. It was circular, an abstract painting on metal with lines of silver, blues, and deep purples weaved in smooth lines. Only a serious artist could've wielded the metal and paint so flawlessly, and I stood there admiring the artwork for a good minute. Something like that would look perfect in my office.

"Excuse me," I said, heading back to the front desk. "Could you tell me where I might find something like that piece over there?"

"Yeah, that's one of our local artists. He sells his stuff at the galleria over at the end of Ocean Avenue."

Looks like I'll be making a stop. "Great. Thanks again, Astrid."

"No problem, Mr. Davenport. See you Thursday."

THE FIRST THING I did after leaving AnaVoge was pick up a rental car, and then I left a message with my father's secretary to let him know my trip had been extended. He wouldn't be happy about the news, but it was better than the alternative—walking away empty-handed.

After grabbing a coffee, I made my way down Ocean

Avenue. There was a Freymond Galleria on the corner, and I was able to grab street parking, which was surprising, considering all the traffic I'd seen on the way there. Granted, it'd been heading in the opposite direction, but still.

There was an older gentleman just outside the store, picking up a pop-up sidewalk sign that told of the specials going on inside the galleria. I checked my watch again. Surely they couldn't be closing at ten in the morning. *Maybe he's just changing out the signage,* I thought, as a sudden gust of wind kicked up around us, causing the man to stumble backward. I ran over and caught his arm just in time, keeping him upright as he clung to the sign.

His eyes crinkled around the edges as he straightened and gave a weary chuckle. "Thank you. I'm not as sturdy as I used to be."

"It's no problem. Can I take that inside for you?" I said, nodding at the sign.

"I'd appreciate that."

I followed as he headed toward the door. "Are you guys still open?"

"That we are, though we're closin' up early since the storm's comin'."

My brow furrowed as I looked up at the darkening sky. "You close when it rains?"

"Rain?" The man shook his head. "That there's Tropical Storm Adelaide. A little early in the season, but not unheard of."

Damn. That was what I got for being so preoccupied

the past couple of days. "I didn't realize…"

"Nah, shouldn't be too bad, but it's picked up speed, so we'd rather be safe than sorry."

"Right. Well, I'll come back—"

"No, no, don't be silly, come on in." He held the door open wide for me to pass by, and as I stepped through, I was greeted by an enormous lion, made entirely of—

"Are those tires?" I asked.

"Sure are. More where that came from, but we keep 'em in the back, since the reptiles seem to scare the kiddies."

Right…

"I appreciate you bringing that in for me," the man said, clapping me on the shoulder as I set down the sign. "I've got to get a few things done before I head out, so look around and take your time. The name's Mike. Let me know if you have any questions or if I can help you find something."

"Thanks, Mike. I won't be too long."

I didn't have to venture far to find what I was looking for. An entire section of the store near the front was dedicated to the artist whose work I'd seen at AnaVoge. From modern abstract table sculptures, to multi-panel wall art, the style was instantly recognizable, brushed metal with a pop of color. The pieces were so beautiful that I couldn't stop staring.

"You like those?" Mike said, coming up behind me a few minutes later. "We get so many requests for his stuff we almost can't keep anything in stock."

"I'm not surprised. I saw a piece at AnaVoge and that's what sent me down here."

"Ah, the abstract. I know exactly which one you mean. Not to show bias, but that's my favorite too."

I ran my fingers over a rectangular wall piece, and while it was stunning, it wasn't quite what I'd come for. "You wouldn't happen to have any of those round abstracts, would you?"

"As a matter of fact, we just sold out of the last one the other day, but let me give him a call, see if he's got any more up his sleeve," Mike said, moving behind the counter.

"That's not necessary—"

"Oh, it's no problem at all."

"Really, you don't have to..." I started, but he was already dialing the number. As he began to speak to the person on the other end of the line, I wandered off a bit to give him some space.

The shop was packed with art, not so much that it seemed junked up, but maybe it was the variety of the designs that made it feel so unusual. Along with the stunning metalwork, there were also framed paintings lining the walls, some with watercolor landscapes, some abstracts, and others along the lines of human caricatures. There were more animals made from recycled tires like I'd seen when I walked in, hidden in the back just like he'd said, and papier-mâché tree spirits littered the tops of tables scattered around.

Eclectic was the word I'd use to describe this place.

"Well," Mike said as he hung up and I headed back

over. "Looks like it's your lucky day. He just finished a couple variations of those pieces over the weekend and said you can swing on by and grab one."

"Swing on by? Like…by his house?" I must've looked as bewildered as I felt, because Mike laughed.

"That's just how we do things down here. If you'd rather pick it up here, that's no problem. It just might take a couple of days before he can drop them off."

"No, that's okay. I don't mind going by to pick it up." *Yeah, it's definitely a different world down here.* Something I found I'd forgotten since I'd been away.

"Great," he said, tearing off some receipt paper and jotting down the address in a messy scrawl. "Oh, and make sure to take cash or check, since he doesn't have a card reader."

I took the address and shook his hand. "Will do."

"You got it. I hope you find exactly what you're lookin' for."

THE SKY WAS A MOODY GREY, and getting darker by the minute. Fat droplets splattered the windshield as I drove down the two-lane road my GPS had directed me to turn on a couple of minutes ago. This was the part of the island I'd always heard referred to as "old money," and driving through it, it was evident why. The houses were larger, older, but statuesque in the colonial style, many with columns or wraparound porches perfect for lazy days and mint juleps. With the section of Spanish-moss-draped oak trees up ahead, curved over the road like they were holding hands, it was easy to forget that sandy beaches lay only a couple of miles away.

As I passed through the overhang, I remembered the first time I'd been driven down this way. At the end of the line of trees, my father's driver had made a right, which led down a long road that took you to South Haven All-boys Academy, the prestigious school I'd been shipped off to for my high school years.

But, if you kept going straight, the way the GPS was telling me to go, the road led to a place I'd been to quite a few times before.

Please don't let me pass by there. Anywhere but there.

Yeah, but that's the thing about cell phone maps—they don't fucking listen.

The farther I drove, the more anxious I began to feel. *No way.* The island was small, but it couldn't be *this* small.

It was.

Stopping in front of the long driveway at 18 Braden, the last one at the end of the road, I couldn't believe my shitty luck. Of all the people and all the places, I had to wind up here. At the house that belonged to Lucas's gram.

I sat there, hands sweating and engine idling, as a surge of nerves came flooding in. Did she still live there? It was highly likely. Although there was a possibility she sold the property to the designer who was now expecting me…

On the other hand, I doubted the home wasn't still in the family, which meant she or Lucas or both might be inside. In that case, I could drive back to town now and no one would be the wiser.

The latter also meant I'd miss my chance to say the "I'm sorry" speech I'd thought about all weekend after I'd failed to utter anything remotely close on Friday. The one that should've come out of my mouth the second I saw Lucas.

Without another second of pause, I pushed on the gas and turned into the driveway.

The old Sullivan house sat back off the road, hidden by thick trees until you drove about a hundred yards in, and then it opened up into a huge clearing with the residence on the far side. A white two-story with oversized double balconies, the house stood tall and regal against the oak and magnolia trees it backed up against. It looked exactly the same as the last time I'd seen it, albeit with a fresh coat of paint.

Putting the car in park behind a black truck, I gripped the steering wheel and took a deep breath. If Lucas lived here, then this was probably a good thing. Being able to talk face to face without the background of an alley or a club or any other distractions. I could still see the indifference in his face from Friday, the cold shoulder he'd given. But was that who he'd be when he was alone with me without an audience?

One way to find out.

The rain was still a steady sprinkle when I got out of the car, not yet enough to warrant an umbrella, though if there was a storm heading this way then that wouldn't be the case for too much longer. Just as I was about to head up the front sidewalk, though, the sound of screeching metal stopped me in my tracks and had me switching directions toward the backyard instead.

Rounding the house, I picked up on the sweet smell of honeysuckle in the air that mixed with the fresh rain and warm breeze. That combination always reminded me of the nights we'd sat in rocking chairs on his gram's back porch and watched the thunderstorms pass before sneaking back to the academy. Back then I hadn't even realized what was happening. That I was falling into something I wasn't prepared for and wouldn't be able to control. And now, more than anything, I needed to understand. To have some sort of closure on that chapter of my life, because years hadn't taken away the way my heart punched inside my chest every time I thought of Lucas.

Gone was the original small shed that'd stored Gram's gardening tools, and in its place was a garage big enough to accommodate a couple of pontoon boats. Judging from the sound of continued whirring and shrieking of machinery coming from the wide-open barn-style doors, though, it didn't seem as though it housed boats or cars.

My suspicions were confirmed as I peeked inside. The man standing at a worktable with sparks flying out in front of him was definitely Lucas. Even with his face covered by protective gear and facing away from me, I could tell by the way the red flannel shirt he wore stretched against his strong back and how the snug fit of his jeans only enhanced his ass— *Wait. Shit.*

Running my hand through my hair, I tried to avert my eyes, but they kept coming back to the lone man in the large space. I didn't need to look at him that way. It wasn't right, and besides, like he'd want me standing there checking him out. Because, shit, that was what I'd been doing—checking him out.

The thought left me stunned. After leaving South Haven, I'd checked out plenty of guys when no one was watching, waiting to feel the same attraction I'd felt for Lucas. But it never came. Sure, I'd notice if a guy was hot, but it was the same way I noticed women were hot—and since it was women who came on to me, women I'd get set up with or pushed toward, then they'd only been the natural progression.

I'd convinced myself it had all been a fluke. That Lucas and I had been the product of being horny teenage guys in an all-boys school who'd grown close and were open to experimenting. Going back to Connecticut, I thought it'd be easier to forget him…

But looking at him now only feet away from me… How had I ever walked away?

Lucas shut off the machine then, throwing the whole room into a deafening silence, and after setting it on the table, he lifted the front of his mask. His back was still to me, but I could tell the moment he knew I was there because his whole body went completely still.

And then, without even turning around, he said, "What are you doing here?"

SOMEONE WAS WATCHING me. I didn't worry, though, because a) I knew everyone on this island, and b) anyone with a lick of sense wouldn't come near Lucas Sullivan with a wheel-belt grinder in his hand. So I took my time finishing off the edges of the steel guitar I'd been working on, smoothing it down on all sides before flipping off the machine. Pushing up my mask, I wiped at the sweat on my brow courtesy of the muggy heat inside the garage, something even the breeze coming in through the open door hadn't been able to cool like I'd expected.

As I took off my helmet, the hair on the back of my neck prickled, telling me all I needed to know about my visitor. I didn't know how I knew, but I knew. That wasn't just anyone standing behind me—it was Jackson.

Fuck, it was a good thing I'd turned the damn machine off first.

Closing my eyes, I said, "What are you doing here?"

Tentative footsteps shuffled along the concrete. "I was told to come by."

"What?" My eyes flew open as I wheeled around. And sure enough, there he was, Jackson Davenport, standing there in grey dress slacks and a white button-up and tie. Even with his sleeves rolled up, he looked out of place in my dusty workshop. Out of place, maybe, but every hair on his gorgeous fucking head was still remarkably in place even with thirty mph winds. I narrowed my eyes. "Who told you to come by? Wait, no. Let me guess. Shaw?"

"Shaw? The bartender guy?"

"Sounds like something that asshole'd do," I muttered, yanking off my gloves. I threw them on top of the workstation and then crossed my arms.

"Actually, I'm here about the artwork. Mike from the galleria called you, and you said to swing on by, so…here I am."

Oh. Right. The piece. *Fuck.* Wait…Jackson wanted *my* work? And he had the audacity to come here and—

"I didn't realize it was you," he said.

Sure you didn't, I thought, even as my gaze traveled over his body. Jesus, did he have to look so good? The rain had caused his shirt to stick to his chest and biceps, revealing just how huge he really was. He looked like he spent all of his time in the gym, not going to business meetings or whatever it was he did now. Though if I had one guess, I'd say he worked for his father. *That had always been the plan…*

"Would that have changed your mind about coming?"

I said, and as soon as the words were out of my mouth, I wanted to kick my own ass. I didn't care what the answer was, and it didn't matter why he was here; it only mattered that he left.

Jackson seemed to think it over for a moment and then shook his head. "No. I still would've come."

And wouldn't you know, my body responded to that with a shiver I prayed to God hadn't been visible. Damn traitor. *He broke your heart,* I reminded myself. *He almost broke* you.

"I should've known it was you, though," Jackson continued. "You're a talented guy. Always have been."

Talented with my hands, you mean? Why, yes, I am, and you would fucking know. Right then, though, I wanted nothing more than to use those hands to rip the bastard apart, to tear his heart out the same callous way he'd done mine. How could he stand there so calm and collected, like there wasn't enough tension in the air to strangle us both? *Because you meant nothing. Because he's a rich daddy's boy who got everything he wanted. Because you trusted him and he lied.*

The blood boiled in my veins, but I tried to keep my face casual. If he didn't care, then neither did I, and I'd be damned if I'd show weakness in front of this man. The sooner he was back out of my life, the better.

I nodded over at the piece I'd set out earlier. "It's over there."

"Great. Thanks." He went over and knelt beside it, and then his big hands ran over the steel with reverence. "This is really beautiful, Lucas."

Keeping my mouth shut, I continued to watch his fingers smooth over the curves, his admiration evident. He stroked it like it was the greatest thing he'd ever touched, and I couldn't tear my gaze away, as much as I wanted to.

"Mike said you've got a big following. That they can't keep almost anything in stock." Jackson's blue eyes, one much darker than the other, flicked up to me, and he smiled.

Ahh, so this was how it would be. He'd small-talk me in an attempt to be friendly, and then he'd get what he wanted and leave. Well, fuck that. He wasn't getting niceties from me.

"I stay busy."

"I believe that." He finally caught on that I wasn't in the mood to chat, because his smile faded and he stood up. "How much?" he asked, pulling his wallet out of his back pants pocket.

"Nothing. It's yours."

Jackson's hand stilled. "I'm here to buy your artwork, not steal it."

"I don't want your money."

He looked down at the bills he held and then back up at me. "Something wrong with it?"

"Yeah. It reeks of your old man." The venom came out before I could contain it, an automatic reaction, like I was a snake that'd been stepped on.

And there goes my poker face. Ah, fuck it.

"Wow." Jackson gave a low whistle and raised his brows, but shoved the bills back inside and tucked the wallet into his pocket. "Okay. Now we're getting down to it."

With a snort, I shook my head. "That's where you're wrong. We're not getting down to anything. You're gonna pick up that piece, get in your car, and drive back to where you belong."

He blinked. "Excuse me?"

"You heard me. You got what you came for, and like I said, I'm a busy guy. Enjoy."

A sudden gust of wind blew in, sending one of my blueprints flying off the table and turning my attention away. I snatched it before it could disappear out the open door and then shoved it inside one of the worktable drawers. The rain was starting to really pick up outside, and as much as I hated to do so, I needed to wrap things up for the day. So much for a few more productive hours. I unplugged all the machinery and put away my helmet and gloves, ignoring Jackson so that he would take the piece and get the hell out.

"No." Jackson's voice rang out strong and clear, and when I turned around, his shoulders were squared and the look on his face said he had no intention of going anywhere.

But I was in a shitty mood now, so I shrugged. "No, you won't enjoy?"

"No, I'm not leaving. Not yet." With his strong jaw locked tight and his eyes blazing, he had my cock leaping to attention like it was starving and only his mouth would satisfy. "You didn't give me much of a chance to say what I needed to say on Friday, and if I have to force you to listen today, I will."

At the word "force," and the image of him doing just that, I had the urge to reach down and adjust myself, but my self-control was stronger.

"Careful, Jackson. You might remember how much I enjoy that."

He swallowed. "Lucas, I need—"

BAM! The wind kicked in one of the garage doors, the heavy wood slamming shut so hard that some of my tools on the wall nearby fell to the floor. With a curse, I ran over to pull the other door closed, but the gusts were too strong, keeping it plastered to the wall outside. I grunted and yanked on it again as the rain slapped at my face, and then Jackson was beside me, his strong arms easily jerking the door forward, and we managed to pull it far enough that the wind helped slam it shut.

I wiped my face on my shirt sleeve, and when I glanced up, Jackson ran his hand through his wet hair and lifted a brow.

"It's getting bad out there," he said.

Yeah, no shit. And the weather worsening didn't seem to motivate him to head toward the door, and if he stayed here any longer—

"I need to talk to you," he said.

"So you've said." I didn't see what could be so important, not right now. Not ever. Jesus, why couldn't he have left ten minutes ago when I'd told him to? With a sigh, I pinched the bridge of my nose and said, "Where you stayin'?"

"Why?"

"Just answer the question."

Jackson hesitated. "The Rosemont."

Fuckin' hell. The Rosemont was off the island, and with the way the storm was beginning to hit, he didn't have enough time to make it back there before things got bad. *Great. Just fucking great.* Anywhere else and I would've sent him on his way, but no. He had to make things difficult. This was the last thing I wanted to do, but now I didn't have a choice.

I swiped the car keys out of his hand.

"What the—" he said as I pocketed the keys and pushed by him to rehang the tools that had fallen to the ground. He stayed close on my heels, protesting the whole way. "What do you think you're doing?"

"What does it look like I'm doing? I can't let you leave now. God forbid a waterspout intercept your ass on the bridge. I don't need that on my conscience."

"Lucas, give me the keys. It's not that far."

"Too fucking bad," I said, flipping off the garage lights and pitching us into darkness. Then I pushed open one of the doors enough to slip through and held it until he reluctantly followed, and then we both ran the short distance to the back porch.

Yeah, I hadn't thought this through. Having Jackson in close quarters while we rode the storm out? This wasn't good. This wasn't good at all, but I wasn't a complete asshole sending people off with a death wish.

Once we were inside, I kicked off my shoes in the mud room and grabbed a couple of beach towels, tossing one in his direction and drying my face off with the other. My clothes were soaked, and I didn't chance looking over at Jackson to see that his were the same. They'd be clinging to every muscle he had, and I didn't need to see that.

Stalking off down the hall without a word, I let him follow. I did have to mentally congratulate myself on the way to the kitchen, though—at least I kept the house clean even though I rarely had visitors.

"Are you mad at me?" he asked.

I opened the fridge, grabbed a couple of water bottles, and then tossed one in his direction.

"Was I supposed to be ecstatic to see you? Happy to spend a few hours stuck in close quarters while the storm passes?" I shook my head and then downed half the bottle in one long gulp.

"You act like I did this on purpose."

"Didn't you?"

Jackson looked at me then with a no-bullshit expression. "You know better than that."

I finished off the bottle and tossed it in the recycling bin. "Wrong. I don't know anything about you. Now, if you'll excuse me, I need a shower before we lose the water. There's another one down the hall and to the right if you want one," I said, already halfway up the stairs to my bedroom. Then I realized who I was leaving downstairs and added, "Stay. Don't stay. Whatever."

"You took my keys."

"Guess you'll have to walk if you wanna leave, then."

"Lucas."

One word from him and I was looking over my shoulder and into his earnest eyes.

"I'm not going anywhere," he said.

Yeah, you've said that before, I thought, before continuing up the stairs.

CHAPTER 9
JACKSON

I DIDN'T KNOW what it said about me that I could swallow down Lucas's bitterness easier than the impassivity. I'd hurt him—that much was obvious. He wouldn't have lashed out otherwise. That revelation had me breathing out a sigh of relief, because the thought of him not giving a shit about me, about what happened between us, hurt worse than any hate he could throw my way. At least now I had pushed a sore, vulnerable spot. At least now I knew he cared. Or had.

The soft sound of water dripping onto the hardwood from my soaked clothes had me moving down the hall toward the bathroom he mentioned. And if I remembered right...

I cracked open a set of retractable doors across from the bathroom to reveal a washer and dryer, brand new, but in the same spot I'd seen Gram folding baskets of clothes years ago. After glancing behind me to make sure I was still alone, I peeled off my shirt, followed by my pants, and put them in the dryer. Then I cranked it on high, grabbed a towel from the overhead cubby, and dipped into the bathroom to shower.

There was still scalding-hot water, even with Lucas showering upstairs, but I rinsed off quickly anyway and then wrapped the towel around my waist.

Out in the hall, picture frames still littered the walls, the same way I remembered them, and I stopped in front of one of Lucas and his parents, taken shortly before he'd come to South Haven. With his black hair and bronzed skin, he was the spitting image of his welder father, especially now, and Lucas always said he got his love of drawing from his fair-haired artist mother.

Huh. He'd combined his parents' jobs of welding and art to make something of his own.

"What the hell do you think you're doing?"

At Lucas's angry tone, I spun around to where he stood at the end of the hall, eyes blazing. And damn. Freshly showered looked as good on him as his rain-soaked clothes had. He'd put on a pair of ripped jeans and a blue Seattle t-shirt, which was so faded he'd probably bought it to remember his hometown before moving south, and his hair was still wet and almost spiky on top. Amazing how hot he still looked. His body was leanly toned in the way where you knew he did physical labor for a living, and there was a confident set to his shoulders that I'd only seen glimpses of in school. He'd fully come into his own at some point, and a twinge of regret twisted in my gut that I'd missed it.

"The fuck are you doing in a towel?" he said, breaking me out of my thoughts. "Lose your clothes somewhere?"

"You told me to shower."

"I didn't tell you to run around my house naked."

Well, no, he hadn't told me that, but judging by the heated stare, he didn't mind as much as he protested.

Holding the towel in place where I'd tucked it in at my waist, I shrugged. "Not completely naked. Besides, did you want me to sit on your couch in wet clothes?" I nodded at the still-running dryer. "They'll be done in a minute."

Lucas gave an annoyed sigh as he avoided my bare chest, but that meant his gaze fell to the only covered part of me, and it lingered there below my waist long enough that my cock stood up and immediately took notice. Lucas's eyes widened at the involuntary reaction beneath my towel, and he coughed before turning on his heel. "Make yourself at home, then, I guess."

Wow… I still make him nervous. A smile crossed my lips at the thought. *I still make this sexy, confident man nervous.* That probably shouldn't have made me harder—but it did. I reached down to get myself under control, pinching the head of my semi. "Will do," I said.

But before he got to the opening of the kitchen, Lucas stopped, and then a second later said, "Hungry?"

The rumble of my stomach answered the question for me, and he nodded before heading into the kitchen.

It was funny…as begrudging as he was about me being

there, Lucas's manners wouldn't allow him to *not* offer food or a place to ride out the storm. So as pompous as he wanted to be, and with whatever angry words he wanted to spew my way, I'd take them, because at heart, Lucas was a good soul. He may be different now, but that part of him would never change. And that made me want to get to know the man I'd lost.

When I followed him into the kitchen, he ignored me and went about setting out sandwich meat, bread, and condiment jars. I took a seat on one of the barstools at the island, and he continued to avoid looking in my direction. But him not looking at me gave me plenty of time to watch *him*, something that was unwanted if the clattering of plates he purposely dropped and the slamming of the utensil drawers were any indication.

"I'm not distracting you, am I?" I asked. *And there I go again, pushing my luck.*

"Yes. You are."

"Is it me or my nakedness that bothers you more?"

Lucas's hand stilled where he'd been spreading mayo on a slice of bread. "Your general presence is irritating and unwelcome."

I stifled a laugh. *Way to be abrupt.* "You're a little more direct than you used to be."

"When I said you had to stay and wait things out, I didn't say we'd be reminiscing."

"So we can't talk?"

"I don't have anything to say to you."

"Nothing nice, you mean," I said. "Well, that's okay, because I have something to say to you."

"Jackson, I don't wanna hear it."

"You're gonna hear it whether you want to or not. It needs to be said."

"See, that's the thing—it doesn't." He pointed at me with a butter knife and glared. "I don't want to hear a half-assed apology or whatever you've got comin', so you might as well save your breath. You're eight years too late, and I'm not interested."

Well, I supposed he thought that settled that. Unfortunately for him, we had a few hours to kill, and I didn't do silence well. He seemed to react only when poked, so I bit back a grin as I said, "You're a bit of a selfish, stubborn ass. When did that happen?"

The knife clattered onto the table. "I'm selfish? *I'm* selfish?"

"Mhmm. Seem to be."

"Well. At least you'd know something about that."

My smile dimmed. "What's that supposed to mean?"

"You know exactly what that means." He folded a few slices of ham, turkey, and cheese onto the sandwiches, shaking his head the whole time.

"Okay. Let's get it all out there. You're upset because I left—"

"No," he said, shoving the plate in my direction with enough force that I had to catch the sandwich before it went sliding off. "You don't get to assume anything about me."

"At least I'm finally getting a reaction. For a little while there, I thought you'd forgotten all about me."

"Wish I could forget," he muttered, grabbing a beer out of the fridge and then slamming it shut. Then he popped off the cap, tossed it aside, and guzzled the beer down.

Jesus. That fucking stings. I swallowed past the lump in my throat. "Really? That easy for you, huh?"

"Yup."

"Wow. Your gram know you turned into such a jackass?"

"Gram's dead."

My jaw snapped shut as those two words made my head spin, and the words that'd been on the end of my tongue disappeared. Shit, his gram was…dead? *Way to stick your entire foot in your mouth, asshole.*

"Lucas, I'm so—"

"Sorry?" He snorted and leaned against the island. "I already told you not to waste your breath with that shit."

"I am, though. I know she meant a lot to you."

His gaze stayed on the window that overlooked the backyard as he took another sip of his beer. He didn't have to say anything for me to know how much her death— whenever it'd happened—hurt. Continued to hurt. God, he didn't have anyone left, did he?

Like he'd heard my thoughts, he shrugged, as if to say, "Shit happens." And then to close out that conversation, he picked up his sandwich and we ate in tense silence. I'd poked the bear enough today. A defensive Lucas wasn't one

I could get through to, so once the angry red flush crept back down below the neck of his shirt, I vowed to rein it in.

Once I'd finished lunch and declined seconds, he took our dishes over to the sink and washed and dried them while I went to check on my clothes. They were just dry enough, so I quickly dressed and hung the towel back over the rack in the bathroom. When I returned to the kitchen, rolling the sleeves of my shirt up my forearms, Lucas was still at the sink. His back was toward me, his hands spread wide on the counter as he stared out as the rain gathered in puddles around the yard.

I had all intentions of leaving him alone to his thoughts, but before I could sneak back out, his quiet voice grabbed hold of me.

"Why're you here, Jackson?"

"Because you won't let me leave." When that didn't get him to look my way or crack a smile, I blew out a breath. "I had a work meeting—" I started, but he waved me off.

"No, I don't mean the bullshit excuse about work or the piece. I mean why'd you go lookin' for me Friday?"

"I…" Why *had* I gone looking for him? It wasn't just to say I was sorry—that hadn't even crossed my mind at the time. But I couldn't even understand the whys of it myself. "I don't know."

"You don't know."

"I overheard your name at a diner that morning, and I… I had to see you."

Lucas lowered his head, rubbing between his brows

with his thumb, and somehow I knew his eyes were closed as if he were in prayer.

"Jackson…" he whispered. "You shouldn't have come here."

Off in the distance, there was a crash, like falling timber, and then…the lights flickered out.

CHAPTER 10
LUCAS

J UST FUCKING PERFECT. *Really, great timing.* I slapped the panel of the backup generator shut and exhaled.

"Something wrong?" Jackson asked from behind me, where I knelt beside the blasted old thing in the basement.

"Generator must be shot." I got to my feet and kicked the side of it for good measure, but unlike in the movies where the machine would magically restart, it just groaned in response. "Hope you're not still scared of the dark."

Jackson rolled his eyes. "I was never scared of the dark."

"Bullshit. You were."

"Nope. Wrong guy."

"You seem to suffer from some sort of amnesia. Or you blocked out a specific incident——"

"If you're referring to the fact that I wasn't the first to want to walk through the woods at night, then you got me. I know all about the alligators on this island."

"They stick to a path, not the woods."

"There's a first time for everything, and between an alligator's jaws is not the way I wanna go."

"But you wouldn't mind if it were between someone else's jaws?" I cracked a smile at the sexual innuendo until I remembered just who it was I was smiling at.

Jesus, Lucas, shut the fuck up.

Snapping my mouth closed, I headed back up the stairs to the wooden hutch where I kept all the candles, and grabbed an armful of the scented jars and a lighter.

"Need some help?" Jackson asked as I set the candles around the living room.

"Nope."

"I can light them for you."

"So can I."

He sighed, but didn't say another word. Instead, he took a seat on one end of the couch and watched as I lit the wicks. The room had grown dark as the wind howled and the rain and hail pelted the roof and windows, but the candles gave off a comforting glow.

"This is cozy," Jackson said when I sat down in the recliner, as far from him as I could get.

I wasn't stupid; no way I was chancing anything by sitting close to him. I was still so damn angry. Even after all this time. I thought I'd gotten over it. Accepted it, moved past it. But seeing him again brought back every ounce of hurt and shame I'd felt back then, which pissed me off because it meant I was still broken. And it was all his fucking fault.

And then for him to tell me he just had to see me? That he didn't even know why? How was I supposed to take that? He'd told me under no uncertain terms that he never wanted to see me again. But he'd shown up not just at Argos, but my own damn house as well. It was almost too perfect how it all worked out, him coming here, getting stuck in close quarters, but, of course, thinking Jackson had somehow masterminded it all to happen this way was ridiculous. It was a coincidence, though in the back of my mind I could hear Shaw telling me nothing was coincidence.

Fuck you, Shaw.

"So if we can't talk, got any other ideas? Checkers… charades…care to lose at a game of cards?" Jackson smiled, attempting to tease me back into shallow conversation.

But I had a different idea, one that would require something to help me bear whatever knowledge came from it, so I went to the kitchen to grab a couple of beers and passed one his way before plopping back onto the recliner.

After taking a long pull of the cold brew, I stretched my legs out in front of me and crossed them at the ankles, getting as comfortable as I could for what was about to come. Casually bracing myself. "You want to talk? So talk."

Jackson's eyes widened, like that was the last thing he'd expected to come out of my mouth. But he must've known he only had a small window of time to say what he'd come to say, because he didn't hesitate. "I'm sorry, Lucas. I was a coward, and I should've told you that night what was happening, but…" He searched for the words. "I didn't want you to get involved."

I peeled at the beer label. "You didn't want me to get involved…"

"Any more than you already were."

"Wasn't really your choice to make, was it?"

Jackson frowned and rolled the bottle between his hands. "Guess not. I just knew what my father would be like, and it was easier to—"

"Leave in the middle of the night without saying good-bye. Right."

"You have every right to be upset."

"Yeah, I do."

"I'm sorry if I hurt you."

Pursing my lips, I nodded and took a drink of my beer. He'd only barely scratched the tip of the iceberg, and I waited for him to continue with the apologies, but he only sat there expectantly. The candlelight flickered across his features, the shadows deepening his chiseled cheekbones and strong jaw. I wondered how many times in a day I could damn him for being so fucking beautiful.

"That all?" I asked.

"No." Leaning forward with his elbows on his knees, he slowly rubbed his hands together and took a deep breath. "Lucas… It hurt me too. Leaving you."

The thud I heard and felt was my heart dropping to my

feet as I took in his revelation. It went against everything I knew, everything I'd been told. He'd left of his own free will, and his actions afterward…well, there was no excuse for what had happened then. And I still hadn't heard an apology for *that*.

Jackson finished off his beer and then set the empty bottle on the coffee table in front of him. "Maybe you don't believe me. I wouldn't blame you a bit. And I know you've moved on from all this, but… being here, seeing you again. I had to at least tell you."

Moved on from it… And here I thought I had too.

Jackson cleared his throat and shifted uncomfortably on the sofa. "There's, uh, something I'm a little curious about, though."

I raised an eyebrow, and his mismatched eyes lowered to my neck.

"How did you get my necklace?" he asked.

Lifting my fingers automatically to the pendant I always wore, I said, "*Your* necklace?"

"Well…unless you made a replica for yourself, which… yeah, I guess that's entirely possible. Sorry. Forget I said anything."

My jaw opened and shut as I tried to process what he was saying. He was trying to tell me he *didn't remember*? The biggest slap in my face, and the source of my humiliation and hurt, and he *didn't remember*?

"Fuck. You," I said, bolting out of the recliner. The urge to hit him was strong, and I forced my legs to move in the opposite direction, which took me to the kitchen. Good. I needed another drink.

This has to be some kind of sick joke.

"Wait up. What just happened here?" Jackson said, coming up behind me as I took out another beer.

"Get away from me."

"What did I say? Lucas, look at me."

"If I look at you, I'll be tempted to break that pretty face, and then what will you tell Daddy?"

"Lucas——"

"I mean it. Go the fuck away."

"Please just tell me what's wrong. Don't make me beg."

"Beg?" I whirled around and pinned him against the refrigerator door so fast that he didn't have time to blink. "*Beg?* You *should* fucking beg. Beg for my forgiveness; beg me not to kick your ass all the way back to Connecticut right now. Come on, beg for me, Jackson. Goddamn beg."

Jackson's chest heaved beneath me, his breath coming out in shaky pants as I held him there with my forearm across his strong pecs. He didn't try to get away or push me back, and as my thigh brushed between his to keep him in place, I figured out why.

He was hard. So very fucking hard.

"You've gotta be kidding me," I said, trying for disgust, but my body betrayed me. My cock strained against the zipper of my jeans to the point of pain, and when I pushed my hips against his so that our erections rubbed against each other, he groaned.

"I'll beg," he whispered, his eyes on my lips. Then his

hand came up between us to finger the pendant I wore around my neck. The steel triskele hung from a thin black cord long enough to be easily concealed under a shirt, and it was such a part of me now that I'd forgotten it was even there. "Tell me where you got this, and I'll beg."

"Shouldn't it be the other way around?"

"If that's what you want."

"What I want…" As I licked my lips, the urge to push him to his knees and make him do exactly that warred with my common sense. Lust made everything hazy, and being this close to Jackson again, pressed up against him so I could feel the rock-hard muscle… *Fuck.* I pushed my forearm harder against him. "What I want…is for you to wake the fuck up."

That seemed to snap Jackson out of his own fog, because his eyes flicked up to mine. "What?"

Jerking away from him, I stepped back, enough that I was no longer touching him. "This playing stupid shit," I said, and held up the triskele. "You mean to tell me you don't remember how this got back to me? Seriously?"

"So it *is* mine."

I dropped the necklace. "Unfuckingbelievable. Did you hit your head at some point in the last eight years? Bad car crash?"

"The hell are you talking about?"

"Have you suffered some sort of *amnesia*, Jackson?" That was the only explanation for his behavior.

Jackson speared a hand through his hair and pulled at

the ends. "No, there's been no fucking amnesia. I remember clearly when I lost it."

"When you 'lost' it." I scoffed. "You 'lost' it in the letter you sent. Or do you not remember that either?" And because I'd had it, I shoved my finger into his chest. "You said you were sorry for being a coward. You're still a fucking coward."

"Lucas, stop," he said, his strong hand gripping my wrist. "What letter?"

W HAT IS HE talking about? I've never written him a letter.

Lucas tried to pull his hand back, but my hold on his wrist didn't allow him to go anywhere. Not until he answered *my* questions.

"Explain," I said.

The glare Lucas shot my way was enough to kill, but behind that anger there was…hurt. Pain. And he seemed to be under the impression I'd put those there.

I loosened my grip on him as a niggling feeling in the back of my skull told me something wasn't quite right here. He was angry, sure, but his reaction had been more extreme than what I'd been expecting. A brief thought flickered through my mind, and I prayed to God that the conclusion I was jumping to wasn't what had actually occurred.

"Lucas," I said, letting go of him, and he backed up against the island so there were now a couple feet between us. "What is it you think I did?"

A humorless smile crossed his face as his thumb stroked over the medallion he wore. "'Dear Lucas,'" he said, and then began to pace around the kitchen. "'I've been told by my parents and staff of your continued visits, and I need to make this clear: I don't want to see you. Not now, not ever again. Whatever you think it was that happened between us was a figment of your imagination, and I want nothing more than for you to forget even the mention of my name. You were a mistake, one that I sincerely regret, and you're wasting your time by coming here. Please do not contact me again, or I'll be forced to call the police and take out a restraining order. Signed, Jackson.'" Lucas let out a snort. "It *was* sweet, however, of you to include this." He ran his thumb over the triskele before tucking the necklace back into his shirt and facing me again. "So. Amnesia miraculously cured yet?"

I couldn't breathe. The air would not physically enter my lungs as I stood there gaping at Lucas. What he was suggesting... That *I'd* ever do something so cruel was beyond my wildest imagination. It was not, however, beyond the imagination of someone close to me.

"Oh my God." I finally managed to suck in a shallow breath as the truth slammed into me with more impact than the gale-force winds outside.

"No? Not ringing a bell? Hmm, I might have to jog your memory with physical evidence, then." Lucas opened a far drawer and rummaged through it before pulling something out. He sauntered over, a cruel smile playing on his lips, and then dropped a wrinkled envelope on the island in front of me. "Go ahead."

The front of the worn envelope had Lucas's name typed out, but there was no stamp or return address, like it'd been hand-delivered and not mailed. I knew without opening the letter what would be inside, but I reached for it anyway, pulled out the paper that had been crumpled and then smoothed out again so that the words on the page had faded a bit in the creases. As I began to read, the tremor in my hand made the letter shake, and I had to use both hands to steady myself.

Nausea rolled through my gut the more I read, and as I came to the final line, I had to go over it once, twice, and then again, my brain desperately trying to make sense of things. "Lucas, I didn't… That's not my…" I couldn't get the words out, as the revelation of what had actually happened all those years ago stunned me to my core, changing everything I thought I'd known. And as my world went into upheaval and I fell onto the barstool, the letter fell from my hands.

MY FATHER DIDN'T BOTHER KNOCKING on my bedroom door before he entered. He never did, and it no longer made me jump when the door flew open and his tall frame suffocated the space. "Jax, look what's just arrived," he said, and the pride in his voice made me look up from where I'd been searching the clutter on my chest of drawers. When I saw the large envelope he held, I refocused on my search.

"Well," he said, waving it at me. "Aren't you curious if you got in? This one's Yale. About blasted time, too."

"Uh... You can do the honors."

I could feel his narrowed stare as I opened the top drawer and rifled through it. There were no strings my father wouldn't pull to get me into the school of his choice, his alma mater, so it was pointless opening the dumb thing. Yale was the one he wanted, so Yale was the one it'd be. I'd already resigned myself to that fact years ago.

"What is that you're doing?" he said, growing irritated at my lack of attention and excitement, but I had more important things on my mind. Like where my necklace had disappeared to.

"Just looking for something," I mumbled, slamming the drawer shut and opening the one underneath.

"Looking for something?" My father wagged the envelope in front of my face. "How about you look at your future? Now." His tone brooked no argument, and I reluctantly took the thick envelope from him and sat on the edge of my bed. Thick envelopes meant one thing —welcome to university life, oh, and here are the housing forms and the classes and the extracurricular activities and the blah blah fucking blah.

"Congratulations, you've been accepted to Yale—" I didn't even get out the rest of the sentence before my father let out a triumphant shout and snatched the paperwork from my hands.

"See? What'd I tell you? A Yalie, just like me." His eyes shone as he looked down at the paper in his hands, and when he looked my way, I tried for a smile, really I did, but all I could think about—all I'd been able to think about for the past two weeks—was the person

I'd left back in Georgia that I'd never see again. Especially on this Yale path, a place he wouldn't be caught dead anywhere near, even though his grades were more than enough to get in.

"What? Aren't you excited? This is what you've wanted your whole life," my father said, trying again to rouse me into the same state of exuberance he was in.

"It's great," I said. "Really."

"'It's great,'" he repeated, his lip curling. "That's all you have to say? 'It's great'?"

"Well, it is——"

"It's more than 'great,' Jax. Do you know how many kids are getting rejection letters right now that would kill to be in your shoes?"

Without thinking about it, I reached up to fidget with the necklace I'd worn for months, but my fingers landed on nothing but the collar of my shirt.

"Stop doing that." My father sneered. "Your mother used to do that."

I dropped my hand and pushed myself off the bed, heading back over to the dresser to resume my search. "Habit. I lost my necklace a couple days ago and can't find it anywhere."

"Since when have you worn a necklace?" he said, curling his lips in disgust at the word "necklace." "Only women wear those."

"No, it's more like a pendant thing on a black cord... I got it from... I mean, I bought it at school."

My father's eyes were like coal as he stared at me. "Well. I'm sure it'll turn up, then."

"Yeah." And then before I could stop myself, I asked, "Is that all the mail I got?"

"What else were you expecting?" He shoved the acceptance letter back inside the envelope.

Nothing. I'd been expecting nothing at all. But I'd held on to some silly sliver of hope that even though I'd left South Haven abruptly, and without giving Lucas any contact information, that he'd somehow find a way to me. It was a stupid idea, us keeping in touch, which was exactly the reason I'd had to leave in the first place, but…I missed the guy. I missed my friend…and whatever else we had become.

At the hopeful look on my face, my father's lips straightened. "Actually, I do have something for you that was dropped off."

I perked up. "You do?"

He nodded at my desk. "Take a seat."

"Take a seat" was code for "you're not gonna like what I have coming for you," but I did as I was told anyway, pulling out the chair at my desk and waiting for the ball to drop. Since I'd been home, there'd been an awkward distance between the two of us, but nothing had been said about why he'd pulled me out of South Haven early, and I didn't dare bring up the subject. Deep down I knew why, and not letting me walk the graduation stage with my peers last week had seemed to be punishment enough.

My father took something out of his inside suit jacket pocket and then dropped the sealed, unmarked envelope onto the desk in front of me and stepped back.

"What's this?" I flipped it over, expecting to see a return address for another one of the colleges I'd applied to, but the other side was unmarked as well.

"Why don't you open it up and see for yourself?"

That was where I should've said no. Nothing good ever came from unmarked envelopes, at least according to crime shows.

After carefully popping open the seal, I pulled out the contents—a stack of photos, and I recognized the handsome guy in the picture on top immediately. It was the slightly shorter guy I couldn't pinpoint.

I felt a sense of foreboding, and I swallowed hard. I didn't want to see the rest. "What is this?"

"Why don't you keep going?"

"I'd rather not."

"Oh, come on. It'll be fun. That's your buddy, right? What was his name...Lucas something or other?"

I met his eyes, and something malicious hid in their depths.

The next photo was much the same as the first—Lucas was standing in the personal space of the guy, leaning in close to his ear as if he was telling a secret. So, they were friends talking. Big deal.

Yeah, then why did my heart seem to be thumping with the treble turned all the way up?

I fumbled through the next few, my vision blurring at the edges as Lucas's lips touched the guy's neck in one shot, and then moved to his mouth in the next. I knew that mouth. I knew the faint taste of butterscotch that came from his tongue, and the way he'd tease and nip at my bottom lip to draw out the anticipation. Those lips were mine. No, correction: had *been mine. For a brief, fleeting moment, one I still couldn't believe or begin to process. It didn't make sense to me that I'd fallen for a guy. A* guy. *The thought of being attracted to a male simply hadn't occurred to me before, but now I couldn't get him out of my head. Two weeks apart hadn't made things easier—they'd only intensified to the point I was ready to tell my father to screw off and hop on the first flight down to Georgia. I wasn't crazy; I knew the feeling had been mutual. All those promises made in the dark, plans and futures and what we'd become. Together had been the only thing we'd agreed on. Which was why I couldn't believe what I was seeing.*

No… Maybe this had happened before Lucas had come to South Haven. Maybe it was all a—

My eyes caught the numbers at the bottom corner. The photos were timestamped yesterday.

Heat rushed to my face as I tried to understand what I was seeing. Why? Why was Lucas kissing some guy, and who the hell was he? No one from school, that much was obvious. Had he been seeing this guy the whole time we'd… No. That was impossible. *We'd spent almost every waking minute together, so whoever this was, it had to be some kind of rebound. Right?*

And then another thought: if my father had pictures of Lucas, and Lucas seemed oblivious to the fact that he was being photographed, then I could only imagine the evidence he had mounted against me from our time together. The thought of my father's beady eyes watching the two of us made me fucking sick. No wonder he'd pulled me out of South Haven. Looking back, our friendship had been leading up to the inevitable, and it was clear my father had hoped to put an end to things before they reached the point of no return.

Too late for that, *I thought, and as my father gave a brisk nod for me to keep going, my hands shook.*

The next photo continued the progression—Lucas cupping the guy over his jeans… Jesus Christ. *Then the blond pulling up Lucas's shirt as he backed him up against a brick wall in the next. It was clear where this was going, and I didn't need to look at the rest. Seeing Lucas with someone else, moving on already, was like a stab through my intestines, the knife twisting and gutting me completely.*

I shoved the photos back inside the envelope and had to breathe through my nose. If I opened my mouth, a choking cry might come out, and there was no way I'd break down in front of my father. He didn't need to know he'd gotten the best of me, that he'd won. His life's work was knowing how to crack his opponent, how to break them and bend them to his will. He always won. This would be no different.

Show nothing. Give nothing away.

When I spoke again, it wasn't until I could keep my voice strong. Steady. Unaffected. "You looked at these?" I asked, keeping my gaze on the desk.

"My private investigator filled me in on the details. I don't need to look at that filth."

"And why would you hire a private investigator to scope out some kid?"

My father stalked across the room and then braced himself over the desk, bringing his face in close to mine. "You see, Jackson, I've got far too much riding on you for you to fuck it all up. You were nothing more than another play toy for this kid. Don't you see that? Just one of many distractions that'll cross his path."

My hands clenched under the table. "That's not true."

"It is true."

"We're just friends—"

"Wrong." He straightened, his large shoulders dwarfing me in his shadow, his voice reverberating off the walls. "You were *just friends. But that stops right now. I didn't send you down to the most expensive school in the country for you to come back a queer."*

Holy shit. There it was. Out in the open, no one skirting around the issue at hand. And all I could do was sit there, my mouth parted, unable to speak.

With a growl, my father said, "He means nothing to you, you hear me? And you mean nothing to him." He glanced down at the envelope on my desk. "You can keep those."

The door slammed behind him, the walls trembling in his wake. It wasn't until I heard the purr of his Jaguar heading down the driveway that my heart split in two and I gave in to the silent tears that'd been blurring my vision. I reached up again for the necklace, but there was nothing there to comfort me, no piece of Lucas left behind to help me know it was real. Because it had been real...right? He'd meant more to me in those short eight months than anyone I'd known in my entire eighteen years. But those pictures... God, they told a different story, one I never would've believed if the truth wasn't staring me in the face.

Why, Lucas? Why?

"I BURNED THEM. Every single picture—I burned them all. I didn't need to see…" Jackson shook his head, like he was erasing the memory of my betrayal. The one he may not have seen but obviously still felt.

Paralyzed where I stood, I struggled to put the pieces of his story together with what I knew to be true. And as what Jackson said sank in, his words boiled down to one thing—we'd been played, nothing more than pawns in his father's fucked-up game. Our lives so unimportant that it'd only taken a couple of scheming moves to set us on new paths—separately. Permanently.

"Lucas, I don't blame you," Jackson said, misunderstanding the horror I knew was written all over my face. "I up and disappeared without explanation, and you…moved on. It was my fault. I should've said—"

"I came to see you," I said, my voice a whisper as I gripped the edge of the counter. "At your house."

Jackson's expression transformed from apologetic to incredulous in the blink of an eye. "You... What? When?"

"The day after graduation. I showed up on your doorstep and was told you didn't want to see me."

The blood drained from Jackson's face.

"So, stubborn ass that I am, I went back the next day. And then the next." I rubbed at the stubble on my jaw as I remembered the way his father and the household staff took turns slamming the door in my face. Not my finest moments, but I'd refused to believe Jackson hadn't wanted to see me. Until... "And then a letter was dropped off at my hotel, along with the necklace. I got the message then."

Jackson had gone stock-still, a beautiful, haunted statue staring down at the marble countertop. What was running through that head of his? He was probably freaked out that I hopped a plane to chase after him, like I was some kind of desperate stage-five clinger. Too late to take back that piece of history, and I didn't regret it anyway. The last thing I'd been thinking was what his father would say about me blowin' in upstate, but maybe that should've been my first thought.

Jesus, he was quiet. Too quiet. The silence ramped my anxiety up to a ten, so when Jackson refused to speak, to even breathe, I finally spoke up. "Say something."

Like he was coming out of a trance, Jackson blinked and slowly lifted his head to meet my gaze. "I can't... believe...you did that."

He can't believe... "You just fucking *left*," I exploded, pushing off the counter, my outrage finally pouring out in a rush meant for his father—but he wasn't here, and it was coming out one way or another. Gripping the ends of my hair, I paced the kitchen without looking his way. "What else was I supposed to do? I didn't know if you were hurt or okay. You just disappeared in the middle of the night... *Jesus.* You fucking—" Turning around, I slammed straight into Jackson's strong, unyielding body, my hands coming up to catch myself on his abs. It was like latching on to the side of a rocky mountain ravine. Goddammit, I didn't need to be touching him like that. I didn't need to know what he felt like under my palms or catch the scent of my soap on his skin. *Which reminds me, I need to stock some generic Irish Spring bullshit in the guest bath. Not that he'll be showering here again. Okay, Jesus, Lucas, move.* Before I could move away, though, Jackson locked on to my wrists.

"You came for me," he said softly, though his breaths were coming faster. Those contrasting eyes of his had dilated so that I could barely see the blue of his irises, making them almost a perfect match for once.

"And you had no idea. This whole time." I didn't know whether to laugh or cry. Hell, I really wanted to fucking rage. At someone or something...whatever would take the edge off the fire coursing through my veins.

I tried to jerk out of his hold, but Jackson's grip on me was tight, and before I could blink, he had me backed up against the counter. He was so close I could feel his breath on my lips, could see the way his eyes fell to my mouth.

The rain beating against the window faded into the background as Jackson became the only thing I could see, and his soft panting all I could hear.

He dipped his head toward mine, pausing long enough that I had time to pull away if I wanted to. And maybe I should've. Kissing Jackson would complicate everything. It was throwing myself out to sea without a lifeboat or a preserver or any damn thing to hold on to to save myself. There'd be no saving this time, but as much as I knew that in the back of my mind, I couldn't stop from moving my head forward, so that our lips were almost brushing.

The truth I didn't want to admit to myself was that I wanted his mouth on mine more than I wanted air in my lungs, but this was a bad idea. I didn't know the man in front of me any more than he knew me, and as the thought crossed my mind, I found myself inching back from him. But Jackson didn't let me get far. He closed the gap between us by jerking me forward by the wrists—and then his lips crushed against mine.

Oh fuck me to hell.

His sudden movement took me by surprise, and my brain lagged for a couple of seconds while it processed what was happening. Jackson was…kissing me. He'd made the first move, and his lips were on mine, warm and soft and urging mine to part for him.

Is this really happening? Maybe I'd hit my head on a flying wrench in my workshop and had gone the way of Dorothy in Oz, because there was no way this was real. I'd dreamed him up, put him in my kitchen amid a storm he couldn't escape from, and twisted our past until it fit with a reality that was better than the one we'd been dealt.

Jackson's teeth nipping at my lower lip brought me back to the present, and the entry he sought. As he dropped my wrists, my mouth parted, giving him the access he wanted, and then my hands were in his damp hair, holding him in place as I angled my head for a deeper feel of his tongue against mine.

God, he tasted so good. He kissed me hungrily, and I gave it right back to him, the urge for more causing us to switch places as I dominated and pushed him up against the pantry door. His fingers clawed at my waist, desperate and wanting, and I obliged his unspoken request by pressing my hips against his, one hard length to another.

I smiled against his lips as a moan, deep and filled with desire, left him. Like he couldn't get enough. Like his body and his mouth were always supposed to be on mine.

I WAS KISSING Lucas Sullivan. And not just in one of the many fevered dreams I'd had in the years since I'd last seen him, but actually devouring him, like the fate of the world rested on our lips staying crushed together. It was fast and frenzied, and the way he'd instinctively taken control and pushed me up against whatever was behind me had me rock hard. With my size, I was always the one to take charge, and I couldn't deny how hot it was for someone my equal to give it back to me as good as I gave.

Lucas's hands trailed down from my hair to the sides of my neck, stealing my breath. It reminded me of the way he'd kissed me for the first time all those years ago, against a rough-barked pine in the woods that separated his gram's house from the school. I had a scraped back for days, but it had been worth it to finally feel his warm mouth on mine, giving in to all that pent-up electricity between us. I hadn't ever kissed a guy before that moment, and Lucas didn't make it easy on me—he took what he wanted, and I went along with it because it felt so damn good and because I wouldn't ever say no to Lucas. And that was the only thing that scared me back then—that I'd never say no to him.

But it seemed like I wouldn't have to stop him now, because all too abruptly, Lucas pulled away, putting far too much space between us. "No. This is not happening."

Dazed, I watched him worry his hands through his hair as he tried to shake himself out of his stupor. He was aroused—that much was painfully obvious by the way his pants were tented, but his self-control was winning out.

How much further would I have gone if he'd wanted to? The possibilities sent a thrill all the way to my balls, and I reached down to ease the pent-up ache, massaging them with a rough hand.

"Christ, what are you doing?" Lucas groaned as he watched me work myself, a tortured look on his face.

I didn't even know I was doing it. My reserve in the bedroom always seemed to surprise my partners, but something about Lucas emboldened me, made me want to tease and share a part of myself I kept hidden away. And let's be real—after that kiss, I needed the relief.

Lucas focused on my hand as I stroked myself over my pants, and he bit his lip. He looked half ready to pounce, half ready to kick me out of the house, and I prayed it would be the former. Indecision warred in his eyes, his body tense as a live wire. It was when my thumb edged over the top of my hard-on and I gasped that Lucas made his move.

His body slammed into mine, his tongue plunging into my mouth to take possession. My hips bucked up at the move, and he reciprocated by letting his fingers trail down between us to bat my hand away and tease my erection.

Oh, shiiit. Every secret dirty daydream I'd had of Lucas couldn't compare to the way he felt against me as he deepened the kiss and massaged me harder. I couldn't believe the way my body was responding, so instantly and without a second thought. Who was I? A man who enjoyed the feel of another man's lips on his more than anyone I'd ever kissed in my life. I didn't understand that at all, didn't know what that made me, but worrying about it was the last thing on my mind as Lucas's mouth moved in perfect sync with mine.

One of his strong hands came up to land on my chest, holding me in place—as if I would go anywhere else—and then Lucas's other hand snapped open the button of my pants. He nipped and teased my lower lip, and I let out a moan of anticipation. I knew where this was going if I let it, and just like back then, I didn't understand all the whys, but I did know that the pull I felt for this man wasn't something I'd ever felt with anyone else. So when I squeezed Lucas's ass to urge him on, he pulled down my zipper and then cupped my erection.

"Shit," I breathed out as he stroked me, the combination of his firm hand and the friction of my boxer briefs making my eyes roll to the back of my head. He wasn't gentle, and there was nothing hesitant about the way he touched me. This was a man who knew exactly what he was doing, and that only made me harder.

"*Jesus*, Jackson." Lucas's words tickled my lips as he shook his head and his fingers skimmed the head of my cock. "I forgot how fucking big you are."

My head thudded back against the door, and I had to reach out for the hand that was driving me to the point of coming all over his palm if he kept it up. "No, you didn't."

Lucas took me by the chin, his eyes twinkling with a devilish light. "You're right. I didn't." Then he dropped to his knees, pulling my boxers and pants down with him in one quick yank.

"Lucas— Ah, *fuck*," I said, as he not only took me in his mouth, but sucked me inside so fiercely that my cock hit the back of his throat. I was vaguely aware of the curses that were flying out of me, but all I could concentrate on was not busting a nut five seconds in. Holy shit, had anything felt this good *ever*? No. Hell no.

As Lucas shifted between my thighs, he pushed my legs open wider, giving him more access to all of me. I felt exposed as I stood there watching the man on his knees, but he wasn't looking at me. He wasn't looking anywhere. His eyes were shut, but his mouth worked like a damn Hoover, taking what he wanted, and I was more than willing to let him.

Somewhere in the back of my mind I had a thought that this wouldn't end well, that Lucas would wake up from whatever trance he was in, realize what he'd done, and then go back to resenting me. But with his warm, wet mouth around my cock, I couldn't bring myself to give one fuck.

My back arched, pushing my hips forward and even deeper inside Lucas's throat, and when he choked, I instinctively pulled back. That was the wrong move, though, because Lucas's hands wound around my thighs, bringing my hips forward, and he licked clean the pre-cum off my dick before greedily devouring me again.

"You taste so good," he murmured around my cock, and I shivered from the vibration.

How many times had I fucked my fist imagining it was Lucas's mouth? More than I'd ever admit to myself, that was for damn sure, but all those empty fantasies had nothing on the reality. I speared my fingers through his hair as Lucas's muscular arms held me right where he wanted me. He brought me to the brink of orgasm and then backed off, sucking the sensitive skin on my sac instead and then moving to tongue my slit.

"You are way too fucking good at that," I said, pumping my hips forward and pushing the head of my erection past his lips. "Lucas… Lucas, look at me."

Something in the air changed then as Lucas stopped moving for a second, like me saying his name had pulled him out of wherever his head had been. *Shit. Don't stop… please don't fucking stop.*

As if he'd heard me, he slowly took me inside again, and one of his hands wrapped around the base of my dick. Twisting and sucking, his mouth and fingers working in tandem, faster and harder, taking, taking, taking from me. Lucas's eyes stayed firmly shut the whole time, even as I willed them to open and look up at me. Did he even know who he was sucking off right now? Did he care? Would he look at me differently when he finally opened them?

I'd find out soon enough, because the small amount of control I'd held on to was wearing thin, and the familiar way my balls pulled taut had me pushing Lucas's head away, trying to get him to move. He didn't budge, his hold on me showing me that he was pointedly choosing to ignore my warning, and *God*, the thought of coming in his mouth had my orgasm roaring to the surface. As I shot my load down his throat, Lucas's tongue massaged the underside of my cock, milking and drinking down every last drop of me until I was shaking, my legs ready to give out from under me.

As the ringing in my ears began to subside, Lucas got to his feet, and I pulled up and zipped my pants. He still wasn't looking at me as he wiped his mouth.

"Damn. Lucas, that was… Wow," I said, my lips curving up as I reached for his hand, but either he didn't see me or he chose not to, because he shoved his hands in his pockets and moved away.

"Thanks," he said, the word short and clipped.

"Thanks?"

"Well, I suppose technically you should be thanking me." His words dripped with sarcasm as the air between us cooled, and a sense of dread filled my gut.

"Did I…do something wrong?" I asked.

"Course not."

"Okay," I said, studying his face for a hint of what had just happened here. "Then what's the problem?"

"There's no problem."

"Obviously that's not true. You won't even look at me."

Lucas finally pinned me with a stare, but there was no emotion behind his eyes. "Did you enjoy yourself?"

My eyebrows shot up. *Did I enjoy… Is he fucking kidding?* "What is that supposed to mean?"

"I'll take that as a yes."

"Like you just did me a favor?" I gripped the back of my neck as his abrupt mood change chilled me to my core. "Wow."

He turned his back on me as he headed toward the stairs. "I'm sure you remember there's a guest room down the hall. You can stay there till the storm passes."

I balked. "That's it? That's all I get from you?"

Lucas stopped with his hand on the railing. "Most would be fucking thrilled if that's all they got from me."

"You fucking asshole."

"I've been called worse."

"Do you think that's why I came here? Because I wanted…*that* from you?"

He gave me a sadistic smile. "Oh, come on, Jackson. It's called a blow job. You can say it."

I opened my mouth to speak, to try to say *something* in that moment, but nothing felt right. It was like we'd had a small window of opportunity, of realization between us, and it was gone almost as soon as it'd come—pun completely intended. I didn't recognize the cold, closed-off person standing there. Where had he come from and why?

"So. Thanks for coming by." Lucas's sarcasm slapped me in the face as he started up the stairs, and I found myself going after him.

"Lucas…"

He looked over his shoulder, and the expression in his eyes was unreadable—whatever was going through Lucas's head, it was nothing he wanted to share with me. One thing I did know, though: I wasn't welcome to follow.

I dropped my hand from the banister, and Lucas's eyes narrowed slightly, a crease forming between his brows. Then, as fast as it had come, it was gone, and he left me standing there, in his house, as he shut himself inside his bedroom.

I T WAS THE day after I'd been "smacked the hell down," as I was now referring to it, and as I drove past downtown South Haven on the way back to my hotel, the town was already up and about, clearing the debris from yesterday's storm from the roads and side-walks. Other than the scattered remnants of trees and small branches, it didn't seem like there'd been much damage. Quite the opposite from what had happened between Lucas and me yesterday. He never came back down the rest of the night, so I'd passed out on the couch while waiting for the storm to roll on by. And this morning my keys were on the coffee table, and Lucas's truck was gone.

He was avoiding me, and I had no idea what had happened. Well, other than the most head-exploding blow job I'd ever had, but I couldn't even enjoy that memory

anymore without thinking of Lucas's inscrutable expression afterward.

What had I been thinking going over there in the first
place? I should've left as soon as I realized whose house I
was at. Being on Lucas's turf, in his home, a place that was
familiar to me and held so many memories as it was, and
then having to be in such close proximity to the man
himself? It had been a recipe for disaster, long-dormant
desire I hadn't even known was there. Lucas probably
thought I'd gone there specifically to seduce him or something. *Jesus.* Had that been what I was doing? God knew it
hadn't been my plan upon coming back to Georgia to even
see the guy, but one second of being in Lucas's presence
and all bets were off. I couldn't explain it. I didn't understand it. And I'd stayed up half the night replaying what
had happened between us over and over, trying to ratio-
nalize the turn of events, because it all happened so
quickly.

One thing that had come tumbling out and shocked
me to my core—the fact that my father had purposely
separated and kept us apart. That information changed
everything. It was like the solid, stable ground of what I
had always known to be true had suddenly cracked
beneath my feet, and how did I trust anything anymore?
What else had he lied to me about?

And how would things have been different with Lucas?
Would I have stayed in Connecticut? Gone back to him? I
already knew the answer to that. I'd been ready to hop a
flight to South Haven until I'd gotten the photos of him

with someone else. Photos my father had engineered to keep me under his thumb.

My stomach lurched as I turned into the self-parking garage at my hotel, and then—speak of the devil—my cell rang, the caller ID displaying my father's direct office line. I hit the reject button and waited as the boom gate lifted.

Not the person I want to talk to right now. If ever.

I drove around searching for a free spot as the phone rang again, only this time I let it go to voicemail.

How could my father have been so vindictive and cruel? I'd given up so much of what *I* wanted to please him, and mostly because I tried to overcompensate for losing Mom. He'd taken her death hard, and being the only family he had left, the responsibility to carry on the family name *and* the family business *and* make him proud landed on my shoulders. But why had I even bothered when he'd been manipulating me my entire life to do what he wanted?

After pulling into an open space, I shut off the engine, just as his number lit up my cell yet again. Frustrated, I slammed my fists against the wheel and took a couple of deep breaths. I couldn't keep ignoring his call, but fuck if I wanted to fake the small talk when I was so pissed. Now wasn't the time to bring it up, though, so I bit down on the inside of my cheek and hit accept.

"Do we have a problem?" my father said in lieu of greeting when I brought the phone to my ear.

I could taste the blood from my teeth piercing my skin, and I unclenched my jaw. "Good morning to you, too."

"You think it's a good idea to send me to voicemail?"

Yes. Yes, I do. "I was in the middle of an important call."

"With Vogel?"

"Of course," I lied.

"I hear there's a holdup."

Thank you, Sydney. "Minor. It's just taken a bit longer than planned to sync our schedules."

He scoffed. "Do I need to remind you how important this acquisition is to the company? I trusted you to knock this one out, so if—"

"It'll happen. I've got a meeting with Vogel on Thursday, and that'll get the ball rolling. Don't worry."

"'Don't worry,'" my father mimicked. "'Don't worry,' he says."

"Have I ever let you down before?"

The silence that followed spoke volumes. He knew as well as I did the answer to that one, just as he knew I'd land this acquisition with my hands tied behind my back. I never let him down. Not ever. And that only fueled my anger.

"Wrap things up as soon as you can and get back here," he said finally. "Your fiancée's getting antsy to start the wedding plans."

Those words were a gut punch back to reality, the one I'd been avoiding since coming down here. "I haven't proposed," I said through my teeth.

"Which is why you'd better get a move on before Sydney wises up and marries me instead."

There's more chance of that happening than with me. Especially now. "I'll be back soon enough."

"You do that. And son? I'm counting on you. Don't let me down."

My jaw was clamped shut so tight I could've spit molars. "Yes, sir."

As the line went dead, I cursed and threw the phone into the passenger seat. Damn him. I'd never resented my father as much as I did in that moment, and I'd never wanted to call him out for something so much. It wasn't the right time to confront my father about the past with Lucas, though, not over the phone, as much as I wanted to. But if I was honest with myself, I didn't know if I ever would. Not because I was scared to, but if Lucas never talked to me again, never wanted to see me, what would it be worth to bring up the past? It wouldn't solve anything. Wouldn't fix what had happened. It would only serve to sever the relationship with the only family I had. And even if thinking about what he did made me want to bash the shit out of something, he was still my father—and my boss.

Almost immediately, my phone lit up with Sydney's number, and I was reminded yet again that there were other, bigger issues to deal with than Lucas Sullivan. Even the limited amount of interaction we'd had since I'd been in town made the thought of never seeing Lucas again settle in my stomach like sour milk—but what could I do? I couldn't force the guy to spend time with me. Hell, I'd already shown up at his house uninvited, and that had gone about as well as a mugging. The truth was that I was leaving in a few days anyway. I couldn't blame him for having a life…without me in it.

As I hit the decline button on my phone to reject Sydney's call and stepped out of the car, I resolved not to seek out Lucas again while I was here.

That didn't mean I didn't hope he wouldn't find me.

CHAPTER 15

LUCAS

THE LIGHTS ON the Body Electric Tattoo Studio sign were off when I pulled my truck into a street parking space hours after I'd left Jackson alone in my house. It was still early, well before the tattoo shop opened, but Shaw always fit my appointments in off the books, and today I was especially grateful for the distraction.

I crossed the street and nodded at several shop owners sweeping out their entryways and putting out tables, chairs, and signs. Shaw had left the door unlocked, and when I walked through, the bells jingled and Shaw glanced up from where he was leaned back in an office chair reading the newspaper, his combat boots crossed on the reception table in front of him. When he saw me, he narrowed his eyes. "You look like shit warmed over."

I batted my lashes and smoothed back my hair.

"Really? I'm glad you think so. It's probably my new foundation."

"What's it called? Hammered shit?"

"Don't remember. I'll have to ask your mom." I had to sidestep quickly as a Sharpie sailed past my head. "Ooooh, the man has good aim after all. I'd heard otherwise." I moved again as he faked me out and then sent a magazine flying through the air like a Frisbee, and it hit me square in the shoulder. "Geez. Is that any way to greet a paying customer?"

Shaw snorted. "I've never charged your ass, but keep it up and I might change my mind."

"Have it your way," I said, shutting and locking the door behind me. "As long as you're not tempted to tattoo 'I love pussy' on my arm. False advertising and all."

"Maybe next time," he said with a wink. "So, will it be coffee or hair of the beast this morning?"

"Coffee. The whole pot, if you don't mind."

One side of Shaw's mouth turned up, and he folded the newspaper neatly back to its original form before getting up. "I don't mind, but Gia might when she comes roaring in for her shift later." He went over to the small station he had set up in the corner for his workers and clients that had a Mr. Coffee and a Keurig, and grabbed an oversized stainless steel tumbler from the cabinet underneath. Then he poured the rest of the steaming coffee from the pot and handed it over.

"Thanks." I didn't bother with the creamer and sugar routine this morning, nor did I wait until it cooled off any, taking a couple of deep gulps and thoroughly scalding my mouth and esophagus. *Good.* After last night's activity, it fucking needed it.

While Shaw took the pot to the back to rinse and refill —because, trust, hell hath no fury like Gia without her brew—I headed over to his workstation to settle into the chair. Body Electric was Shaw's labor of love, a small business off Ocean Avenue downtown, and the only one on the island. He and his four tattoo artists stayed busy, since vacation seemed to make the tourists want to ink their skin in a way they'd never do back home. It was how I'd met him a little over seven years ago. I'd come in, completely wasted, and he'd promptly kicked my ass right back out.

I chuckled at the memory as I looked around the space. Each artist had their own station, but there were no partitions to separate each area, so the whole shop was wide open. The walls were painted a midnight blue, setting off the silver gleam of the steel designs lining the back wall. Some of my best work. Damn, I'd really nailed those. It was a good trade-off: I decorated the shit out of his shop, he decorated the shit out of my skin.

"Doesn't look like Adelaide hit you much yesterday," I said, as Shaw headed over to one of the sinks set up at the back.

He turned on the faucet and set about scrubbing his hands and wrists with a thick lather of soap. "Nah, not too bad. I came down early to clear out some branches from the road before the crews came through, but that's about it. Your place fare okay?"

Had it? One of the smaller pines had fallen in the front yard away from the house, no biggie, but the real damage had been done inside. In my own damn kitchen.

I'm such a fucking idiot. What had I been thinking going anywhere near Jackson? Regardless of the past shit we'd dredged up and the miscommunication of it all, it didn't change the fact that we'd both gone on with our lives. We were different people now—well, I was. Jackson, however, still seemed firmly trapped both personally and professionally by his old man. Nothing would ever change as long as that bastard was around, and I wasn't fooling myself again by getting involved with a man who'd be leaving town in a few days. Not gonna happen. My life was just fine without Jackson Davenport getting tied up in it.

"Lucas?" Shaw laughed and shut off the faucet. "Damn, man, finish that coffee and then we'll resume conversation."

I took another long draw and found myself wondering if Jackson was still asleep on my couch. The storm had passed sometime in the middle of the night, and I'd left right before dawn and headed to my favorite spot on one of the private beaches to watch the sunrise. It was something I did often, and it felt necessary this morning especially. With his shirt off and half covered by one of my throws, a sleeping Jackson was almost too tempting to resist, and neither of us needed me crawling on top of him for an early morning wake-up call. I shifted in my seat at the thought.

"Shaw…have you ever believed one thing and come to find out it was all a lie?"

If my question surprised Shaw, he didn't let it show. He ripped open an alcohol swab packet and wiped the part of my arm that he'd be adding ink to eventually. Today he'd just be giving me a preview of the design he'd drawn up for me and deciding on placement.

"It's happened before," he said.

"What did you do about it?"

His expression turned serious. "I killed the person who lied to me."

"Because that's an option." I said as he cracked a smile.

"Nah. It's not a big deal now, but my mother lied about who our father was."

"What?"

"Yep. Found out when I was fifteen that it wasn't the baseball MVP she'd always told us he was. No, my father had been some rich European who'd passed through town on a holiday, knocked her up with me and Kev, and then refused to see any of us again. Classy guy."

"Holy shit. How did I not know this?"

Shaw shrugged as he opened a box of surgical markers. "He doesn't exist to me. Nothing to say."

"And your mom? She lied to you."

"She wanted us to have a better role model as a father than that fuckhead. Can you blame her?"

"Guess not."

"I think we turned out okay. We're not crack addicts in

an alley, and it could've easily gone that way. I didn't take the news well at the time."

"Ah, yes, the rebellious phase. Now I feel sorry for your mom."

"You should. We put that woman through hell. Explains why we were such shit ball players, though."

I laughed, settling back in the chair as he began to free-hand the design. It wouldn't be an exact likeness of my gram, more an abstract portrait from Shaw's memory, surrounded by her favorite flowers, magnolias. He'd be weaving them into and around the triskele design I'd gotten after my parents passed. I'd been meaning to do it for a while now, and with it being the third anniversary of her passing this week, the time seemed right. When it rained, it fucking poured, so of course Jackson had chosen now to come back into my life.

"You know, whatever you were lied to about, you get to choose the outcome and how you move on from it," Shaw said, as if he'd sensed I'd gone back into my head.

"Wise Master Yoda. I think you chose the wrong profession."

Shaw raised a scarred eyebrow. "Considering I'm gonna be marking your skin somethin' permanent soon, you'd better hope I chose right."

Before I knew it, I was telling Shaw all the details of what had happened the day before, from the letters and the truth coming out, down to me on my damn knees. This was what happened around the guy, the spilling of the guts, which was why I'd learned not to fight it and let it happen.

I'd known him long enough to know he was a vault, so whatever I told him in confidence always stayed between the two of us. And he did give the best damn advice, even if I wanted to slap him shitless in the process.

When I was done with my confession, Shaw nodded. "That all?"

"Is that all? Shaw, I took advantage of the situation, got what I wanted from him, then got the hell out."

"So you haven't talked to Jackson since? Just pussied it upstairs to hide until he fell asleep? Doesn't sound like the Sully boy I know."

"The alternative was fucking him all night, which would've been an even bigger mistake."

Shaw's forehead creased. "I'm failing to see how that's a problem…"

"Well, I would've missed this quality time with you, for one."

"You would've been forgiven."

"You're a shit, you know that? If it wouldn't fuck up my arm, I'd kick your ass right now."

Shaw chuckled, because he knew as well as I did that no one his size was getting trampled, and definitely not by the likes of me. The guy lifted cars for fun.

"So, you talked," Shaw said. "What's he in town for?"

"Business shit, I guess. I didn't ask."

"Kind of important, isn't it? Maybe he came for you."

"Not in a million fucking years."

He shrugged. "You never know."

"Trust me, I know. A guy doesn't just fly in after a few

years to check in with someone he used to know. And definitely not a straight guy."

Shaw pulled back in surprise. "He's straight?"

"He's not out, and I'd bet my savings he's never been with another guy."

"Huh. I didn't catch that vibe from him at Argos. A little innocent, sure, but he eyed me good and well."

"Excuse me?" I said sharply, and Shaw laughed.

"Relax; he wasn't lookin' because he was interested. More…curious. Like he'd never been around so many men in his life."

"He went to an all-boys academy, dumbass."

Shaw rolled his eyes. "That doesn't translate to all-gays, babe. Give him a break."

"Defending him now?"

"What's the real problem, Lucas?" Shaw asked, his eyes intent on the line he drew on my bicep. "That you might actually still care about this guy?"

"What are you, my therapist?"

Shaw leaned back to inspect his work. "Sometimes."

I thought about all the times I'd ended up in this shop or in Shaw's condo upstairs, fully intending not to say a word but pouring my damn heart out instead. The guy had a way about him that just poked at you until the truth came streaming out, like a hole in a water balloon, whether you wanted it to or not.

"You know what your problem is?" Shaw said.

"I have a feeling you're gonna tell me."

"You're a self-absorbed ass stuck in your comfort zone."

"And that's taken years to perfect. Why fuck it up now?"

"For something special," Shaw said softly as he began to sketch out one of the blooms. "I remember when I met you and you were still mooning over that guy. I don't think you've ever gotten over him." I opened my mouth to protest, but before I could say anything, Shaw said, "And before you say otherwise, remember I can see through your bullshit. He hurt you. Now you know it wasn't actually his fault. So, Lucas, man. The fuck's the problem?"

What is my problem? Seriously? My head was beginning to throb, and I didn't like the conclusion this conversation was leading to.

"I don't see you running to get in a relationship," I said.

"That's not because I'm a stubborn bastard who's anti."

"Then why?"

Shaw shook his head. "We're not talkin' about me. I'm not the one smashing hearts like the Hulk over here. It'd take a special guy to put up with my shit, and I haven't met any of those."

"What shit? You're the most has-his-shit-together person I know, and that includes Bash."

Shaw's eyes flicked up to mine. "You only think that because I haven't fucked you."

"You think I don't know you're a kinky bastard? You're built like a fucking ox. I'd be disappointed if you weren't."

With a laugh, Shaw continued to work in the color. "Look. You don't have to listen to me. You should, but that's up to you. If you don't go make things right with this guy, you're always gonna wonder, and by the time you get up your nerve, he'll be married to some Sally Sue with five kids and you'll still be fuckin' every new face at Argos."

Closing my eyes, I focused in on the strokes of the pen on my skin, but my mind kept popping up pictures of Jackson like it was showing me flash cards. Maybe Shaw was right, and damn him. My obstinate side wanted nothing more than to sulk in silence, but when had that ever gotten me anywhere?

"I hate you," I said.

"Nah. You hate being wrong."

"I hate that too."

"Mhmm. Where's he staying?"

"The Rosemont," I said, and Shaw's lips twitched.

"Ah." When I looked at him in question, he said, "The bar's decent. And, you know, the beds there aren't bad either. Might be worth a trip."

I shook my head, because of course Shaw was familiar, the dirty bastard. "Why do I get the feeling that if I don't willingly drive myself over there that you'll do it for me?"

The grin he gave me was Cheshire Cat wide. "Now you're thinkin' smart, my man."

FUCK ME, I was doing it. Shaw's little "go get him" speech had my ass driving over the bridge to where I sat now in the Rosemont's guest parking lot looking up at the rising Savannah hotel. Maybe I should've checked for Jackson at my place first, but it was closing in on noon, and I was sure he'd hightailed it out of there the second he woke up. I was taking my chances, assuming he'd be here, and if he wasn't, I'd come back later.

Like a fucking stalker.

After setting the alarm on my truck, I headed toward the revolving doors of the hotel's entry. I hadn't thought much past tracking Jackson down, and I sure as shit had no idea what I would even say if I did see him.

"Sorry about the blow job?" Because I wasn't.

"Hope you don't mind me showing up, because I can't stay away from you." Because that was more than I wanted to admit out loud.

"I was a dick and I apologize." Yeah, that was more like it.

My curses echoed off the revolving doors, and as it spat me out into the ornate lobby, I glanced around to get a hold of my surroundings. The hotel itself was circular, so the lobby was one giant open space with the bar, restaurant, and shops hugging the sides of the curved silhouette.

Right. I'd just ask the check-in desk for his room number and they'd hand it over, easy enough. Unless they didn't. In which case, thank fuck you could see the lobby from the bar.

Fuckin' hell, my palms were sweaty as I headed toward the front desk attendant, and I shoved my hands in my pockets instead of letting my nerves come out for everyone to see.

The woman behind the desk smiled at me. "Checking in, sir?"

"Uh, no. I'm here to see a friend of mine, but I don't remember which room he said he's in, and he's not answering his cell. Would you tell me where I can find him?"

Her smile slipped. "I'm sorry, sir, I can't give out guest information."

Yup. Figures. "I understand. Maybe you could call his room directly to see if he's available to come down?"

She started to respond in the negative, but I couldn't tell you anything specific she said, because out of the corner of my eye, I saw the familiar profile of just the man I was looking for. Through the windows of the hotel's restaurant I could see him, a plate of food in one hand, pulling out his chair with the other.

"Never mind. Thank you for your help," I said, already heading in Jackson's direction. He'd changed into a freshly starched suit, and the thought crossed my mind that maybe I'd be interrupting a business meeting. But he seemed to be dining alone, and even if he wasn't…too bad. I didn't plan to leave until I did what I came to do.

I got halfway across the lobby when Jackson glanced up, mid-bite, and then did a double take. He dropped his fork without even seeming to notice as he watched me close the gap between us, and a nervous flutter of energy, utterly unfamiliar, passed through me.

No turning back now.

CHAPTER 16

JACKSON

I WAS SO stunned when I looked up and saw Lucas staring at me from across the lobby that I dropped my forkful of chicken, sending it clattering down to the plate, turning heads in my direction.

What was he doing here? Lucas was heading straight toward me like he had a purpose. I hadn't expected to see him again, but I couldn't deny the relief that flooded through me as he walked inside the restaurant. Dressed in a loose linen shirt and shorts, and with his black hair lying flat instead of spiky, the way he'd worn it every time I'd seen him, he didn't cut quite as intimidating a figure as the Lucas who owned the nightclub scene. Instead, he seemed…nervous? The thought was laughable. Lucas Sullivan and nervous didn't go together in the same sentence. Never had, never would. But the apprehension on his face was undeniable as he approached my table, his whole body tensed up like he was bracing himself.

As he came to a stop, Lucas cleared his throat and gestured toward the empty seat across from me. "Mind if I join you?"

Did I mind? This was the same guy who'd left me high and dry this morning, and now he wanted to have lunch with me?

Curiosity won out, and I nodded slowly. As Lucas pulled out the chair and sat down, I wiped my mouth with my napkin and watched as he tried to get comfortable, first leaning back with his hands in his lap, then holding on to the armrests, and then finally setting his elbows on the table and interlocking his fingers.

"I'm a bit of an ass," he said.

My eyebrows shot up. *Not where I expected him to go.* But he wasn't wrong, so I nodded. "Yes. You are."

"Selfish…arrogant…"

"That too. I don't know when that changed, but I get it."

His eyes narrowed a fraction. "Do you?"

"Self-preservation. You don't open yourself up, never let anyone get too close. After all, you've got a reputation to live up to, right?" One side of my mouth quirked up as I brought my coffee cup to my lips.

"Looks like you've got me figured out."

"Nah. That's just what you let everyone see. The Lucas I knew is somewhere under all that bravado."

"The Lucas you knew has been gone a long time. I'm afraid he's probably gone for good."

"If that was true, you wouldn't have taken my keys."

Lucas snorted. "That was hardly a good deed after—" He stopped himself, clamping his mouth shut, and I chuckled.

"What? Blow jobs aren't a good deed? Shame."

Lucas jerked his head around to see who'd heard me, and when he faced me again, his voice betrayed his surprise. "Who are you?"

"Still the proper kid you knew; don't worry. Maybe a little frayed around the edges now."

"You always did look good when you let go and didn't give a fuck," he said, a smile curving his lips.

"I suppose I had you to thank for that back then."

"That's me. Always the bad influence."

"Don't do that."

"Do what?"

"Pretend like you weren't the only good thing in my life back then."

That seemed to stun Lucas, because he reared back and stared at me, and I stared right back. A thousand words were said in those moments of silence, and most of them began with, "I'm sorry." All of the anger and hurt and resentment washed away as we sat there making up for our offenses without saying a word.

"I know," I said finally. It had taken a lot for Lucas to show up here in the first place, and that alone was bigger than any "I'm sorry" he could say, and I knew he didn't want to hear an apology from me either. Actions spoke louder than words, after all.

Lucas nodded, and then caught the attention of a passing waiter to order a water. When it came a couple of minutes later, he drained more than half the glass before he spoke again. "Can I ask what brought you here?"

Straight to the point. "We're looking to acquire a tech company that's based here."

"We, as in your father's company," he said. "I'm assuming that's who you work for."

"Yes."

"And once you acquire this business…then you'll go back?" he asked, and when I frowned, Lucas shook his head. "Never mind. Don't answer that."

He knew as well as I did my days in South Haven were numbered, and speaking it out loud when I'd just gotten here seemed somehow like a slap in his face. Wanting to change the subject, I nodded at the purple lines that peeked out from beneath the sleeve of his shirt. "Been coloring?"

Lucas looked down and stretched out his arm, and then I could see the hint of a freshly drawn outline of flowers and what looked like an artistic rendition of his gram that hadn't been there last night. "Just a little addition coming soon."

"Looks like it'll be painful."

He laughed. "You're supposed to say it looks hot."

"Hard to tell with it covered under your sleeve like that, but I'm sure it'll look as good as the others I remember."

With an exaggerated eye roll, Lucas threw his hands up. "Jesus, Jackson, if you wanted me to take my shirt off, you only have to ask nicely."

And just like that, the awkward tension between us faded as a glimpse of the man I once knew came through. The one who was confident without being arrogant. Kind when there wasn't steel armor to get through. I liked this guy. Missed him, even.

"Maybe later. You naked in a public place might cause mass hysteria, and then I'd never get time with you."

"And you'd like...*time* with me?" A slow, creeping smile lifted his lips as he caught my drift, and the fact that I'd been the first to admit wanting to continue to see Lucas had me squirming in my seat.

"I mean, I'd like to...you know...get to know you again," I said. "Catch up. For whatever time we have..." *While I'm here* was the unspoken rest of the sentence, but he already knew that.

"Huh." Lucas tapped his lips, as if he was debating with himself whether to make the effort, and I found myself holding my breath as I waited the drawn-out seconds for his answer. "Well, I guess it would be considered rude not to take in an outsider who's come all this way."

I nodded. "Terribly rude."

"Mhmm." He drummed his fingers along the arm of his chair. "So. You busy now?"

CHAPTER 17

JACKSON

"YOU'VE GOTTA BE kidding me," I said, pulling my shades down so I could get a clear view of exactly where Lucas had taken me.

Lucas shut off the engine of his truck and looked over at me. "What?"

"Of all the places we could go and things we could do…" I shook my head. "This is not where I thought we'd spend the day."

Lucas glanced at the brick facade of the South Haven All-boys Academy and shrugged. "Thought you could use a bit of nostalgia."

"I'm good, thanks. Maybe we could hit the beach instead?"

"Sure. Later." Lucas got out of the truck and slammed the door behind him as I groaned. I hadn't set foot in my old stomping grounds since I'd left there before graduation, and it wasn't on my list of priorities. Not because I had bad memories of my time there, but who ever wanted to return to high school?

Lucas shielded the sun from his face as he looked back at me and inclined his head toward the building, a clear indication that I needed to get my ass out of the truck.

Yeah, yeah, I'm coming. Though it wouldn't have been on my top twenty choices of things to do, I didn't regret coming with, even if my curiosity was piqued. It was even more so as Lucas bypassed the main doors and walked through the perfectly trimmed front lawn toward the back of the school. Everything was in such pristine condition, you couldn't even tell a storm had come through.

That's what money buys you. A perfect illusion.

"This way," Lucas said, and I glanced around to see if anyone was noticing the creepers hanging around, but the campus was quiet.

"What are we doing here? Breaking and entering?" I asked, as I followed Lucas around the side of the main building to a back door. His keys jangled as he picked a key fob out from the assortment on the ring, and then he scanned it on the pad by the door. There was a loud click and flashing green light, and Lucas winked at me.

"No need for any breaking," he said, opening the door wide for me to pass through first. A rush of cold air greeted us, and as my eyes adjusted, I could see that we were in the electives hallway, the one I'd spent my time doing public speaking and business management while my friends made art and played instruments.

"Ahh, just stealing, then. Whose key was that?"

"It's mine."

I snorted. "Yeah, and I came to South Haven for the mountain view."

"Don't believe me?" He raised an eyebrow. "You should know Principal Stewart gave it to me personally."

"Was he intoxicated at the time?"

"It's entirely possible." Lucas led us down the empty hall to the first door on the right, and then he procured another key and unlocked it.

"So…you're a teacher in your spare time?"

"God, no." He flipped on the light inside, and it became instantly clear he'd been telling the truth about the keys being his. The room had the same singed metal smell his shop did, and there were at least twenty finished sculptures lined along a table pushed up against one long wall. "I was asked to do a seminar on metal sculpture for the shop class. I guess Principal Stewart figured having an alum might inspire the students…and wiggle loose a few dollars from some of the parents." Lucas grabbed a notepad and pen from the desk in front of a whiteboard and headed over to the sculptures. "Classes just ended, so I've got to get these scored and choose a winner." With steady hands, he held up the first object on the table, a small octopus replica, admiring the long legs that had propped it up a good six or so inches.

"What do they win?" I asked.

"Me."

"What?"

Lucas chuckled and carefully set the octopus down. "A summer apprenticeship with me."

"Oh. Right." *Head out of the gutter, Jackson.* "That's big of you to take the time to help someone out. Pay it forward."

He continued to move down the line, studying each design with keen eyes. "Nah, it's entirely selfish. I can't create as fast as the demand lately, so I've been trying to find someone with a bit of a knack for this kind of thing to join my business. Who better than impressionable high school students?"

"You're right, that is selfish."

Lucas smirked. "Unfortunately, as with most things, the one I want the most is…unavailable. This one," he said, picking up a 3D profile of a man's face made of stainless steel ribbons that far and away stood out as the most unique and technically challenging piece of the bunch. "The kid who did this? Talented little motherfucker. And he's completely out of the question."

I came to stand beside him to admire the piece. "Why? Bad attitude?"

"Football scholarship. He's *that* guy, you know the one. The all-American quarterback with the charming smile and the— Oh, wait. He's a mini you."

"Very funny."

"Nah, he's a little rougher around the edges than you were, though you both seem to share parental…challenges." He set the sculpture down and moved to the next. "Speaking of which, who's the poor bastard losing his company that you came all the way down here for?"

"Well, it's not a done deal yet, so I shouldn't say."

"Shouldn't? Or won't?"

"Both?"

"Ah. Well, this *is* the *getting to know you* part you said you wanted, so…"

He was right. It wasn't like our takeover would be a secret for much longer, and I didn't want to hide anything anymore from Lucas, not when I wanted him to open up to me too. So I said, "I'd appreciate the discretion until things are finalized, but I'm here for AnaVoge."

Lucas's head jerked up and surprise lit his face.

"You've heard of it, then."

"Uh, yeah," he said, rubbing his jaw. "I mean…who hasn't around these parts, right? I didn't realize it was on the market."

"It's not. Not officially, anyway, but I plan to make an enticing offer they can't refuse."

The line between Lucas's brows deepened. "Because that's what you do, right? You use that charming smile and appeal to *entice* others so that they can't say no to you. And I'm assuming you have a pretty high success rate." When I didn't say anything, he tsked. "Doesn't quite seem fair."

"It's business."

"Granted, I'm not a corporate kinda guy, but coming down here to push a business into selling to you when there's not a For Sale sign in their front yard seems a little fucked."

"You seem mad all of a sudden—"

"What if I asked you to leave them alone? AnaVoge. Would you do it?"

I searched his eyes, trying to understand why he'd ask me to do that and why he even cared. "No, you know I can't do that. And I wouldn't want to."

Lucas's expression hardened. "Can't and won't because you're just the *messenger*. The one who does the dirty work for someone else." When I blinked, confused at the vitriol in his words, he pinched the bridge of his nose and blew out a breath. "Sorry. I'm sorry. It's none of my business."

"You're right. It's not."

Lucas bit his lip and nodded just as the sound of the bell indicating class change sounded from the speakers overheard.

A scatter of loud footsteps and voices chattering into the hallway overtook the tension that had cropped up again between us, and I was almost grateful when the door flew open and two students barged inside.

"Yo, Mr. Sullivan," the blond one said as he got a good look at Lucas's casual attire. "Beachin' it already without us? Bonfire's not till tonight."

"Bonfire?" I said. "You guys still do those?" As soon as the words were out of my mouth, the memory of what happened the night of our senior bonfire hit and my cheeks flamed. We hadn't exactly made it there…

The blond eyed me strangely. "It's a tradition. Who the hell are you?"

"Ross, I'm positive your parents taught you to respect your elders, especially an alum who's giving me a hand in judging your final projects." Lucas nodded in my direction. "Say hello to Jackson Davenport."

"Jackson Davenport?" Ross said, squinting at me. "Dude, you're one of the Davenport Worldwide guys, right?"

I nodded. If there was one thing that remained true, it was that all rich kids grew up knowing the lineage and history of all their rich peers, both past and present. This kid was no exception.

"Damn, that's cool. My dad says you guys are cutthroat, but all the biggest CEOs are." Ross looked back at Lucas. "You picked my piece, right? Come on, please. I'm not ready to go back to Minnesota yet."

"You did have an interesting take on the female form, but will it be enough?" Lucas pretended to lock his lips and throw away the key.

"Aw, man," Ross said. "Justin can't win everything. He won't even be able to do the apprenticeship, so you should pick someone else. Someone who'll tell jokes all day and is badass company." He elbowed his friend, and they laughed as some secret left unsaid passed between them.

"If you find such a person, do let me know so I can stop wasting my time with this"—Lucas picked up a garbled mess of steel and flipped it over—"melting blob, is it?" Ross's friend stopped laughing, and Lucas smiled at him. "I feel the words 'nice effort' will be a bit too strong in this case, Mr. Klapeer."

That only made Ross laugh harder, the sound echoing in the large room as his friend's face went crimson. The noise was loud enough to catch the attention of his peers, because several stuck their heads inside, and when they saw Lucas, grins spread across their faces and they walked in, greeting him with unmasked enthusiasm. It was clear he was well liked, and Lucas's sarcasm seemed to be a perfect match for smartass teenagers.

I stood back as they circled Lucas, pointing out their pieces, asking him questions, joking around. It was strange to think that only a few years ago that had been us, and now here we were. For someone with so many walls around him, Lucas certainly didn't have a problem letting them down with his students, and that only made me more determined to get this side of him when we were alone. Before we'd been interrupted, you could've cut the tension in the air with a knife, and I didn't want to spend what little time we had together fighting.

Lucas didn't like my line of work—fine. He didn't have to. Whether his dislike stemmed more from my father, who wasn't exactly on my good list either at the moment, or whether it was because Lucas didn't approve of our methods, I wasn't sure, and it didn't really matter. Hell, I wasn't even sure I *liked* my job when it came down to it, but it was the only thing I knew, and I was damn good at it. Once I got back home and possibly confronted my father about his hand in screwing up my life, well, then I'd have to go from there. But for now, until Thursday, my career was the last thing on my mind.

Another bell sounded, this time a warning bell that you had two minutes to be in your seat, and the boys gave

Lucas a quick wave before darting back out into the hallway.

"You're a natural with them," I said, leaning against the counter as Lucas went back to grading the designs.

"Eh, they're pains in my ass," he replied, but he was smiling when he said it.

"Not unlike someone I know."

"You mean used to know. Unless you're implying I'm still a pain in your ass."

Oh, all the implications with that sentence. And because I knew it'd get a reaction, I grinned and said, "Depends. Did you want to be?"

Just as I thought, Lucas fumbled with the sculpture in his hands, cursing as he set it upright and then pinned me with those intense eyes. "That sounds an awful lot like an invitation."

Shrugging, I turned my attention back to the projects at hand. "Looks like you've got a tough decision. Who's it gonna be?"

"Uh uh. You don't get to change the subject." Lucas stalked toward me, and a familiar thrill of anticipation shot through my body, the kind that always happened when he was near. His solid chest grazed my arm, daring me to move away, but I wasn't budging, not even when his breath tickled my neck. "There something you want, Jackson?"

Two could play that game. I'd already seen what effect I had on Lucas, so if he wanted to knock me off balance, I could try to do the same. Turning my head toward him, I saw just how close he was, and I twisted my lips. "Actually…there is something I want. Badly."

Lucas's head moved toward mine a fraction. "Oh yeah? Tell me. Or show me, if you prefer. I'm an equal opportunist."

"Mmm. I want"—I leaned in close, like I was going for his lips, and then, at the last second, brushed the skin of his cheek instead—"to get wet." I heard Lucas's soft intake of breath and let that little piece of info soak in for a second before adding, "At the beach."

Lucas groaned and pushed me away as I laughed. "Fucking tease," he muttered.

"What was that?"

He plastered a fake smile on his face. "I said do you like any of these?"

"Ahh." I scanned the long row of designs, and when my eye caught on a rising flame made of twisted metal, I pointed at it. "That one."

"Hmm. Not a bad second choice." Lucas made a note on the pad, flipped it shut, and then turned to face me with his arms crossed. "So."

I mimicked his pose. "So."

"Since you seem to have an affinity for flames, care to attend a bonfire this evening? If I recall correctly—and I do—we were a little too…*preoccupied*, and missed ours." A devilish gleam lit Lucas's eyes. It was the night I'd decided to give myself over to the man staring at me now, and it had been the first *and* the last time.

Jesus, that was the last thing I needed to think about

right now. Especially while in such close proximity to Lucas and alone, not to mention mere steps from his old dorm room. So, yeah, maybe a bonfire surrounded by others was a smart idea.

"Sure," I said, but my voice was too husky, and I had to clear my throat. "I think a bonfire sounds great."

A slow smile spread across his face. "Good. Maybe this time we'll actually make it and see all that we missed."

"AW, COME ON, Mr. Sullivan. Just one game."

I rummaged through one of the coolers near the fire pit and pulled out a couple of sodas, shaking the ice off them before handing one to Jackson. "Nope."

Nathan crossed his arms and smirked at his classmates before facing me again. "It's not like you're gonna break a hip or something. Or are you that old?"

I narrowed my eyes at the little shit trying to taunt me and Jackson into a game of beach football. "You haven't graduated *yet*, Nathan. I'd keep the smartass comments to yourself before I feel the need to pull some strings. You like Burger Barn, don't you?"

Oohs and laughs rang out among his friends, and I had to admit, the image of Nathan flipping burgers made my lips twitch. Kid needed someone to knock him off his damn high horse.

"Tell you what," Nathan said. "We'll even go touch."

My eyes shot over to Jackson, who was biting back a grin. Yeah, I'd bet these little fuckers wanted to touch.

"Or tackle works too, if you're not worried about sand burns and breaking bones," he continued.

I took Jackson's soda before he could pop the top, and tossed them back in the cooler. "We kick off and I get to choose my team."

"We usually flip a coin for—" Nathan stopped short when I crossed my arms. "Yeah, okay, fine."

"Good." He threw me the football, and I handed it to Jackson. "Care to be my quarterback?"

Jackson's eyes dilated at my suggestive tone, and after a moment he gave a nod. "Love to."

I picked out the guys I wanted for my team, making sure to pad it out so I wasn't left with much to do. Not that I couldn't play, but I hadn't been much of a sports guy growing up. I did, however, have a secret weapon—Jackson. He'd wipe the beach with their asses singlehandedly, so I was feeling pretty confident, even if it had been a few years since he'd been on the field.

It was skins versus shirts, and the other team lost their shirts, since there was no way I'd be able to focus if Jackson took his off. And though I was pretty sure most of the guys playing didn't bat for my team, I didn't want them looking his way either. Might inspire a few ideas, and I'd hate to have to break someone's face.

One of the skins kicked off, sending the football flying high in our direction. Jackson caught it with ease, and then, in an explosive burst of power and strength, he shot forward toward the opposing team, and I stopped what I was doing to watch. Damn, the way he dodged past each set of outstretched hands was nothing short of impressive, his long legs eating up the sand, and before I knew it, he'd crossed the line drawn in the sand that indicated the end zone.

"Touchdown shirts," called our official referee, a boy I didn't recognize who sported a cast on his right arm.

"Holy shit, how's that fair?" Nathan cried out, his face a perfect picture of shock that had me snickering.

"You wanted us to play," I said.

"Play, not demolish."

"Guess you'd better step up your game, then. Unless, of course, you've changed your mind and wish to forfeit?"

Nathan glared hard, stubborn thing, and then grumbled, "We'll play."

"You're evil, you know that, right?" Jackson said from behind me, his hand landing on my shoulder as the other team huddled together to come up with a game plan.

"I do. I just wish we'd placed bets now."

"Hmm. We still could…"

"Hey, genius—we're on the same team."

Jackson tossed the ball high up in the air and caught it with one hand. "Maybe just a little wager between us, then."

That caught my attention. "Tell me more."

"We can bet on the number of touchdowns. Whoever's closest wins. And as for *what* they win, that can be left up to the victor."

Now that sounded dangerous, which also meant it was something I needed to win. "Anything the winner wants?"

Jackson lifted his chin with an air of confidence that told me he wasn't planning on losing. "Anything goes."

The low chuckle that came out of me then sounded almost evil even to my ears, and I held out my hand. "Deal. Five-nothing, us."

"You don't think much of me, do you?" Jackson teased. "I say ten-nothing, us. Deal." His shake was firm, and just before he let go, he squeezed my fingers, and that small action wasn't lost on me. Then Jackson winked and went to take his place on defense so the other team could attempt to get past us.

Good luck, boys, I thought, as one of our guys kicked off. Nathan caught the ball and started to run toward us, but Jackson had him in his sights. Nathan dodged right, then left, attempting to fake him out, but Jackson didn't take the bait. His hands came out to strike him in the arm, quick as a viper, and Nathan's shoulders sagged in defeat as he came to a stop. On and on it went, Jackson a one-man team with the rest of us as backup as he took away every attempt the other team made to score.

"Touchdown! That's five for shirts, less than nada for skins," the ref said, as Jackson scored yet again.

"Dude, I'm ready for a fucking drink," one of the skins muttered, wiping the sweat from his brow. Nathan looked over at the rest of his team, out of breath and utterly defeated, and then tossed the ball at me. "All right, we're out."

"Out?" I repeated. "Already?"

"Yeah, yeah." Nathan rolled his eyes, and after putting their shirts back on, he and the losing team stalked off to where the rest of their classmates were hanging out around the fire pit.

"Good game," Jackson called out after them, which was met with a grumble of "who invited that guy" and "fucking showoff." Jackson turned to me with a huge grin on his face, and I laughed.

"You look awfully proud of yourself for beating a few pipsqueak high schoolers," I said.

"It's been years since I've done that." He popped open the can of soda I handed him and guzzled half of it down before adding, "And *you're welcome*."

"I'd rather thank you for the hot show you put on. I think handling that ball so well might've converted a few of those guys."

"Did I really just hear a compliment about my ball handling from you? Damn," he said, and took another swig, clearly amused at my word choice.

Jesus, now all I could think about was the way those large hands of his could handle even more of me, including the erection threatening to tent my shorts. A hard-on was the last thing I needed out here with a bunch of high schoolers and staff, so I quickly wheeled around and headed up to one of the sand dunes to give us a bit of privacy—and to give my dick a chance to *down, boy*.

As I toed off my shoes, Jackson did the same, and then he sat down next to me and dug his feet deep into the soft white sand. I chanced a look at him, and my cock shifted at the drop of sweat that had fallen down to his jaw. It lingered there, on the precipice, for a moment, and then began a slow slide down the length of his neck. I wet my bottom lip, wanting to lean over and lick the drop away. He'd taste salty on my tongue, and it would only ignite the hunger stirring in the pit of my stomach.

Forcing my eyes away, I took a deep lungful of air and focused on the small waves lapping at the shore. Having Jackson so close made it hard to get my body under control. I needed to remind myself that he wasn't some no-name I wouldn't remember tomorrow. He wasn't a fling. He was fatal. The damage he could do to me if I let him would be irreparable, so I didn't need to think about the way he looked at me, with some misguided sense of hope, and I sure as fuck didn't need to think about the muscular thighs he was currently stretching out beside me.

Goddammit, his body was a work of art, and I knew exactly what I'd do with it if he let me. Correction—if I let myself. *Which I won't*, I thought, as my gaze locked on the substantial bulge behind his jeans. *Really*.

"Have you ever thought about leaving?" Jackson asked out of the blue.

"Leaving…South Haven, you mean? No."

"Really? Not even when…"

"Gram died?" I filled in. "You'd think so. I've traveled, but nowhere feels like home. Well, I guess Washington does a bit, but I don't have the memories there that I do here. And we sold my parents' house, so…nowhere I'd rather go."

Jackson nodded. "I always liked it here. Being near a beach, the small-town feel. I can see why you'd stay."

Why didn't you? I wanted to ask, but the answer to that was redundant.

Jackson knew it too because he cleared his throat. "Back in Connecticut, the winters are brutal. Sixteen inches in twenty-four hours last year. I would've prayed for a beach day then."

"Damn. I'm not usually one to complain about inches, but—" Jackson pushed me over before I could finish, and I let out a loud bark of laughter.

"You'd complain when your balls shriveled up and fell off from hypofuckingthermia."

"Nah, I'd just find a hot body to make sure that didn't happen," I said before I could stop the words from coming out, and then I wanted to kick my own ass. *For fuck's sake, Sullivan, shut the hell up and don't talk about all the guys you'd fuck —including the one you can't.* "I've never, uh, seen that much snow."

"You'll have to come visit. I'll take you tubing at Powder Ridge." He was keeping the conversation light, not acknowledging my foot-in-mouth disease, and not delving into anything either of us would object to. It was enough to distract my body from noticing his…for the moment.

I mimicked his pose and kicked my legs out, crossing them at the ankles. I'd worn shorts, and more than half my legs were covered in sand. "You'd just like to kick my ass in a snowball fight."

"Damn right I'd love to do that. And you'd deserve it."

"No one would say I didn't." A roar of laughter from over by the fire pit sounded, and I looked over to see a new addition to the crowd. "See that kid over there?" I pointed at a tall, dark-skinned mountain of muscle laughing with a couple of guys as they stood in front of the fire roasting marshmallows.

"Kid?" Jackson shook his head. "I don't see a kid; I see a behemoth."

I chuckled. "Now you know why I called him a mini you. Fucking arms as big as the Hulk."

"Ah. So he's the football star-slash-secret artist."

"That's the one. Justin. His father played for the Falcons, so that kid's primed for the NFL."

"And that would be a bad thing?"

"A good ass in tight pants is never a bad thing."

"Of course," Jackson said, his mouth curving up on one side. "Where was he earlier when the other team needed him?"

"Told you. Parental challenges."

"Huh." Jackson fell silent as we watched them sandwich their marshmallows between chocolate and graham crackers. "Has he ever talked to you about it? Having to choose between sports or art?"

"Like that matters with you richies. You don't get to choose, remember?"

"*Us* richies?" Jackson said, raising a brow. "Not including yourself in that statement, even though your gram owned one of the biggest houses on the island, which is now yours…" He took a swig of his drink. "Huh. Makes sense."

"My parents weren't rich. Dad left South Haven to make it on his own terms, and that's only 'cause Gram didn't try to control his life. *Unlike* you richies."

"Trying to insult me?"

"It's a statement of fact. My own observation. If you take offense, then that means you have your own issues with it."

Jackson put down his soda and faced me. "Can we not talk about the shit that pisses us off?"

"Because that would be a little too much realism for you, huh, Jax?"

He tensed. "Don't call me that."

"Why not? Everyone else did."

"I don't like it."

"But—"

"Not. You." He practically growled those two words, and I had to admit, his take-no-shit tone had my cock taking notice once again. *Just perfect.*

"Fine. *Jackson*," I said, trying not to notice how his shoulders relaxed a little at that.

"Lucas…" He stared out at the ocean. "I don't wanna fight with you."

"Yeah." *I don't want to fight with you, either. Unless it's in bed. Ah, hell, Sullivan, come* on.

"What did you say?" he asked.

"Uh…" Surely my brain-to-mouth function hadn't short-circuited on me now. "Fuck. I said that out loud, didn't I?"

Jackson let out a surprised laugh and nodded.

"Not like the semi I've been sporting since you came around doesn't tip me off."

"Feel free to do that more," Jackson said, and my eyes went wide. "I mean say what's on your mind." He laughed. "It'd be nice to know what you're thinking."

"I tell you."

"The censored version. You used to tell me everything. Even the *in bed* thoughts." He gave me a playful nudge.

"That wouldn't do either of us any good. Trust me."

"I do trust you." Four simple words, said with complete and utter sincerity, and not one part of me doubted them to be the truth. It made me wonder…*why me?* This beautiful, strait-laced boy could've had anyone, and yet he'd gravitated toward the loner, the new kid who'd just lost his family. He'd befriended me, no questions asked, and then he'd made me fall in love with him.

Even sitting here now, it felt like no time at all had passed, like we'd just snuck out of the academy for a few beers at the beach. Back then, Jackson hadn't even seen it coming. He thought I was just his best friend, someone he could confide in and spend time with, and I let him believe that for a while. For me, I'd known the first second I saw

him that I would never have merely a friendship with
Jackson Davenport. It was a knowledge that weighed heav-
ily, until one day when I couldn't take it anymore. It had
been Gram's birthday and I was determined to show up
with the gift I'd made. After failing to stop me from
sneaking out, Jackson followed me into the woods that
separated Gram's house and the academy, and it was his
constantly voiced worry over getting caught that flipped
the switch. That was when I'd had enough of holding back
with him.

Without warning, I'd pushed Jackson up against a tree
and had my lips on his before he could protest. And then I
had the shock of my life when he kissed me back. I thought
he'd push me away, hit me, tell me we couldn't be friends
anymore. Instead, the next night he kissed me again, on
the beach not far from where we sat now. Hidden by one
of the sand dunes, Jackson had been the one to initiate
things that night, and we'd gone a helluva lot further than
just kissing.

My dick swelled as I remembered the first time he
touched me, the way his hands shook as they unzipped my
pants, but his eyes had remained steady and sure on mine.
Christ, calm the fuck down.

"Do you remember?" Jackson said softly, his gaze
locked on the same spot mine was, as if he were reliving
the memory too.

"Yes."

"That…was a good night."

Every night with you was a good night. Every fucking day, too.

"It was. Lucas…I—"

An explosion of light burst into the sky overhead suddenly, startling the shit out of us, and we looked up to see fireworks shooting off from the academy's campus to celebrate the end of term. Boisterous laughter and voices carried over from the bonfire as the night lit up in streaks of every color.

Jackson gave me a small smile as he lay back onto the sand to watch, and I did the same, similarly grateful and annoyed for the interruption in conversation. *What had he been about to say?*

I half watched the pyrotechnics above us, half watched Jackson, wondering how in the span of hours he could have me reverting to the Lucas whose entire life had revolved around him. If his father hadn't intervened, would that still be who I was? Would I still be a happily lovesick fool over him, or would one of us have gotten tired of the other and wanted to play the field? Maybe it was a good thing he'd left when he did if I would've gotten heart-smashed either way. Or maybe I'd just grown cynical and jaded in our time apart.

God, there'd been so many guys. More than I could fucking count, and right now I couldn't remember a good goddamn one of them. But I could remember the exact sounds Jackson had made when I'd kissed him in the woods, and I could still see the mussed-up sex hair he'd sported as he left my dorm the last time I saw him. That had been the memory ingrained behind my eyes every night I fell asleep…until he'd shown up at Argos.

Loud whoops and claps sounded as the fireworks came to an end in a stunning display of color, capturing my attention again, and when they were over, Jackson blurted out, "I miss you." Jerking my head in his direction, I saw him swallow, his eyes still firmly locked on the dissipating smoke overhead. "I miss my best friend."

And just like that, I knew. I would've gone to the ends of the earth for that man, and the scariest thing about that realization was the fear that I still would.

"I always felt so damn alone, and then I met you and I wasn't anymore. It was like you were always supposed to be there. Like I'd always known you. And when that was taken away from me…" Jackson let out a heavy exhale. "I don't have anyone. Not to talk to, not to go play touch football with on a beach. I work. And I have what would be considered friends, people I see at work functions, but they don't know anything about me, not really. It's like… God, it's like I don't feel right in my skin. You know? I don't feel like me. Does that even make sense?" He let out another sigh, and his hand came up to where his eyes were shut. "It doesn't make any sense. And I don't know why I'm saying all this, and you probably don't care, but I just… It meant something to me. Our friendship. You in my life. It meant everything. And I miss you every goddamn day, Lucas."

I couldn't breathe as a hot sting of tears pricked my eyes and my chest grew heavy. Without a word, I reached for his hand, needing to reassure him I'd felt the same but unable to find any words—a fucking rarity if there ever was one. I laced my fingers through his and had the fleeting thought that mine were rough and callused, but if that bothered him, he didn't show it. His strong hand squeezed mine, answering what I couldn't say.

We lay there in comfortable silence, still linked as the clouds passed and the stars came out to play. Eventually, I broke the ice, pointing out my favorite constellation, Ursa Major, and then telling the story behind a few others when Jackson admitted he wasn't familiar with them. He asked about my sculptures, how I'd built up my metalworking business, and there was a genuine curiosity behind his questions. He seemed to have developed an appreciation for art, something I could've guessed by the piece still sitting in my shop. Then I told him how I'd found his address—stealing our teacher's grade book—and that made him laugh.

We shared stories of the things we'd done that filled in some of the gaps from our time apart—minus the obvious man-whoring on my part—and since talking about his job or family life were sticking points, and therefore off-limits, Jackson chatted instead about the places he'd visited. He'd been all over North America, across Europe and to Asia, seemingly on his own. He told me about visiting the Louvre in Paris, eating sushi in Japan, hiking up the Great Wall, and I felt a sting of jealousy that I hadn't been there to experience those firsts with him.

And while his travels sounded amazing, I got the feeling there was something else Jackson wasn't telling me. I could sense a weight on his shoulders, and whatever the cause was, he wasn't saying. I didn't want to push for that information, not now, and especially not when it might be something I didn't want to hear. I was content for the first time in a long time just to be there, lying with him under the same sky with the summer breeze blowing and the sound of the waves falling—even if that peaceful interlude was a short-lived illusion. No matter the feelings he stirred up, the fact was Jackson would leave again soon, but at least this time I knew it was coming.

Jackson's thumb brushed across my skin where we were still connected. "Don't you care if anyone sees you?"

"Sees me do what?"

"You know. Be here. With a guy."

For some reason, that made me chuckle. It was easy to forget how almost innocent Jackson was when he looked the way he did. How he came from a completely different world than I did, and how he probably hadn't been around anyone comfortable with their sexuality in years.

"I'm pretty sure it's not a secret," I said. "I've seen some of those kids sneak into the clubs, and if they've done that, they know enough about me. Word gets around, remember?"

"Oh, I remember. But they don't seem to care."

I knew what he was thinking. Back when we were in school, it seemed like every last one of them were judgmental pricks, and at least one of them had tipped off Jackson's father, unless it was a teacher. "Things are different now. I'm sure there are still a few assholes in the bunch who fuck with their peers, but what are they gonna say to me?"

"'Mr. Sullivan's a homo'?"

Snorting, I shook my head. "I'd drown them in the ocean first. Or maybe throw 'em in the fire with the fuckin' marshmallows."

Jackson looked over at me and smiled. "You've never cared what anyone thought of you. I've always admired that."

"That's not true. I cared what Gram thought." I had to force the next words out. "And you."

Though that didn't seem to surprise him, Jackson stayed quiet for a while, like he was debating with himself. And then he asked, "Why me?"

The same damn question I'd asked myself in regard to him, only this time words carried a weight to them, because he wasn't just asking me why I'd respected what he thought about me. He was asking a hell of a lot more than that, and I held back all the reasons he wanted me to say. That he was the only one back then who hadn't judged me, the sad new kid with a chip on his shoulder. Who'd seen the real me and had cared enough to. How to tell him that he'd felt like home since the first time I'd sat next to him in biochem and he'd smiled at me, and when he'd offered me a seat at his lunch table later that day, he'd inadvertently offered me so much more than that.

But I didn't say any of those things, because if I did, he'd see right through me and realize I'd never gotten over him. And that was a truth I wasn't ready to face until he left again. So I said, "I don't know," and tried not to notice when his smile wavered at my non-answer.

Jackson's gaze flitted away, over to where the fire had long been snuffed out, and he sat up. "Shit, what time is it?"

"Late."

"I didn't even know they'd all left," Jackson said, getting to his feet and wiping the sand off his jeans.

Sure enough, the part of the beach that had been packed with students what felt like only minutes ago was now empty, which meant they'd had to go back to the academy for mandatory curfew. It also meant several hours had passed as Jackson and I tuned out the world.

I stood and looked up and down the beach, and when I didn't spot another living soul, I said, "Need to go, or up for something else?"

"What do you have in mind?"

"I was thinking a midnight swim would be nice."

"A swim, huh?" Jackson looked down at his clothes and then back up at me.

"You can wear those. Or nothing at all…" I shrugged and began to walk backward to the ocean.

"What are you doing, Lucas?"

"Gotta get the sand off."

"Bullshit." Jackson's hands were low on his hips as he watched me undo the top button on my shirt. I could've easily whipped it over my head in one go, but I happened to like Jackson's eyes on me, and since teasing him had been one of my favorite pastimes, I took my time. With each button I undid, his stare grew heated.

"You gonna join me or keep staring?"

"Keep staring."

I laughed as I finished off the buttons and let the shirt fall down my arms, dropping to the sand. Then I flicked open the button of my shorts. "Don't be a chickenshit, Davenport."

"Peer pressure. Exactly what you tell those kids not to fall for."

And aren't those the magic words…

"Oh, come on, Jackson," I dared, unzipping my shorts and shoving them down my hips. "Fall for me."

CHAPTER 19
JACKSON

F ALL FOR ME…
Those words coming from Lucas's mouth as he stripped for me right there on the beach were like a slingshot to the heart. It didn't help when he kicked his shorts off, leaving him in nothing but a pair of boxer briefs that clung to the thick bulge between his hard thighs. Every inch I could see now was nothing but tanned, hard lines of muscle, with tattoos covering his entire right shoulder, creeping across his chest and down his arm. My pulse jumped, and suddenly it was too hot to stay fully clothed.

Yeah, I didn't need to fall for the guy again. Something told me I already had.

Lucas backed up another couple of steps, inching closer to the water. "You can't say no. I won the friendly little wager from earlier, so I'm cashing in. You said anything goes. This is my *anything*."

"You only won because the other team gave up."

"Tough shit. A bet's a bet."

Cheater. I wasn't ever one to back down from a bet, but losing my clothes after my confession earlier and diving into the ocean alone with Lucas? That was asking for trouble. But... *Ah, fuck it.* Maybe a little trouble was what I needed in my life.

I pulled my shirt over my head and tossed it on the sand before I could think better of it, just as Lucas's feet hit the edge of the water. With his gaze roving over my naked torso, Lucas's lips parted, and then a slow smile crept across his face.

Oh yeah. He likes this. Any doubt I had about whether Lucas's attraction to me had diminished in the time we'd spent apart dissipated as he licked his lips, and then his eyes dropped to where my fingers rested on the button of my jeans, as if to urge me on. I complied by unbuttoning and slowly unzipping, drawing out the rest of Lucas's patience.

"Get in the fucking water, Davenport," he said, his voice hoarse, and I noticed the way he quickly backed up into the ocean to hide his growing arousal. And dammit, that didn't do anything to help my own, and I had to reach down and adjust myself before I dared to kick off my pants.

Nerves hit me full force as Lucas watched me with hungry eyes on my way toward the water. Fuck, it wasn't like I had anything to be embarrassed about. He already knew how I'd felt about him before, and if either of us had thought that was a fluke, our kiss—not to mention the blow job—last night would've put those doubts to rest.

Yeah, I was attracted to the guy. So much so I was willing to wade into the Atlantic Ocean toward a man who had the ability to change my life in ways I couldn't think about right now, even if he only saw my being in town as a fun fling. So I wouldn't think, not tonight. Because right now, no one else was around, not on the beach, not in the ocean, and sure as hell not in my head.

The water was warm and inviting as it lapped at my ankles, and the farther I walked in, the more Lucas swam backward, until the water was at his chest.

"Come here," he said, crooking his finger at me, and I responded to his request by submerging myself underwater. I swam in his direction, giving a couple of strong kicks before I surfaced.

Even though the water was mild, it cooled me off just enough, and as I ran my hand over my face and through my wet hair, I said, "Peer pressure and bets work. I'm here. You happy now?"

One of Lucas's legs hooked behind mine, knocking me off balance and jerking me forward, and then his hands were on my waist and his lips grazed my jaw.

"Yes," he said, his mouth moving lightly along my skin, and just when I thought he'd kiss me, Lucas pushed me completely underwater.

As I resurfaced to the sound of Lucas's laughter, I wiped the water from my eyes and lunged for the shady fucker, but he jerked away, splashing up a spray of water in my direction.

"You're gonna pay for that," I said, growling as I reached for him again.

Lucas's grin was wide as he darted away. "I fucking hope so. Better make it worth my while."

My cock kicked behind the thin material of my boxer briefs, my thoughts immediately straying to what I wanted to do once I got my hands on him. I ducked back under the water and wrapped my arms around Lucas's legs before he had the chance to move away. He struggled against me as I pulled him under, his hands pushing against my shoulders, but as I lifted my head to swim back up, my face brushed against his erection and Lucas went rigid. Taking advantage of his momentary surprise, I used my hold on him to shove him down as I propelled myself up and broke through the surface.

Come and get me.

A few seconds later, he roared to the surface, and I didn't even bother trying to get away. "Looks like someone's asking for it," Lucas said, as he roughly grabbed my waist again, threading his other hand through the back of my hair. "Is this what you wanted?"

"Pretty sure I just wanted you wet."

Lucas's eyes flared and then dropped down to my lips, and when I licked them, the hold he had on the back of my head tightened. Between one breath and the next, he took possession of my mouth, his tongue tangling with mine in a delicious slide. The sexual tension between us had been building all night, and Lucas kissed me until I was dizzy, effectively erasing the memory of any other who came before—and after—him.

Our legs intertwined as he pressed his body to mine, so that every part of us was connected, and the sheer intensity coming off him left me trembling. This. *This* was what I'd been waiting for all night, and Lucas didn't disappoint. Not even close. When he sucked my tongue in his mouth, I groaned with the need to be even closer. I reached for one of his legs and held it up beside my hip, and when his erection throbbed against mine, he began to rock his hips.

"Oh God," I said, breathless already. It didn't matter that we were out where anyone could see. There was no thought in my mind other than how fucking good he felt and how I never wanted the moment to end.

Lucas swallowed my words, biting and nipping at my lower lip. "Touch me," he said, taking one of my hands and sliding it past the waistband of his boxer briefs. The smooth head of his cock brushed against my knuckles as I slid my hand down to cover the hard length of him, and when I squeezed, he let out a throaty moan. His reaction made me feel powerful, and I wrapped my fingers around his cock, relishing the thick, solid feel of him in my hand.

It had been so long since I'd touched him this way, but as I began to stroke him, it was like no time had passed at all. Using my shoulders as leverage, he drove his hips up greedily into my palm, and the fingers he had in my hair pulled tight.

"That's perfect... Oh fuck," he said, and the way Lucas

was falling apart had me wishing we were no longer in the ocean so I could get my hands, mouth, and dick where I wanted them, because I couldn't get enough. His moans and gasps overrode the need to see his body flexing and straining beneath my hands, though, but it was what he said next that struck me speechless.

"I want to feel you," Lucas said on a shuddering exhale. "Together." Before I could ask what he meant, he tugged down my boxers to free my cock and wrapped my hand around the both of us.

Oh shit, I thought, as he thrust his hips up, and as his dick rubbed against mine, my eyes practically rolled to the back of my head.

"Fuck," he said. "Fuck, yes, just like that."

The tortured groan of ecstasy coming from Lucas amped up my need to hear him calling my name as he came from the pleasure of my hand. I squeezed our hard lengths together and pumped my fist up and down around us, and holy fuck, nothing had ever felt so good in my entire life. Was this what I'd been missing? What I could've had with Lucas every damn day for the past eight years?

"God*dammit*." The cords of Lucas's neck strained as his head fell back, his fingers and nails digging into my ass so hard I knew I'd have bruises tomorrow. "You're gonna make me come so fucking hard."

He bit into my shoulder, and it was that sting of pain that I felt all the way to my balls. There was no way I could hold back anymore, my self-control fast approaching its limit. The hand I had around us moved at an uneven pace as my orgasm crested and I continued to pump us through my slick fist, but then I felt his cock jerk and it was all over. The tidal wave crashed over me first, my release tearing out of me so hard my vision went fuzzy, and then Lucas was coming, his dick pulsing in time with mine.

He recaptured my mouth as we came down from the high, and I let go of the grip I had on us so that I could wrap my arms around him and hold him. As the frenzy died down to a low simmer, his kisses became unhurried, Lucas exploring me as I explored him.

Lucas had once been so much a part of me that I'd felt like half of myself when he wasn't around, and as we reconnected with each other, it was like finding a part of myself I'd forgotten I'd lost. The arrogant facade he'd put up when I'd first seen him again melted away, until the boy I knew emerged, eyes full of warmth and the trademark hint of mischief.

"Jesus, Jackson," Lucas said when he pulled away, a devious smile turning up his lips. "I didn't realize you were so into water sports. Touch football seems like a waste now."

"Nah. You did have to win a bet to get me in here."

"No, I only had to dare you." He tilted his head to the side. "I wonder what else I could dare you to do…"

"I'm a little scared to find out," I said, laughing.

"Hmm, the possibilities…"

"Don't you dare." I curled my finger underneath his necklace and kissed him again.

"Oh I dare. But Jackson?"

"Hmm?"

"We have a problem." There was a wicked glint in his eyes as he leaned forward to whisper in my ear. "I think your massive cock is scaring the fish."

I rolled my eyes and pushed him away. "Oh God. Be serious."

"I am. You're so big I got lockjaw last night—"

Shaking my head as I bit back a smile, I sent a splash of water his way and treaded out of the water.

"Jackson, where you going with your huge dick?" Lucas's teasing laugh echoed off the water behind me.

"Fuck off," I called out over my shoulder, which only made him crack up harder.

"You fucked me off good and well. I think I'm spent now, but thanks."

"Shut up, Lucas."

"I think what you mean is, 'When did you get so damn sexy, Lucas?'"

I chuckled as he followed me out of the water, and we fell back into the easy ribbing that had always been the foremost part of our friendship.

Some things never changed.

CHAPTER 20
LUCAS

W ELL, THAT HAD escalated faster than I'd expected. Not that I regretted it, because who in their right mind wouldn't want their hands and mouth all over a man like Jackson? No, the problem was that now that I'd had a taste, it wasn't enough. Instead of sating my lust, I'd only made things worse, because now I craved getting Jackson in bed and putting all that foreplay into good use as the opening act.

But fuck, I'd already tempted my self-restraint to the breaking point tonight, so as I parked with the engine idling in front of the Rosemont, I tried to tell myself this was the right thing to do. Leave Jackson here and go back home—alone. Even though I wanted him in my bed so badly it had me clutching the steering wheel to keep from reaching for him.

"Well," he said, suddenly coming off shy and nervous,

even though an hour earlier I'd seen the brazen side of him I knew was in there. "Tonight was…fun. Thank you." Jackson's fingers wrapped around the door handle, but he didn't pop it open.

"Pretty sure I'm the one who should be thanking you." I knew my smile had to be immoral, because Jackson blushed—actually blushed. And it was so endearing that the next words were out of my mouth before I fully thought them through. "You free tomorrow?"

What the hell, Sullivan? He's leaving soon. Don't get fucking attached, you idiot.

But I'd already thrown down the invitation, and when Jackson bit his lip and then nodded, I felt more relief than inconvenience.

"Good. I'll pick you up at ten," I said, and then gave him one last once-over. "And don't dress up."

I STIRRED THE NEXT MORNING, tossing and turning in my bed as light filtered through the blinds in my bedroom. I had the vague thought that I needed to wake up, but at the edges of my mind hovered a memory of Jackson back when we were teenagers, and sleep claimed me again before I could open my eyes…

THE SAND WAS soft against my bare back, the night breeze coming off the ocean chilly, but there was no way I was putting my shirt back on. Jackson had pushed up onto his elbow beside me and was staring intently at the inked lines that covered my arm and shoulder.

I held my breath as he reached for me. His touch was tentative on my skin…so light I could barely feel it. And just when I felt him start to pull away, I put my hand over his and increased the pressure of his fingers where they'd begun to trail my tattoos.

Jackson met my eyes.

"You can touch me," I said, my voice wavering. I hadn't meant for my words to come out sounding unsure—they were anything but. There wasn't one damn thing I wanted more than for him to keep his hand on me, but just below the surface of my skin lay the panic that at any moment he'd realize what he was doing and stop. Please don't stop, *I begged, sending up a prayer that would probably be shut down the second whoever was up there saw my name attached.*

But just this once I was proven wrong, because slowly, ever so slowly, Jackson's fingers began to move again, tracing the swirls that lined my collarbone. I shuddered under his touch.

"What does it mean?" he asked, following the outline that rounded over my shoulder and down my arm.

"They're Celtic knots." I cleared my throat. "They don't have a beginning or an end, so they're used to represent infinity…eternity. I got it after…" I couldn't say the words "after my parents died," but Jackson nodded like he knew anyway. He never made me talk about the car crash that had taken them from me only months earlier, sending me to live with my gram, and for both of those things, I was grateful.

Jackson's finger came to a stop on the inside of my upper arm, and then he lightly ran over the symbol. "This one's my favorite."

I closed my eyes. There was no way he could've known that was the one part of the tattoo I'd designed. The one part I'd been insistent on having on the inside, where it wouldn't be front and center. The reminder I'd made for me and me alone.

"Is this a knot too?" he asked.

"It's a triskele. A triple spiral." I took his hand and guided it over the three curls. "It's one continuous line that represents life's movement. Past...present...future."

"Looks almost angry."

A small smile turned my lips up. "A triskele represents strength. Moving forward, no matter the obstacles."

"That sounds like you."

I blew out a breath and shook my head. "I'm not strong. I feel... lost sometimes." Until I'm with you, *I thought.* And then I feel like I have a purpose in staying alive after all.

"You're the strongest person I know," Jackson said. "You don't think so, but you are."

"So are you."

He jerked back. "Me? No." Jackson scoffed, and then peeked up at me with a half-grin. "Just a rich boy on Daddy's plan. Isn't that what you said when we first met?"

"I'm sorry. I was wrong—"

"No, you weren't. Not really. I mean, that is *the plan. Going into my father's business. Always has been."*

"It doesn't have to be. Not if you...want something else."

Jackson gave me a sad smile. "Some of us aren't as strong as others." Then he trailed his fingers down my chest, following the line of my abs down my stomach and lower...lower... "But there is something else I want."

I STARTLED AWAKE as my alarm went off, the station set to a horrible rap station to entice me to get my ass up on time, and I sat up and hit the snooze with my fist. Figured my dream would be cut off before the good part. Fucking cockblock alarm.

Yawning, I scrubbed a hand over my face and thought back to the memory that had presented itself in my dream. It was no wonder it'd been brought to the forefront after last night. Right after Jackson traced the markings on my skin had been the first time we'd fooled around, right there on the beach, something I'd thought about last night as we lay under the stars.

I thought back to what he'd said, about not being strong enough to have a choice, and back then, I, stubborn shit that I was, had been determined to change his mind. My hand came up to finger the weathered cord of my necklace. I'd spent a week perfecting the triskele pendant in my gram's basement just to give it to Jackson and prove him wrong. It had been my very first piece, the design that had later given me the idea for a business, and Jackson had loved it, wearing it every day under the collar of his uniform. At least, until the day it'd been returned to me.

But for now, Jackson was here, in South Haven, with me.

Maybe there was hope for the lost little boy yet.

CHAPTER 21
JACKSON

I T WAS TEN on the dot when I stepped out of the Rosemont to see Lucas's truck idling a few feet away. Wearing a pair of Aviators and a lazy grin, and with one arm on the wheel and the other slung over the passenger seat, Lucas looked every bit the part of a sexy islander-slash-chauffeur. He lowered his sunglasses, and his eyes roamed over me. "I see you take orders well."

I hopped inside the truck and slammed the door shut. "Surprised?"

"Pleasantly," he said, his grin turning sinful. "Though you look like a proper tourist in that getup."

"Hey, it was either this or another suit." I hadn't planned on a beach day while I was here, thinking this would be a quick work trip, so I'd had to go to one of the souvenir shops down the street that morning to purchase something casual. I'd come away with a pair of overpriced flip-flops, shorts, and the salmon-colored Savannah t-shirt I sported, among other things.

"Ah, that reminds me." Lucas pulled a brightly colored pair of swim trunks out of the beach bag in the rear floorboard and tossed them in my lap. "Figured you didn't bring any, and you might need 'em."

"That's okay. I'll just go bare."

Lucas slammed on the brakes and whipped his head around.

"Or I could wear these." I pulled up my shirt and lowered the waistband of my shorts to reveal the blue swim trunks underneath.

He shook his head. "You fucker. It's not nice to tease," he said, heading out to the street, and I smiled at his reaction. As we crossed back over the bridge to South Haven, I watched him out of the corner of my eye, trying not to be blatant about it. He seemed more at ease today, singing along softly to U2 with the windows down and the wind blowing through his hair. I also noticed how the tank top he wore showcased his suntanned skin and powerful arms, the same arms that had been wrapped around me last night.

As Lucas took us in the direction of the east side of the island, I said, "Aren't the beaches back the other way?"

"Yup."

"So this isn't part two of last night that you've got planned."

"Nope. Well...not exactly the way you're thinking."

I peered out my window. "Planning on dumping my body in the marsh?"

"Not *planning* on it…"

"Then you're taking us to swim with the crocs?"

"Alligators," he corrected. "And I didn't say you'd be swimming with them, but by all means." Lucas turned into a driveway, and I stared at the prodigious house before us. Compared to the other Southern-style mansions built up along the marsh, this one looked completely out of place, with its sleek modern lines and glass walls that reflected the sun in a way that, even being see-through, made it look inaccessible.

I whistled in admiration. "Damn. Who does this belong to?"

"Friend of mine. But that's not where we're going." Lucas drove past the garage big enough to house at least a half-dozen cars and toward the marsh where a large pontoon boat was anchored to a dock. After putting the truck in park, he popped open his door. "Let's go."

"Go?" I asked, as Lucas grabbed the bag and a cooler from the back seat and headed down the dock. "Hold on. Are we stealing your friend's boat?"

Lucas pursed his lips. "Stealing is such a negative word."

"What would you call it?"

"Since I fully plan to return it, I'd call it borrowing. Don't worry; he doesn't mind." Lucas climbed into the boat and dropped the cooler on the deck. Then he looked up to where I still stood on the dock. "Better hurry and get in before he changes his mind."

Glancing at the name of the boat scrawled across the back, I laughed. *"Hard and Full of Seamen."*

"Complete perv, obviously. Come on."

Against my better judgment, I climbed aboard and looked back at the immense house, waiting for someone to run out and threaten us. Growing up around rich bastards like my father, I knew those types like the back of my hand, and there was no way in hell they'd let a boat this extravagant out of their sight.

When Lucas stood up and caught the direction of my stare, he laughed. "Oh, live a little. Just think how fast this baby'll get up to once the cops start chasing us."

I shook my head. "You're trouble, you know that?"

I thought he'd laugh again at my comment, but as he went about untying the boat from the dock, his forehead scrunched up. "Yes, I do." He then went over to the other side and lifted the anchor.

"Can I help?" I asked.

"Yes, actually. Take your clothes off."

Laughing, I shook my head. "I meant with getting the boat ready to go."

"That's part of it. Can't set sail until we drop trou. Those are the rules."

"Damn. Not even any foreplay this time," I joked, grabbing the back of my shirt and pulling it over my head. Lucas visibly swallowed as his eyes roved over my chest, stomach, and arms, and, without looking away, he reached down to fumble inside his bag.

"I need you over here," Lucas said, pulling out a small bottle, and I froze for a second, thinking it was a bottle of lube. But as he poured the contents into his hand, I realized like a dumbass that it was only sunscreen.

Shows where your mind is, Davenport.

Lucas licked his lips, never taking his eyes off me, as I went to stand in front of him. "Can't have you get burned on my watch," he said, rubbing the lotion between his hands before sliding them over my shoulders. They were strong and a little rough, proof he worked with his hands, as they massaged the sunscreen into my skin, never letting me forget that it was a man touching me, feeling his way down my chest and abs.

"That feels good," I said, and Lucas smiled as I enjoyed the way he took his time, making sure he got every inch. A couple of times he dipped his fingertips just under the band of my shorts, but he removed them quickly, teasing me juuust enough to have my dick reacting—and it had definitely taken notice.

"There," Lucas said when he finished, his lips hovering only inches away from mine. He angled his head, and I thought he'd kiss me, but then he faked me out and backed away, grinning as he wiped off the leftover sunscreen on a towel.

He drove us down the marsh, winding around the tall grass and pointing out houses of note, owned by old classmates or teachers, as well as a couple of celebrity vacation homes. It was a warm and sunny spring day, and several boaters were out enjoying it, fishing and sunning themselves and waving as we passed. Lucas didn't slow down until we'd passed them all, and then he stopped the boat in the middle of an extensive clearing away from any other residences. The fact that he wanted privacy wasn't lost on me, and as he walked over to where I sat, he grinned.

"I've got a long pole, just for you," he said, as he unbuttoned his shorts and kicked them off. "Stand up."

My eyes grew wide at the implication, and as I got up from the long bench that ran along the side of the boat, he came closer, and when he was only inches away, he ran his hand down my side, starting at my ribs and working his way down over my hips, then farther, until—

He flipped open the top of the bench and pulled out a fishing pole.

"It's a bit thin, so it may not be what you're used to, but I think you can catch something with this," Lucas said, winking at me as he handed me the pole, and I cursed.

"You're not right."

"Oh, I'm all kinds of right, but you don't think I'd take advantage of you without letting you catch us dinner first, do you?" He took out another pole and a tackle box, and then shut the top. "I didn't think you'd want to get your hands dirty, so no worms for you. Do you prefer the red or yellow grub-tailed jigs?"

"Uh… I've never done this before, so I'll take your word on what's good."

Lucas looked up. "Seriously?"

"My father wasn't exactly the bonding type, and I was too busy with sports." I shrugged. "Guess you'll have to give me another first."

Lucas's eyes darkened and he bit his lip as a growl came from his throat.

"You like that?" I asked, holding out my pole so he could put the bait on. "Being my first?"

He looked down at the way his shorts had spiked behind the zipper. "I think you know the answer to that."

"Good. Just one thing." When he lifted a brow in question, I said, "Don't go easy on me."

CHAPTER 22

T HAT JACKSON DAVENPORT was a goddamn fucking liar.

"Whoo, what's that, seven? Eight? I hope you're hungry, Sullivan," he called out, as he opened the cooler of ice and tossed in another flounder.

I looked back at my own bobber, the one that hadn't moved once, and narrowed my eyes. "I think there's something wrong with my pole."

"I promise, there's nothing wrong with your pole," Jackson said, laughing as he bent down over me like he was going to kiss my neck, but then he hesitated.

"Thanks for the reassurance, but the least you can do is kiss me, since the fish are all bypassing my pole. Otherwise, this is all bullshit."

Jackson smiled and leaned in, his lips a warm caress on my neck, and I shivered. "You're kinda cute when you pout. Also a bit of a sore loser. You know this is just getting you back for last night, right?"

"Yeah, yeah, and here I thought we both won last night." I put the pole down and got to my feet, stretching my arms over my head, and that move made Jackson stop and stare until a vibration from his shorts pocket had him reaching down to turn it off without looking. Again. "Want another soda?" I asked.

"That'd be great," he said, and I grabbed a couple from the mini fridge. As I came back over, movement caught my eye, and I set the drinks down and went over to where Jackson was baiting his hook again.

"Look," I said, caging him in against the side of the boat with my front pressed to his back. I put my chin on his shoulder and pointed over by the bank a good thirty yards away. "You see it?"

"See what? I don't— Oh, holy shit."

An alligator that had to be over twelve, thirteen feet long was crawling out of the water and up onto the bank, and Jackson's eyes were big and round as he watched the prehistoric creature.

"Now that's something you don't see every day," he murmured.

"Not a rare occurrence around these parts. Whaddya say? Want to lure him back in and have gator tail for dinner?"

He looked back at me over his shoulder. "You've lost your mind."

"Tastes like chicken."

"I'll pass."

"How do you know you don't love it till you try it?"

"I don't mind trying it. What I *do* mind is wrestling an alligator into this boat so we can *have* gator tail. I'll pass on that."

"Where's your sense of adventure, city boy? Five-hundred-pound alligator? Pshh. Easy." I sat down and picked up my pole as Jackson cast his line out again.

Just as he took the seat beside me, his cell vibrated, and he sighed as he took the phone out, glanced at it, then powered it off.

As the screen faded to black, I said, "Do you need to get that?"

"Nah, it's not important."

"Uh huh. Okay." I was silent for a minute, but as something played at the back of my mind, I had to ask. "Is it work-related? Something you need to go take care of? Because they've called a few times, and I can take us back to—"

"No, no work today, and there's not an emergency, so it's fine. Nothing that can't wait until tomorrow."

"If you're sure."

"I'm sure." Then an arrogant grin slowly tipped his lips. "Don't think because you haven't caught anything that I'm letting you give up that fast. I never said I'd share with you, and—" His pole jerked in his hand, and we both looked out at the water in time to see his bobber disappear. "Oh shit."

"No. No way," I said, as Jackson and I both got to our

feet and he quickly began to reel the line in, laughing the whole time. "You've *got* to be kidding me."

Nope. Not kidding. A seatrout dangled from the hook, and he removed it from the line and held it up proudly before tossing it in the cooler with his other winnings.

"That's it. I'm calling it," I said, and then I hooked my fingers on the inside of his shorts and pulled him toward me. Jackson had definitely gotten sun today, as evidenced by the light pink flush on his cheeks and nose. It set off the blue of his eyes, one light, like the color of the Bahamas, and one dark, like a turbulent storm. It was a combination that served as a decent metaphor for his inner struggle— the good-natured man with the sparkling personality who could light up a room that warred with the bad intentions of those closest to him. "I think you've sufficiently kicked my ass today. I'm taking you back to my place."

Jackson's hands roamed over my bare back and settled at my waist. "I have to say, I thought you were a better fisherman."

"I'm gonna call this beginner's luck. Rematch anytime."

"Deal," he said, flashing that gorgeous white smile. He could win wars and impregnate women of the world with that smile. Seemed wasted on me.

"Well. I suppose we should return the boat before the owner realizes it's gone. Tell me, Jackson. You up for a fish fry?" Then I bit down lightly on his lower lip before sucking it in my mouth. "And you will share with me. But *only* me."

CHAPTER 23
JACKSON

L ATER THAT NIGHT—and completely stuffed from dinner—I lounged on Lucas's patio swing, pushing it back and forth with my foot, as he put away the dishes inside. I could hear him clattering about as my eyes adjusted to the falling darkness. It was a fair trade —I'd caught the flounder and seatrout we dined on, and he cleaned up after.

As I brought the last of the white wine we'd polished off to my lips, I imagined what it would be like if this was my normal. It was so peaceful here, with only the sounds of nature filling the air. Crickets, frogs, and something else I couldn't put my finger on. What would it be like to have days spent on the water, evenings watching the sky light up with fireflies, and nights next to the man I found myself falling for further with every passing minute?

Down here, life seemed so simple and easy. Here, the

only people that mattered or existed were Lucas and me, and it had me wondering what if... What if it could always be this way?

"Mmm. Please feel free to fish for me anytime," Lucas said, as he came back outside with an uncorked bottle of white wine.

I lifted my glass, and he poured a refill. "Now that's a change in tune. Not sulking anymore?"

"Hell no. This has turned out to be an even better deal. You can do it all—catch, clean, and cook."

"And what will you do?"

"Sit here and look pretty?"

I smiled as he sat beside me on the padded swing, and he laid his arm across the back without even thinking. It was a move anyone else would think he'd done hundreds of times, but he'd never done it before, even though we'd sat on this same swing years ago under his gram's watchful eyes. I pushed the swing back and forth as we sipped our wine and enjoyed the quiet of the moment. He was so close that I could feel the heat radiating off his skin, but we didn't touch. It was enough just to be.

"The fireflies came out to play," I said. "I forgot how much I loved those."

"You mean lightning bugs." He smiled. "I take it you don't have those in Connecticut?"

"If we do, I've never seen them."

"You're missing out, Yank," Lucas said, leaning forward and cupping his hands around one of the fireflies. Then he brought it toward me and let go. It hovered in the air, its abdomen lighting up like it was putting on a show before flying away.

"Seems I miss out on a lot being away from here."

Lucas looked over at me and didn't say anything, but I could feel his fingers lightly running over the neck of my t-shirt. And then I had an irrational thought: *I wish he'd ask me to stay.* Jesus, that would be asking a lot. I'd been in town a week and already I expected him to turn his life upside down to accommodate me? Being here with Lucas felt more like my home than my actual home did, but how to say that without him thinking I was crazy? *Shit, maybe I am crazy.*

"You okay?" Lucas asked, and by the stillness of the swing, I realized I'd stopped pushing.

"Yeah, was thinking." *Don't say it, don't say it.* My gaze drifted away from him and over to the row of flower boxes that hung off the porch. They still housed bright, happy blooms, and that had been around since his gram had been alive. Clearly, Lucas had gotten his green thumb from her. "Can I ask…how did she die?"

Lucas knew exactly whom I was referring to and didn't skip a beat. "Complications from a stroke. Three years ago this week."

"I'm so sorry."

He shrugged as if to say it hurt like hell, but what could he do? "I'm glad I got a few good years with her."

"She was an amazing lady. I'm glad I got to know her."

"She was the best," he agreed. "And she really liked you."

I felt a stab of pain that I'd never gotten to say good-bye, and lifted the wine to my lips again. I wondered if she'd still liked me after I left her grandson without so much as a warning. She would've also known about his trip up north and the disaster that'd happened there, and it made me cringe that she might've thought the worst of me before she died.

Lucas pointed with his glass over to a magnolia tree far down the property. "She's over there if you want to say hi later."

"I'll have to do that." *And apologize.* Then something he'd said earlier niggled at my brain. "Did you say three years ago this week?"

"Mhmm."

Wait a second. It'd been eight years to the week since I'd left, and his Gram had also passed the same week five years later? No wonder he'd boarded himself up good and tight. And now, here we were, getting ready to do it all again when my time in South Haven was up.

"Funny you should choose this week to come back, wouldn't you say?" Lucas said, reading my mind. He gave me a humorless smile that did nothing to hide the pain behind his eyes. "God or the fates surely have a fucked-up sense of humor."

I didn't even know what to say to that. It didn't seem fair that this man had gone through so much in his twenty-six years.

"I know I was an asshole when I saw you again, but do you know what it's like to lose everyone you care about?"

Lucas held up his fingers to tick off a list. "I lost my parents. I lost you. Then Gram passed. Putting up walls is the only way I know how to cope at this point."

"I hate it. I hate that you've had to go through all that. I hate that I've contributed."

"It wasn't your fault."

"No, it wasn't. But I never want to be someone who's hurt you. And Lucas…" *Say it. Now, just fucking say it before you back out.* I held his gaze as I said, "I don't want to hurt you."

"You may not have a choice," he said, smiling sadly.

I didn't think that was true. Not anymore. I wasn't eighteen without a penny of my own to my name. Actually, I had quite a few pennies put away now, enough that I'd never have to work again if I didn't want to.

But there was something else, something I needed to tell him while we were on the subject of all things unpleasant. "There's something you should know."

HERE IT COMES. Whatever it was Jackson was about to get off his chest was nothing good, I could tell, so I braced myself the best I could.

"Okay, so tell me," I said.

He avoided my gaze. "It's about the phone calls today."

I fucking knew it. But I tried to stay nonchalant as I asked, "What about them?"

"It's not what you think."

Maybe it's exactly what I think.

"There's a woman back home. Sydney."

A woman. What a surprise.

"She works with me, and she's also a…friend."

"A friend," I repeated, squinting at him. "Like we're friends?"

"No," Jackson said quickly. "There aren't any romantic feelings on my side, not like that, but it's…complicated."

"Is she your girlfriend?"

"I've never called her that, no."

"Then what's so complicated?" I asked, trying and failing to keep the jealousy at bay.

"I'm supposed to marry her."

My heart plummeted to the ground as I struggled to comprehend the bomb he'd just dropped. Jackson was getting married? *No. Fuck no. And to a woman?* "You're not fucking serious right now."

"Yeah. I am." Jackson paused. "But Lucas...I don't have any intention to marry her."

"You'll have to excuse me if I'm a little confused."

"It's sort of a..." He searched for the words. "An arranged marriage sort of thing."

My jaw fell open for all of two seconds before I pushed up off the swing. "Okay, now I know this is a joke," I said, but Jackson grabbed my arm before I could move past him.

"Why would I joke about that?"

"Because no one has an arranged marriage anymore, Jackson. For fuck's sake, grow some balls."

Jackson bristled as he stared up at me. "You think I'd get pushed into something I don't want to do?"

"I know you would. You have."

"This is different. Sydney, she's..." He sighed. "She's a good girl. An even better friend. I've known her since we were kids, and she'd do anything for me, us. It's always been sort of hanging over our heads that eventually we'd end up together. It's what our parents want, and it's what Sydney seems to want."

"Is she what you want?"

Jackson hung his head and let go of my arm. "No. And I've done everything to discourage her but flat-out say no, and I never have a good enough reason to tell her that."

"Uh, how about you don't *want to*."

Jackson rested his elbows on his knees and steepled his hands in front of him. "Lucas, I never thought I'd see you again."

"Surprise, motherfucker. Here I am." God, I was being an asshole again and I knew it, but what the fuck was I supposed to say? Congratulations?

"Yeah, here you are. And the thing you have to understand… I thought my time with you had been a fluke. That it was some exaggerated version of events that had happened when I was a hormonal teenager. I spent all this time thinking I was nothing to you, and since then, I haven't met anyone, male or female, who made me feel the way I did back then. Or thought I did." He looked down at his hands. "So you'll have to forgive me if I considered living a decent life with a good person and making her happy."

"Aren't you a fucking martyr."

"That's not fair."

"So it's fair for you to settle? To not *try* to be happy and do something for yourself?"

Jackson's cheeks reddened. "What are you implying? That I should've come down here sooner when I thought you were fine playing the field?"

"Yeah. Sure. Why not?"

"I get this is surprising, but you don't get to be pissed off about this. Surely there's been somebody for you since…"

Since you broke my fucking heart? I smirked. "There've been many somebodies."

Jackson's eyes bugged out. "What?"

"Hey, you asked."

"You're not supposed to say there's been many. Are you serious?"

"What am I supposed to say? That I've been celibate since you?"

"Of course not. Sorry… I didn't realize you'd had that many relationships."

"I haven't." When a confused expression crossed Jackson's face, I said, "Well, you didn't say relationships, did you? The answer to that would've been zero." Leaning against the balcony railing, I crossed my legs at the ankles. "I fuck, Jackson. I don't let them in. I don't let anyone in."

Jackson turned positively green, and he looked back down at his hands, like he was trying to come to terms with that fact. "Many somebodies and no relationships," he said in a low voice. "That explains the sex god comment, then."

"The what?"

He sighed and sat back in the swing. "At the diner I overheard a couple of guys mention your name, which is how I knew where to find you at Argos. They called you a sex god. And there was something about 'that hottie with a body Lucas ignoring his twink ass.'"

"Flattering they know I've got standards."

"Apparently you also have a reputation." His eyes turned to slits. "What, do you go out and party every night and bring guys home? Is that your life now?"

"No," I said. "I never bring them back here."

"Lucas—"

"And I haven't been out partying for days now, so that's not an accurate conclusion either."

"You're a little fucking slut, aren't you?"

"Hmm, would we say little..."

"Jesus Christ," he muttered, running a hand through his hair as he got to his feet. "Lucas, be serious. Why all the men?"

"What does it matter? I'm single; I'm allowed to do that. You, on the other hand, just admitted you're practically engaged. Maybe we should talk about that for a second."

"There's nothing to say. I'm not engaged, nor will I ever be, at least not to Sydney. She thinks this trip is me taking time to think things over and plan a proposal, when it's really me trying to figure out how to break it to her without being an insensitive jackass." He looked up at the ceiling and took a deep breath, and on the exhale, he said, "Like I told you, it's just our families trying to meddle—"

"But you've slept with her."

Jackson's mouth clamped shut, and as he stared at me, his silence confirmed my statement.

"Right," I said, breaking eye contact. "Well, I think that calls for a drink."

"You're already drinking," he pointed out, nodding at the glass in my hand.

"Something stronger, then." I flung open the back door and stalked through the kitchen to the shelf I kept the liquor in. I grabbed the gin and an empty glass and didn't even bother with the ice or a mixer.

"For fuck's sake, Lucas," Jackson said, coming up behind me. "I don't want to fight with you."

I unscrewed the cap and poured the gin into the glass. "This isn't fighting. This is a distinct difference of opinion."

"You know what this is, right?" Jackson said. "We couldn't have each other, so we fucked others to try to chase the other one away. Did it work for you? Because it sure as shit hasn't worked for me."

I spun around, ready to make up a lie to dispute that, but Jackson was right there, a wall of muscle right up on me, not backing down and not letting me get away. His voice was a low growl as he said, "If you think I haven't thought about you every day and wondered what would've been, then fuck you."

My chest moved up and down with my rapid pants, and the fire in my veins had me bursting forward. "No. Fuck *you*," I said, pushing him back until his hips hit the island, and then my hands curled around the fabric of his shirt and we both attacked.

NEITHER OF US held back as our mouths crashed together, an epic tangle of lips and tongues, fisting each other's clothes as we tried to consume the other. Soon, we were kicking off our flip-flops as I pushed Jackson in the direction of the staircase, but our lips never left each other for long in our frenzy to get the other one out of their clothes and upstairs.

As I walked backward, my teeth scored Jackson's lip and then my tongue came out to soothe the sting, and he smiled against my mouth before angling his head for a deeper slide. I staggered up the stairs, practically tripping over myself in my rush to get my shirt off as Jackson did the same, and as we discarded them without another thought, he reached for me again, wrapping his arms around my waist so that we were skin to skin. His hands came down to grip my ass, as I let mine roam all over the smooth, solid expanse of his back, and then I moved to the front of his shorts and made quick work of unbuttoning and unzipping. Then they were gone, nothing but a pile at his feet, and I had him up against the wall with his covered cock in my palm before he could react.

He groaned as I licked and sucked my way down his neck, his pulse beating out of control under my lips, and I couldn't wait anymore. I slipped my hand inside his boxer briefs, rolling my thumb over the pre-cum that had gathered at the plump head of his dick. When I'd gotten it good and wet, I held my hand up to my lips and swiped my tongue across my thumb before sucking it deep inside my mouth.

Jackson drew in a jagged breath as he watched me, and then, quick as lightning, he ripped open my shorts with his hands, sending the button flying down the stairs, and when he saw what he'd done, he gave me a savage smirk.

"Ooh, you're fucking asking for it," I said. My shorts fell the rest of the way down my legs, and then I kicked them his way. As I slowly backed away from him and up the stairs one by one, I said, "Tell you what…if you can get me naked before I do it myself, I might fuck you."

Without warning, Jackson pushed off the wall toward me, but I bolted out of the way just in time, pounding up the stairs as he followed. It had taken us forever to get to my second-floor bedroom, too busy leaving a trail of clothes in our wake, but now that I ran toward my king-sized, I was more than ready to have Jackson all the fuck over me.

I soon got my wish, because Jackson's massive arms wrapped around me, pushing me down onto the bed as he pinned me from behind. His voice was a breathless whisper in my ear as he said, "I think you've forgotten I can also play defensive tackle."

With his powerful body holding me down, I could feel every hard line of him—including his cock, which was exactly where I wanted it. "No," I said, lifting my ass so that it cradled his erection, eliciting a moan from him. "I didn't forget."

Jackson froze above me for half a second before he relaxed again, and he rocked his hips forward, sliding his rigid length between the curves of my ass. Our boxer briefs were now the only barrier between us, and it was still too much. I needed to feel his skin on mine, and I needed it now.

"Hmm. You seem to have me in a compromising position," I said. "Whatever shall you do—"

Jackson flipped me over onto my back before I could get out the rest of the question, and I sputtered a laugh. "Impatient as my dick," I said, running my palm down between us, but he stopped my hand.

"I know you wouldn't deprive me of the chance to have you inside me again. And if *I* don't get you naked, then I lose my chance. Wasn't that the deal?" His voice had turned husky with lust, and I blinked back my surprise at his words.

"I don't remember you being quite this vocal last time…"

"That a problem?"

"Fuck no," I said, lifting my ass as he slid my boxer briefs down over my hips, and as he pulled them the rest of the way off, his breathing became unsteady. I grew even harder under his gaze, if that was even possible, and I palmed my cock and gave it a rough squeeze.

I was so damn hard, and with the taste of Jackson still on my tongue and his watchful eyes following my every move, I began to fuck myself for him, showing him exactly what he did to me.

"Take them off," I said, glancing down at the thin grey material doing nothing to stop his straining erection.

He did as he was told, getting rid of his boxer briefs, but never taking his eyes off what my hand was doing, and when he was completely naked, I stopped and sat up. Jackson's body was a work of art, his unmarked skin flawless, every inch of him sculpted and shaped to mouthwatering perfection. His balls lay swollen and heavy beneath his huge, thick cock, and he wrapped a hand around the base of it and gave it a firm stroke. That plump head of his I'd tasted earlier begged to be licked again, and my tongue came out to wet my lips.

I had an overwhelming need to be inside him, pinning him to the mattress like I had before, only this time fucking him so hard he'd never be able to walk again without thinking of my cock lodged deep in his ass as I made him come again and again. I didn't think I'd ever get this chance again, and I needed him seared into my memory and myself into his body so I could remember it always, even when he'd long gone.

My hands shook as I opened my bedside drawer, whether from the anticipation or the knowledge that I needed to make this moment last, I wasn't sure. After taking out the lube and condoms, I tossed them on the bed, and Jackson looked at them and then back at me with heat in his eyes. He'd looked at me that way before. Right after I'd slipped on a condom and hovered over him for the first and only time we'd come together. I should've known something was off then, but I'd been so desperate for him that I hadn't been able to think straight, to see the signs. But even knowing what would happen would I do it again? *Yeah*, I thought, as Jackson crawled onto the bed toward me. *Fuck yeah.*

CHAPTER 26

"*JESUS*, JACKSON. YOU are so fucking sexy," Lucas said, coming up on his knees to meet me halfway across the bed. It didn't escape my notice the way his body shook slightly, like he was vibrating with need. It only served to make me harder, and as our mouths met again and he laid me onto my back, he said, "I don't think I can wait."

"Then don't."

Lucas lifted up to grab the bottle of lube, and as he sat back on his legs, he said, "I want to see all of you."

Without a second thought, I spread my thighs wide, and as Lucas's gaze on me grew hungry, I felt no hint of embarrassment, no shame, only pure need, an ache dying to be filled.

"No one's been inside you but me?" he asked.

"Only you."

Lucas's eyes flared, and he flipped open the lube cap and coated two of his fingers with the liquid. Then he poured some on me as well before snapping it shut and tossing it aside.

"I want to hear you," he said, leaning down over me and massaging the cool liquid down the crevice of my ass, focusing on my hole, but not yet pushing inside. "Tell me if it's too much or not enough. I want to know what turns you on."

As I uttered, "Yes," Lucas wasted no time in sucking my erection deep inside his mouth, and my breath hitched. "Oh fuck..."

With one hand holding the base of my cock steady, he tongued and flicked my slit, driving up my need to have him inside me. Then Lucas deep-throated me again, only this time, one of his lubed fingers probed at my tight hole. I instantly tensed up, but remembered the last time as clear as if it'd been yesterday. *Relax*, Lucas had said. *Breathe out.* As soon as I did that, Lucas's finger pushed inside, pausing to make sure I was okay, and then his long digit breached the first ring of muscle.

Oh hell, the sensation was so unfamiliar, yet because it was Lucas, I greedily wanted more.

"All the way," I told him, and he complied, licking his lips as his finger went as far as it could go.

"God, you're so fucking tight. I can't wait to have my cock inside you."

The visual of that was almost too much, and I clenched my ass around his finger.

Lucas's eyes shot to mine. "More?" he asked. "Can you handle more? Talk to me."

My hips bucked as he bent down to suck on the head of my cock. "Yes... Yes, I want more."

As Lucas devoured me back inside his mouth, a second finger joined the first, pushing deep into my ass, and then he began to move them in and out, stretching me by scissoring his fingers while inside, getting me ready for him. And fuck was I ready for him.

His fingers reached, feeling for my prostate, and when he grazed it, I cursed so loud that the sound echoed.

"Damn," Lucas said. "I need to fuck you. Now." He pulled his fingers free, and I instantly felt the loss of him. Desperate and needy, I fisted my cock as he reached for the condom, and when he saw the way I arched into my hand, he sucked his bottom lip between his teeth, and his eyes glazed over.

"Fuck. Jackson, what are you doing?"

Those words echoed in my mind, so familiar, like déjà vu, and then I was lost...

"JACKSON," LUCAS WHISPERED, as I reached for the top button of his uniform. "What are you doing?"

What I was doing was crazy, but we didn't have much time, and I wouldn't be able to live with myself if I didn't do this. Show Lucas how much he meant to me.

"I want to be with you."

"But…people might find out. Teachers. The other students. Your father."

"I don't care." I leaned forward to kiss him, but Lucas pulled back.

"Jackson…wait. Are you sure about this? This is what you want? You can't take it back and—"

I cupped his chin and hushed him with a brush of my thumb over his lips. "I want this. With you."

"But—"

"You want to be with me too, right?"

"Fuck." Lucas let out a strangled sound. "You know I do."

Lowering my forehead to his, I closed my eyes and said, "Then please, Lucas. Please. Tonight, just be with me."

I didn't have to ask again, because then his hand was moving up my neck to grip my hair. He pulled my head back, his eyes searching mine, making sure I knew what I was asking for, but I had no doubts. The moment he saw that, he loosened the hold he had in my hair and I kissed him in a way that told him I was surer of him, of us in this moment, than I'd ever been of anything in my life…

"HEY." LUCAS LOOKED down at me as concern filled his eyes. "Where'd you go?"

As the past merged into the present, I stared up at the man I'd been forced to leave behind. If I thought I'd wanted Lucas back then, then it had only grown tenfold in the time we'd been apart.

"I need you," I said, my words coming out strangled.

"You have me—"

"Inside me."

Without a word, I reached for the condom in his hands and ripped the packet open with my teeth, and the whole time Lucas stared at me, his eyes only fluttering shut briefly when I began to roll the condom on his erection.

"Jackson," he whispered, like he was holding on to the last bit of his self-control.

"Please."

That one word, and Lucas got up onto his knees, situating himself between my spread thighs, and then he pushed my legs back so that I was wide open for him. I held them there as he poured more lube onto his sheathed dick.

The tip of his cock nudged against my opening, finding resistance, and Lucas took his time sliding inside, letting me adjust to the size of him. Sweat beaded on his forehead as he held himself back from going at me like I knew he was dying to. Lucas had been so careful with me that first night, too. But I didn't want careful now. I wanted him to take me.

"God...Lucas. I want..."

"What? Tell me what you want," he said.

"More. I want all of you."

Lucas obeyed my request, and when he'd gone balls-deep inside me, he stopped moving, holding us there in that perfect moment where we'd finally come together, joined in every way that was possible.

"You feel unfuckingbelievable," Lucas said, and God help me, he looked so hot above me, flushed, and with the cords of his neck straining. A bead of sweat trickled down the side of his face, and I hooked my finger under his—*our* —necklace and pulled him down to me. When I kissed the drop away, Lucas took my lips with his again—and then he began to move.

The feel of his cock inside me was almost too much, the pressure a pleasurable pain that I seemed to crave, and he gave no mercy, pounding into me with a pace that felt desperate.

"Keep touching yourself," he said, as he held my legs under my knees to get a better angle, and I pumped my cock in time with his hips.

What started as fucking had turned into something more, something intense and profound. It was intoxicating to know how out of control I could make this man, and I knew beyond a shadow of a doubt that he had every bit the same kind of hold on me. I couldn't get enough of the sound of skin slapping skin, the noises he made in his throat as he tunneled into me deeper, faster. And watching him? *Fuck.* Those almost-black eyes looking right back at me, the muscles of his arms and ripped abs flexing as he fucked me like he'd never have the chance again. All those things added up to an erotic visual, and it had my eyes rolling back.

"Look at me when you come," Lucas said, and I was utterly helpless to disobey that command. I snapped my eyes open as my orgasm built, surging down my spine at the same time Lucas's movements became frantic, and as his climax hit, he called out my name, his eyes staying on mine even when they went heavy-lidded with pleasure.

Fuck me, that did it. Game over. My dick throbbed so hard I thought it'd burst, and hot ribbons of cum shot out all over Lucas's abdomen, and there was something primal about the way I was marking his body that made me think, *You're all mine, Lucas Sullivan.* Then his mouth was back on mine, his kiss dominating, and it felt like a claiming.

After grabbing a towel, Lucas wiped us both down with gentle strokes that belied the beast of a man who'd taken me so completely, and when he was done, he pulled me to him, his spent cock finding its home again in the crease of my ass, but the way he held me now wasn't sexual; it was affectionate.

"Will you stay?" he said, yawning as sleep began to claim him.

"Mhmm."

"Promise?"

This time nothing could've pulled me away from him. This time I could say the words I wasn't able to before. Smiling even though he couldn't see, I said, "I promise."

THE CLOCK ON LUCAS's bedside table read four thirty, and with every minute that ticked by, I felt even sicker to my stomach.

"I don't want to go," I whispered.

"Good," Lucas said, smiling into my shoulder. "Stay."

"I wish I could." He had no idea how much. How was I supposed to leave him now? Would I ever see him again? I had a

sinking feeling there wasn't a good answer for that. Not one I wanted to hear. Not one I could accept.

Lucas's lips pressed lightly against my skin, and I blinked back tears I was glad he couldn't see. With our naked bodies joined, my back to his front, and our hands intertwined against my stomach, we lay there, my mind racing a mile a minute, trying to figure out some way to turn back the clock and make this moment last forever. But as the alarm clock flipped another minute, then another, then an hour, I knew my time was up and I had no answers to show for it.

"The sun'll be out soon," I said, trying to keep my voice steady, even when all I wanted to do was cry. "I should probably go."

"Mmm."

"Did you fall asleep?"

"Mhmm, maybe." Then, with a move that belied his drowsy tone, he had me flat on my back and straddled my hips. But as soon as he caught my expression, he frowned. "Hey," he said, brushing away the crease between my brows. "Are you sure you're okay? I didn't hurt you?" He was mistaking what I knew had to be sorrow written all over my face for something he did, but I couldn't hide it if I tried.

"Never better," I said, lifting up off the bed to kiss and reassure him. "I promise. You could never hurt me."

"You look upset. Did I do something?"

"God, no. Lucas, look at me," I said, as I sat up on my elbows. "Being with you is…" I couldn't even find the words. "More than anything I could've imagined. And the past few hours have been the best of my life. Please believe me when I say that."

"Okay," he said warily. "Will you come back tonight? After my finals?"

His question lodged a boulder into my chest. How to answer that *without lying? I wouldn't ever lie to him, but I couldn't tell him the truth now, either. So I didn't say anything at all, instead letting my lips do the talking as I brought him back over me and we explored each other with one final kiss.*

"I wish we had more time," I said, linking my fingers with his.

Lucas brought our hands to his lips and brushed a kiss against my knuckles. "We have all the time in the world, Jackson. You and me."

CHAPTER 27
LUCAS

JACKSON HAD KEPT his promise. He was still there the next morning, lying beside me on his stomach with one of his arms draped over my chest as he slept soundly. I didn't want him to wake and me not be there, so I stayed in bed watching him like a complete creeper. Every once in a while, he'd mumble something incoherent that made me laugh, but mostly he was silent, and I took the opportunity to memorize his face and the lines of his body. He really was the most beautiful man I'd ever seen. It took all my strength not to trace the outline of his strong jaw or kiss his full lips.

When he woke not too long after, though, I quickly remembered what I'd forgotten from our school days—Jackson Davenport was *not* a morning person. Well, not without strong coffee, and stat.

I remedied that by heading downstairs to get a pot

brewing, while Jackson took care of making fried eggs and toast. Damn, was this what people did after they stayed the night? Wake up together, cook breakfast together, head off to work with a kiss on the cheek and an ass grab?

Huh, I thought, as I watched Jackson butter a piece of toast, wearing nothing but his boxer briefs. *Yeah, maybe I could get used to this.*

"Grape or strawberry?" he asked, interrupting my ogling. When I met his eyes, he winked at me.

"Neither. I like the pear preserves on the second shelf, or the blackberry."

"Ah, never had either," he said, opening the fridge and taking out both jars, and I came up behind him and wrapped my arms around his waist. Because I wanted to and because he was too damn irresistible.

I kissed the back of his neck and took a deep inhale, breathing in his scent. "How do you take your coffee?"

"Black."

I scrunched up my nose. "Really? Not even sugar?"

"Really," Jackson said. "What is it with you Southerners putting sugar in everything?"

"That's what makes us sweet."

"You including yourself in that?"

"Hey, I was pretty sweet last night," I said, and playfully bit him on the shoulder to show just how nice I could be.

"That was you sweet? Damn. I'd love to see how you play dirty."

"Mhmm." The timer for the coffee went off and I

slapped his ass and went over to grab a couple of mugs out of the cupboard. "So, what's on the agenda today?"

"I've, uh, got the meeting this afternoon."

The hand I had pouring the coffee jerked, sending a splash of scalding liquid onto my finger, and I shook off the excess. "Shit. Right." The meeting. The whole reason Jackson was in South Haven in the first place. I'd conveniently forgotten about that in the last twelve hours.

"You okay?" he asked, taking my hand and looking at the burn. It was minor, but he still flipped on the faucet and made me hold my finger under the cold water for a minute.

"Thank you," I said, and then picked up the mug of plain black coffee and handed it to him.

"I've got to prepare a few things beforehand, so I should probably get back to the hotel soon, but…can I see you? After?"

The way he seemed so uncertain that I'd want to see him had me grinning like a fool.

"Tell you what," I said, "I'll swing by the hotel once I finish up a couple of orders that need to go out, and we can do dinner tonight. Anywhere. Wherever you want." Then I added, "I'll even wear a button-up. This means you should definitely take advantage."

"You could wear nothing at all and I'd take advantage," Jackson said, and my stomach did the somersault I'd grown accustomed to when he was around. But I was also a little anxious and conflicted about what would happen when Jackson walked into that meeting later. He didn't know it, but he was walking into the office of one of the closest friends I had in the world, and I didn't want him losing his company any more than I wanted Jackson to fail at something he wanted and believed in.

"So this work thing… Do I say good luck or…?"

Jackson took my chin between his thumb and forefinger. "Just say you'll see me tonight."

A smile played at the corner of my mouth. "I'll see you tonight."

"Good," he said, and gave me a soft kiss. "Then that's all I need."

TWO O'CLOCK ON Thursday, and I was sitting in the lobby of AnaVoge for an appointment that the receptionist had assured me was still on. Finally. But, unlike the other visits, my head wasn't in the game. All I could think about was Lucas. The way I'd woken up beside him as he watched me with eyes that betrayed more than a passing attraction, and the fear I felt coming off him when he dropped me off at the hotel. And last night? God. The sound of him as he came, the visual of his strong, lean body straddling mine as his dick disappeared deep inside me, and the way he'd looked at me after, dazed and drunk off the high. I'd needed to get focused and ready for this meeting today, but all I could do was keep replaying our time together in my mind and wonder where we went from here.

"Mr. Davenport? Mr. Davenport, he's ready for you."

Blinking, I shook my head to clear it and realized Astrid was standing in front of a side door, waiting for me to follow her.

"Oh, sorry," I said, and then flashed what I hoped was a smile that said I had my shit together. Getting to my feet, I buttoned my suit jacket, picked up my briefcase, and then followed her through the oak door that separated the lobby from the offices. The back was nothing like what I'd expected. Whereas the lobby had an elegant, traditional feel, the back was modern, all glass walls for the offices of equal size that lined one side of the room, while the rest was an open space with several tables in the middle in place of staff cubicles. It was an inviting, open-door setup that I hadn't seen in any of the companies we'd acquired, and it made me even more curious about the man I was about to meet.

I was led into one of the minimalist offices, and nothing about the space boasted of a CEO at all. Speaking of which, there wasn't anyone in the room, and as I looked at Astrid, she smiled. "He'll be right with you. You can take a seat."

Then she left, and I stood there, waiting in a room full of see-through walls where I could feel eyes on me from every direction. *Well, this is awkward.* Which I'd venture to guess was the point. Keep me on my toes and off guard, giving the home team another advantage. I was beginning to think this guy had a flair for the dramatic.

My guess was right on as the sound of my name had me turning to face... *Holy shit.* The man standing in the doorway holding a stainless steel travel mug was the last person I'd ever expected to see—again. My mouth parted in shock as I took in the oversized collar of his white shirt that was paired with a cropped black jacket and slim-fitting pants. It looked like something Prince would've worn, right down to the high-heeled snakeskin boots. The only thing different about this—Bash, had he called himself?—was the lack of red lipstick, and his inky hair was parted instead of slicked back.

He held out his hand toward me. "It's nice to officially meet you, Jackson Davenport."

"Uh..." I blanked, completely thrown off as I shook his hand. "Sebastian Vogel?"

Sebastian cocked his head. "You seem surprised."

"You're not who I was expecting."

"Should I take offense to that?" he said.

"No, of course not. I just didn't realize we'd already met. *Un*officially, I guess."

He smiled as he let go of my hand. "Yes, well, I make it a point never to talk shop after hours. Too many other fun diversions. I take it you enjoyed yourself Friday?"

My face burned as the first thing I thought of was Lucas's naked body under mine. *Did I enjoy myself? Uh, yeah. You could say that.*

Clearing my throat, I tried like hell to remember this was an important business meeting with a company we had a vested interest in purchasing. "I'd like to focus on the point of why I'm here today, if we could."

"Ah, of course. That was none of my business. Just making sure our locals treated you well during your stay." He walked around his glass desk and sat down in the leather chair behind it. "And I do apologize for the wait. I've had a few things to attend to this week of a personal nature, as I'm sure you can understand."

Do I ever. "I do. I appreciate you meeting with me."

"It's not every day a company of your prestige comes calling. I'm flattered." Sebastian gestured to the chair opposite him. "Please."

Unbuttoning my jacket, I sat down and placed my briefcase on the floor beside my chair. Hopefully I'd be needing the contents before the meeting came to an end.

"Flattered, but not curious?" I asked.

"The rumor mill talks, but I rarely listen to gossip." Sebastian leaned back in his chair and crossed his legs. "The floor is yours. What can I do for you, Jackson?"

As I launched into my pitch, quoting facts and numbers, I felt confident that Sebastian would be easily sold. Davenport Worldwide did come with a reputation for getting what we wanted, and with the amount of money we'd be throwing his way, anyone would be hard-pressed not to take the deal.

When I wrapped things up, Sebastian said, "I assume you've drawn up a proposal?"

"We have." I unlocked the briefcase, pulled out the

contract, and slid it across his desk. "As you can see, we're prepared to offer you a substantial sum to acquire the rights to your company."

Sebastian glanced down and then did a double take at the figure. "You came here to play," he murmured as he picked it up and flipped through each page.

"That we did. Analytics in social media marketing is something many companies are desperate for, and the market is practically untapped. We believe in your business and would like to help AnaVoge become the go-to in your field."

"Hmm." Sebastian dropped the contract back on to his desk. "It's clear you've done your research, and as such, you would also know I'm not in the market to sell."

"We do. But we also know you're a smart businessman. Davenport Worldwide can offer your company the connections and resources it needs."

"Who's to say I couldn't do that on my own?"

"Maybe in time, but with the way things are shifting so quickly, there's no way to know if you'll be relevant two years, three years, five years from now. You've got to strike while the iron is hot. We have the means to do it, and fast."

Sebastian steepled his hands and tapped his fingers on his lips. "And to do that, reach those numbers you project, you'd use your father's signature approach, I assume? Divide and conquer?"

"Assuming we acquire your company, we'd have to do a full assessment and analyze the best strategy."

"That's not a no."

"It's not a yes."

"Hmm," Sebastian said, and rocked back in his chair, his kohl-rimmed eyes studying me. "Well, it's an offer many would jump at. Good of you to come all this way for little ole me."

"A fifty-million-dollar company isn't exactly little."

Sebastian's smile grew. "Yeah, I do okay. But here's the thing, Jackson. May I call you Jackson?"

"Of course."

"What I've learned in the years I've been doing this is that no amount of money is worth it if your people aren't happy. You're not going to keep the best and brightest by focusing on the bottom line."

"Surely you don't mean to tell me you don't care about money."

Sebastian chuckled. "We've been lucky enough that I have more than I'll ever need. But there comes a point when ambition turns into greed, and that isn't such a good look for me. It would also come at a price, I think, and it's my job to look after the best interests of my company and my staff."

"So your answer is no?"

"Can I ask you something? What do *you* like about my company?"

"I respect your work ethic, and your ideas are inventive. You've captured a niche that needs to be filled, and you've made savvy business decisions." I looked over my shoulder at the dozens of people working at tables in the open space.

"The way you bring everyone together on a level playing field is also admirable."

Sebastian's expression turned thoughtful. "Do you agree with the methods *your* company dishes out when they take on all these companies?"

No was my immediate reaction, and my brief hesitation was all the answer he needed.

"I didn't think so." Sebastian stood and came around to the front of his desk, and then he leaned against it, crossing his ankles. "Jackson, you seem to be an intelligent man. Good instincts, remarkable skills of persuasion…plus I like you. So I'm gonna be real with you."

I'd never been so bowled over by another in a meeting before, but I'd also never had someone read me so clearly before either, and I was curious what would come out of Sebastian's mouth next.

"You hate your job," he said.

Okay, not what I expected. "Excuse me?"

"What's more, I think you strongly disagree and/or dislike your father. Perhaps both."

"What the—?" I said, unable to hide my shock at his audacity. "I'm not sure what's prompted you to make assumptions about my life. You don't know anything about me or my father."

"Well, that's not exactly true. See, I've read up a bit on you, too, Jackson, and I've got a theory about you."

He cannot be serious. "I can't wait to hear it."

"You graduated from South Haven Academy, did you not?"

"You know the answer to that if you've done an internet search."

"Fair enough. There's just one thing my search didn't tell me." Sebastian narrowed his lined eyes. "Did you attend your graduation?"

"Excuse me?"

"Your graduation. Were you there?"

"That's what you want to know about me? Whether I walked at the ceremony? What kind of question is that?"

Sebastian shrugged. "A simple one."

I debated whether to answer him, but I was still curious about what all these questions were leading up to. "I left a few days before the end of classes. Why?" He nodded like he'd expected that answer. "Care to explain what that has to do with anything?"

"I just needed confirmation of exactly who you are, and now I know. I apologize for bringing up things of a personal nature, but I appreciate the clarification."

"A personal nature…?" I wondered what the fuck he was talking about, but then it hit me. This guy, Sebastian, Bash, whatever his name was, was a friend of Lucas's, which meant he knew all about our history together and exactly what my father had done. If Lucas had confided in him, that explained why he would know who I was based on the fact that I'd left South Haven before graduation. This had been no level playing field after all.

"You're a friend of Lucas's," I said.

"Yes."

"A close friend, I take it."

"Yes."

Fuck. It all made sense now. Sebastian being defensive of Lucas at the club, the sculpture in the lobby, Sebastian not wanting anything to do with my father's company. Yeah…this suddenly felt like a coup.

"I assume that was your boat yesterday?" I said. "Your house?"

"Guilty as charged. I apologize for not saying hello. I thought it best not to get involved."

"And this is you not getting involved?"

"A mere curiosity."

"So this is why you're turning us down. Because you've been talking to Lucas?" Hold on, had Lucas purposely sabotaged things with AnaVoge? Was this some vendetta against my father? Against me? He wouldn't do that… surely he wouldn't.

One of Sebastian's eyebrows arched. "I would never make a business decision based on my personal life. Or my friend's personal life."

"That would be wise if it were true."

"We don't get to where we are by being irrational hotheads, now do we?"

"No, we do not." I scrubbed my jaw. "How long have you known who I am?"

"I recognized you the moment I saw you. Like I said, I've done my research, and photos of you aren't hard to find."

"Unlike yours. You're quite the enigmatic CEO. No pictures anywhere."

"Maybe I'm shy?" Sebastian winked. There wasn't a shy bone in his body, and he didn't seem to dislike attention, so whatever his reasons, he wanted his identity to stay private. "What I didn't realize, though, was who you were in relation to Lucas. He was never very forthcoming in telling us any details about the man who'd broken his heart, only the circumstances surrounding your...quick departure. And the aftermath, of course."

"Who's 'us'?"

"Shaw and myself."

"Ah, right. The bartender. Seems I walked into a trap that night at the club."

"Pure coincidence. This is not part of some elaborate setup, I assure you."

"Doesn't fucking feel that way."

"You're angry," Sebastian said. "At Lucas?"

"Did he call you? Tell you not to take our offer?" *Please say no. Please tell me Lucas had nothing to do with this.*

"You know as well as I do Lucas would never do that. I haven't spoken to him in days, but Shaw let me know that the boy who'd broken his heart was back in town. It was easy to put the pieces together."

The boy who'd broken his heart... At those words, and the confirmation he hadn't been involved, my anger abated, but the guilt over something I'd had no control of took over instead. Actually, scratch that—I was angry. Angry as hell, but I'd been taking out my frustration on the wrong person. How could I blame Lucas for anything, even if he *had* warned Sebastian, when it was my father's fault I'd never sought Lucas

out, and it was my father's actions that had caused the heartbreak of the only person I'd ever had romantic feelings for?

Shit, I thought, the realization of what was happening
similar to being dunked under by a rogue wave. The feelings I'd had for Lucas hadn't been snuffed out just because
I thought he'd found someone else, and they hadn't dissipated in all the years that had passed since, even though I
thought I'd moved on. They'd always been there, lying in
wait until the timing was right, and now that I was here...
Why would I ever think about going back to Connecticut?
For my job? For what was left of my family? The family
who'd lied to me. Who'd manipulated lives to get their own
way. Who'd tried to keep me apart from someone I loved—

Christ, that was it. I loved Lucas. I *loved* him, and being
here only made that truth more evident. We'd only just
reconnected, and I knew. I could feel it in my bones that
this man, this place was exactly where I was supposed to
be. I didn't know how, and I didn't even know if Lucas
would *want* more, but I knew I had to try. Time had been
taken away from us, but here was our second chance, and I
owed it to Lucas to show him how important he was in my
life. How vital.

"Jackson? You look lost in thought."

I shook away my wayward thoughts. I'd have to come
back to those later. "Sorry."

"That's quite all right. Something on your mind?"

"You just...reminded me of..." I waved him off.
"Never mind. I should be going."

"Wait. Before you go, I'm curious," Sebastian said, taking advantage of my distraction as he leaned against his desk and drummed his black nails along the top. "*If* you were to gain control of my company…what would you do?"

Hadn't we already discussed this? "I told you. We'd have to assess——"

"No, no, don't give me the spiel about what your father would do. I want to know what *you* would do."

Huh. So Sebastian was testing me, wanting to know whether I agreed with my father or if I had my own ideas. Looked like a wicked smart brain lurked behind the flamboyant facade, and I almost had to smile at his gumption. As the silence between us grew, I thought back to how my father had handled previous acquisitions and what I would've done differently.

What the hell. I'd already lost the account. May as well be honest.

"I think the company should stay as it is," I said. "But to move forward, it would be smart to hire a liaison to speed up negotiations. Someone with experience and contacts who can make it happen before you lose the edge."

Sebastian's eyes sparkled. "And where do you suggest I begin my search for such a person?"

I scrolled through my mental Rolodex, and a few names came to mind. "I could send over a list of recommendations. People I've worked with in the past. No guarantees they'd be available or interested, but I'm sure you could make an offer many wouldn't refuse."

"That's generous of you."

Shrugging, I reached for the contract and tucked it back inside my briefcase before snapping the locks shut. "It's no problem."

"You have an immaculate track record. I imagine this will not go over well."

You mean facing my father's wrath for losing out on a fifty-million-dollar deal? The image of my father's head exploding would've made me laugh if it weren't the soon-to-be reality. But at this point, I couldn't care less. Maybe he'd fire me. *Huh. Would that be so bad?* "You imagine right."

"Should I apologize in advance?"

"I wouldn't stay up worrying about it. Whatever happens happens." Getting to my feet, I grabbed my briefcase and held out my hand toward Sebastian. "But I wish you and AnaVoge well. Thank you for your time."

"I do hate that we won't be working together on this venture, Mr. Davenport," he said, shaking my hand in a firm grip.

"Somehow I think you'll do okay."

Sebastian gave me a sly smile. "As will you. Goodbye for now, Jackson."

After saying goodbye, I headed out of his office, and where I should've felt the weight of failure heavy on my shoulders, I only felt relief. *That's strange. How could I be okay with what just happened in there?* Somehow, though, I was, even though I never would've predicted the outcome.

Two things were certain: my father *would* be furious, and Sebastian's company would stay intact.

Exiting into the lobby, I waved goodbye to Astrid, and as I walked out into the heat from the midday sun, I smiled.

CHAPTER 29
LUCAS

I T WAS HALF past seven when I stepped into the Rosemont's lobby. I'd kept myself physically busy with orders all day, but my thoughts had been solely focused on what was happening in the meeting between one of my best friends and my...well...whatever Jackson was. And I had to admit, I was antsy because I hadn't been able to get in touch with either of them until Jackson responded with a text.

I had no idea what to expect as I scanned the lobby, and when I didn't see him, my eyes shot over to the bar. Hell, that was where I'd be if things hadn't gone my way, and knowing Bash as I did, I knew there was no way Jackson had gotten what he came for.

Sure enough, there he sat at the bar, his collared shirt unbuttoned at the neck and his tie undone and hanging down either side. He was sipping on a glass of amber liquid and didn't notice my approach until I said, "What's a gorgeous thing like you doing at the bar all alone?"

Jackson startled and looked up at me. "Hey."

"Hey," I said, unable to read his expression. "Thought I'd find you here."

"You ready to go?" He went to stand up, and I put my hand on his shoulder.

"Finish your drink first," I said, taking the empty seat on the other side of him. "Should I ask how your meeting went?"

Jackson brought his drink to his lips. "I think you know the answer to that."

"You're right. Knowing Bash, I can guess. And even if I didn't, the fact that you're drinking at the bar would've tipped me off."

Rolling the glass between his hands, Jackson stared straight ahead. "I've never failed before. At my job. But today I just…lost it."

"To be fair, you were facing an impossible task. Long as I've known Bash, he's never been one to sell out. Not at any price."

"So I learned," he said, and took another sip. "But you know what?"

"What's that?"

"I've never felt better."

My brow furrowed as I studied him again. He must've been drunker than he let on. "Come again?"

Jackson turned to face me, and then a slow smile lit up his face. "I lost the account today. Millions of dollars, gone. Do you know what that means?"

"You're broke and I should start planning your funeral now?"

"It means that's millions of dollars my father doesn't get."

A beat and then I said, "Yeah, he might kill you for that."

"Maybe. It's not like he needs it. The bastard's got more money than he'll ever know what to do with." When he saw the shock on my face, he laughed. "Yeah, I said it. He's a bastard, and I'm the idiot who thought his dad could do no wrong. I was just too scared to do or say anything and lose what was left of my family." Jackson reached for my hand and set it on top of his strong thigh.

"I think I like you on whiskey," I said.

Jackson laughed again, but this time, his eyes dropped down to the slacks and button-down I wore, and his stare turned heated. "I'm suddenly feeling hungry."

I raised my arm in the bartender's direction. "Check, please."

"I thought you'd agree," Jackson said, tossing down a couple of bills on the bar. Then he squeezed the fingers I had resting on his thigh and licked his lips. "What do you say we do dinner up in my room tonight instead of going out?"

"You want to hide me away when I took the time to

dress up for you?" I said, feigning annoyance, and then I slid my hand up his leg, winking when he stopped me just before I could cop a feel. "I say lead the way."

"Damn trouble," he said, shaking his head, but there was mischief in those contrasting eyes. After downing the rest of his drink, Jackson stood and then held out his free hand to me. "Shall we?"

It wasn't his words that made me sit there, stupefied and blinking at his outstretched arm. It was that this man was reaching for me like it was something he did every day, a natural gesture he didn't give a second thought about. With his shirt unbuttoned to show just the slightest bit of skin, Jackson looked like he'd just gotten off from a long day of work, ready to head upstairs like we did it every day.

Sliding off my barstool, I took his proffered hand and let him lead us out of the dimly lit bar and into the bustling lobby. If there were stares or whispers, I didn't notice them, my gaze stuck on the profile of the man beside me, the one I still couldn't believe was here. How was it possible that I was even thinking of Jackson in a way that suggested things would go further than this week? It was stupid and made me foolish to let myself get carried away yet again, but with every minute I spent with him, I craved more. Just another minute, another touch, another kiss, building up to the inevitable—another heartbreak. Complete devastation I knew was coming and had resigned myself to because I couldn't stay away, and I couldn't let him go. He'd have to be the one to leave again. And when he did, I'd deal with it, same as I had before, which was to say not well.

Stop, just fucking stop. Shut the fuck up and enjoy him while you have him, you morbid asshole.

Jackson punched the up button for the elevator, and opened his mouth to say something, but frowned when he looked at me. "Rethinking coming with me already?"

"Just wondering if you're not taking me upstairs to kick my ass because of Bash," I said, trying for a light, teasing tone.

His lips twisted up into a cocky grin. "Is that not a foreplay you'd enjoy?"

"As long as I have a heads-up about it."

"You're asking for it with that pun." As Jackson interlaced our fingers, I looked down at our joined hands and my stomach twisted into knots. It was the first time I'd ever held anyone's hand in a public setting. Jackson and I never had that luxury before, and I hadn't exactly reaped relationship benefits since. It was a comforting thing, his hand in mine, and when he tugged me forward, he cupped my cheek. "I promise, no ass kicking unless it's a special request."

When I nodded, he leaned in and kissed me, softly and with no hesitation, even though we were in the lobby surrounded by people. I melted into his kiss as my fingers curled around the belt loops of his dress pants, holding him in place, but I needn't have bothered, because Jackson's mouth moved leisurely on mine, taking his time.

If only I'd known what was about to happen, maybe I would've somehow seared the memory more deeply into my brain. I didn't know that this time when our lips touched, our world would be forever changed once again.

"JAX?" THE FEMALE'S voice was unmistakable, and as I opened my eyes and leaned back to look at the woman over Lucas's shoulder, my blood ran cold.

What the… Oh my God. Shit, shit, shit, what is she doing here?

"What is this?" Sydney's words rang out louder this time and echoed through the lobby, causing heads to turn in our direction—not that she paid any attention. "Jax, what are you doing?"

There was confusion and disbelief written all over her face as she looked between me and Lucas, and then her gaze dropped to where we still stood with our arms wrapped around each other.

"Oh my God," she whispered, shaking her head and moaning. "Oh my God."

I let my hand drop from Lucas's face. "Sydney," I said,

moving toward her, but she took a step back and held up her hand.

"Don't you get near me. What the hell is going on?" Her eyes filled with tears as they shifted to the man behind me. "Who is that?"

"His name is—"

"No, never mind, I don't want to know." Sydney's hand went over her mouth like she might be sick, and then she swallowed and shook her head. "This isn't happening. This is some kind of sick joke. Oh my God, I'm gonna pass out."

"Sydney, I…" I didn't even know what to say in that moment, as she paced back and forth. "What are you doing here?"

She whirled in my direction. "What am *I* doing here? Gee, *I* thought it might be nice to surprise you to celebrate winning the AnaVoge account today. I even thought maybe we could stay and spend an extra couple of days on the beach. You know. *Couple* stuff. But I seem to have inter-rupted something."

I could feel Lucas's eyes on me. He was probably wondering why she was under the impression I'd acquired AnaVoge. I hadn't had the chance to tell her I'd lost the bid; she'd just assumed, wrongly so. *Fuck.* What was I supposed to say to her right now that would in any way make up for what she'd just witnessed? There were only two words that came to mind, so I said, "I'm sorry."

"You're sorry? Really?" She rubbed at her chest as she went back to pacing. "You're sorry for kissing a man while you're supposed to be down here planning a proposal to *me?*"

I heard a couple of audible gasps from somewhere behind us, and I took a deep breath before answering. "No, I didn't say that. I'm sorry this hurts you, Syd, and I'm sorry you saw us before I had a chance to tell you. But I'm not sorry for my actions. Not anymore."

Her mouth opened and shut a few times like a gaping fish as she stared at me. "A man, Jax? You've been down here this whole time with a guy? Are you kidding me?" Then her eyes caught on the elevator we stood in front of. "And what, you were going upstairs with him? To your *room?*"

"Syd—"

"No, stop. I'm gonna be sick."

Jesus, this is a shitshow. I lifted my head to Lucas, apology in my eyes, but he was watching Sydney intently as she tried to catch her breath. More people were looking in our direction, unable to stop eavesdropping on such a juicy scandal, so I kept my voice low and said, "Can we go somewhere in private to talk about this?"

"I'm not going anywhere with you. Or with *him.*"

"Leave Lucas out of this, please. This is between you and me."

Sydney's pacing stopped, and she blinked up at me before her eyes traveled to the man still as stone beside me. "Did you say…Lucas?"

For the first time since she'd arrived, Lucas moved, taking a small step toward her. "Lucas Sullivan," he said, holding his hand out toward Sydney, who stared at it as the blood drained from her face.

"Oh my God," she said so softly I could barely hear it, and then she was backing away again.

"Sydney, wait—" I started, but she put up her hand.

"Don't you follow me, Jax. Don't you dare follow me." Then she turned on her heel and fled across the lobby and through the revolving door, vanishing into the Savannah night. No doubt she'd have my father on speed dial already, telling him what a pervert his son was, like he didn't already know. But it wasn't my father's reaction I was worried about now. It was hers. She'd never been anything but thoughtful and kind, and how had I repaid her? By being a total dick and not owning up to who I was and what—and whom—I wanted.

"Shit," I said, running my hand through my hair and gripping the ends. "Shit, shit. I can't just let her leave like that. Lucas…"

Lucas shoved his hands into his pockets and gave a curt nod. "Then I guess you'd better go after her."

I blew out a breath, pacing just as Sydney had, while I debated what to do. I couldn't take Lucas with me, since that would only rile things up again. Besides, she and I needed to have the conversation I'd long put off, even before Lucas had been in the picture. Dammit, the timing couldn't have been worse. "I'm sorry, I don't want to do this, but—"

"Go," Lucas said, inclining his head toward the door. "Before she gets too far."

I put my hands on either side of his face and gave him a quick kiss. "I'll make it up to you," I said, and then I was running across the lobby and pushing through the revolving door. I looked to the left and didn't spot anyone in a pink dress running down the sidewalk, but when I looked to the right, there she was, crossing the street as fast as her high heels would take her. As I broke into a sprint, I took one last look toward the Rosemont, and through the window I could see Lucas staring after me, still standing rigid with his hands in his pockets in the same spot I left him.

"**S**YDNEY!" I CALLED out, closing in on her as she crossed the street. "Sydney, wait up. Please."

"I told you to leave me alone," she said without turning.

"You know I'm not gonna do that."

"You should, Jax. You really should." She hopped up onto the sidewalk and went to move, but her foot seemed stuck on something, and she lurched forward. I reached her just before she hit the ground, catching her and lowering her slowly to the pavement.

"You okay?"

"My shoe," she said, pointing behind me, and I turned to see a spiky high heel wedged between a crack in the sidewalk. I tried to pry it loose, but the heel tore off from the rest of the shoe, and when I finally pulled it free, it dangled off the edge, ruined.

"Great," she said, her voice cracking as she threw her hands up. "Now my favorite pair of shoes breaks? Someone up there hates me."

"No one could hate you," I said gently. "We'll get it fixed. Where were you running off to? Where's your hotel?"

Sydney stayed stubbornly silent, but when she got the hint I wasn't leaving, she inclined her head toward the building behind her. "That one."

"Come on, then. Let's get you up." I handed her the shoe and then scooped her up off the pavement so she wouldn't have to walk barefoot on the dirty sidewalk. She put her hands around my neck, holding on tight as the hotel's doorman let us inside.

"You don't have to do this," she said, her voice low.

"We need to talk about a few things. What floor are you on?"

"Wait. Not my room."

I looked down at her in confusion.

"I mean…" She bit her lip. "I could really use a drink."

AN HOUR AND a few drinks later, and lightweight Sydney seemed to be feeling no pain. Well, obviously it hadn't erased the events of the evening from her mind, but at least it had numbed her enough that the tears had stopped and she'd calmed down a bit, even as I'd told her everything. All of it, from the first time I'd ever met Lucas to everything that had happened since I'd been here. She listened quietly, taking it all in, and every once in a while she'd interrupt with a question, which I answered honestly.

I could see her bare feet swinging back and forth from under the table as she pulled a cherry off her drink umbrella with her teeth. "Jax, you don't really have to marry me, you know." The alcohol was getting to her now —she was beginning to slur her words.

"No?" I laughed. "Thanks for letting me off the hook."

"I mean, I always thought we would. Get married. My parents pushed it and your parents pushed it, and I never once questioned that we'd end up together. I just figured it was a matter of time."

"Yeah," I said, swirling the whiskey around in my glass, the same one I'd been nursing since we'd sat down in the hotel bar. "Our parents and their master plans for us."

"Mmm, yes. Thank God for them."

I grinned at her sarcasm before turning the conversation in a more serious direction. "Do you ever think about... Well..."

"Think about what?"

"What you'd do if your life hadn't been planned out the way they wanted it?"

Sydney's forehead crinkled as she cocked her head to the side. "I don't know. I like working for Davenport Worldwide, so I feel like that was a good decision...on their part," she said. "But if I could do anything... I don't know. I think I'd want to be a mom."

Her words took me by surprise. "A mom? Really?"

"Yeah." Her cheeks flushed. "I want a family. A husband, kids, the whole shebang."

"I didn't realize…"

"Well, we haven't exactly talked about it. I'm not one to put the carriage before marriage," she said, and then laughed at her rhyme. "Have you ever thought about it?"

"What, having kids? No," I said. "Not to say I never would, it just…hasn't crossed my mind."

"I wonder if Lucas wants them," Sydney said casually, and took another sip of fruity martini number three, and the thought of that was an electric shock to my chest. As she set down her martini, she giggled too loudly. "You should see your face right now. You look horrific. Wait, horrific?" She tested the word out, like she was searching through the alcohol haze for the right one. "Horrible?"

"Horrified?"

"That's the word. Yep, you look horrified. But I wasn't really asking about kids. I meant, have you ever thought about what you'd do if you weren't your father's son?"

Not my father's son… That was an interesting way to put it, and not something that had ever occurred to me.

"Look at you, asking the hard questions tonight," I said.

"Maybe I should be a reporter detective person."

I'd never seen Sydney on anything more than a glass of champagne, and I had to admit, she was amusing. And fun. Some guy out there would be a lucky fucker to be able to call her his. It just wasn't me.

"The job thing I'm good at—"

"Obviously," she said. "Except for today."

"Yeah, yeah. Except for today. But if I could do anything…" I didn't even have to think about it. The words came tumbling out like it was the most natural thing in the world. "I love it here. Well, in South Haven, just over the bridge. It's so laid-back and peaceful, it's got that small-town feel, and…"

"And it's got Lucas."

"Yeah. It's got him. Being back here made me realize that I never would've left. Part of me feels angry about that, because I feel like there's so much lost time to make up for, but then the other part of me wonders if it was all for a reason. Like we had to go through all this shit to appreciate what we have even more."

"That makes sense. I think it's also the most romantic thing you've ever said," she said, and then turned serious. "Jax, I'm sorry for causing a scene earlier. You just…surprised me."

"Uh, I think your reaction was more than justified. You could've added a slap in there somewhere and I wouldn't have blamed you."

"Nah, I don't wanna hurt my hand on that strong jaw of yours."

"Broken shoe, broken hand…we could be having this conversation in the ER right now."

"This is a better alternative," she said, and drained the last of her cocktail. Then she held up the glass. "Could I get another one of these things?"

"You sure you want the hangover tomorrow?"

"Ugh. You're right. A water's fine."

I caught our waiter's attention and ordered one for her and one for me, since I didn't feel much like drinking tonight. All this talk about Lucas only made me anxious to see the guy, but I wasn't leaving Sydney without getting on the same page. I owed her that.

"This explains so much, you know?" she said. "I don't know how I didn't see it when it was staring me in the face. The way you didn't want to commit... I felt like I was practically forcing you." She covered her face with her hands. "God, I almost feel relieved. I thought something was wrong with me. That it was just me you didn't want, and I was determined to find some way to make this work."

"That wasn't it at all, I swear."

"I know. I mean, you didn't seem to want anyone else either..."

"Listen to me. There is absolutely nothing wrong with you. You hear me? Nothing. You're amazing, and you deserve someone who can see that about you and love you the way you love them. Just because that's not me, doesn't mean any other guy wouldn't be jumping over himself to get to you."

"I am quite a catch, aren't I?" she said, brushing her hair off her shoulder. Then she caught a glimpse of her bare feet. "Okay, clumsiness notwithstanding."

"Hey, that makes you more endearing. Just don't make it a habit or you'll turn into one of those damsels in distress."

Chuckling, she accepted the iced water the waiter set in

front of her. "I do have a question, though, and I hope it's not offensive."

"Shoot."

"Are you...you know...*gay*?" She whispered the last word like it was a secret. "I mean, have you always known you were? What about all those women you dated? What about *me*?" A stricken look crossed her face, and I had no doubt she was thinking of all the nights we'd spent together —and there were quite a few of those. And while they'd been a good time, nothing could hold a candle to even five minutes with Lucas. It was like he'd wiped the slate clean and I could hardly remember anyone who came before him. Of course, I wasn't going to tell Sydney that, because there was no reason to be an asshole and hurt her feelings. She didn't need to know I'd been going through the motions the last few years. But she did have a point—was I gay?

"I haven't exactly figured that out yet," I admitted. "Maybe? The only person, male or female, that I've ever felt strong feelings for is Lucas, and he happens to be a guy, so..."

"That sounds pretty gay to me."

I caught her sly smile and returned it with one of my own. "I guess it does, huh?"

"Yeah. But you don't have to put a label on it yet if you don't know. I was being nosy."

"S'okay. It was a good question. One I'll have to deal with soon. But Syd?" Covering her hand with mine, I said,

"Don't think I haven't enjoyed my time with you. Please get that out of your head right now."

Sydney chewed her lip again and then nodded. "Okay."

"I mean it. You're the best woman I know, and any guy who wants you is gonna have to go through me first."

"Not a bad idea. From lover to big brother. Wait." She wrinkled her nose. "That sounds a little gross. Strike that from the record."

"Stricken. We'll say overprotective friend —how's that?"

"Much better."

She smiled to herself as she drew a heart into the condensation on her glass. "You seem different down here. More relaxed."

"I am."

"And happy?"

"Yeah. Yeah, I'm really happy down here."

"Good. That's good, Jax." She erased the designs on her glass and then wiped her hands off on her dress. "This is so not what I expected to walk into tonight."

My smile dropped. "I'm sorry—"

"Nope, no more of those. It's okay. *I'm* gonna be okay, so don't you worry about that. And you... I think you're gonna be much happier now, Jax. I want that for you."

"I want that for you too."

"What are you gonna tell your father?"

"I have no fucking idea, but it's not gonna go over well."

Sydney's gaze dropped. "So, you said you knew Lucas was the one back in high school, right?"

"Yeah, that's where we met."

"Jax, I…" She paused. "I think there's something you should know."

"Okay," I said.

"The day you came back from South Haven? Your father was at our house, and I overheard him telling my parents that some guy had become obsessed with you and that's why he had to pull you out before graduation. He was concerned for your safety."

My jaw went slack, and my heart stopped for a couple of beats. "He said he was concerned for my *safety*?"

"That's what he said. And I remember he called the guy Lucas."

"Holy shit," I said, my brain close to exploding. But of course my father would've said that. Better to have his friends think I had a delusional stalker than to let it get out that his son had developed something more than a friendship with another man. "That's not… That wasn't true. Ever."

"I can see that now, but at the time I was scared for you. That's why when I heard Lucas had shown up at your house after that, I believed what your father had said. It didn't even occur to me that you might've…returned his affections."

Hold the fucking phone. "You knew he came to Connecticut?"

A look of shame came over Sydney's face. "Well, yeah.

I saw him once on the front porch. I think we'd had a tennis lesson that day, and your father let me in and told me not to say anything. That it would scare you to know the boy had found you."

"Oh my God."

"I didn't know, Jax. I thought I was helping to protect you." Sydney's eyes pleaded with mine for understanding, but it wasn't her fault. It was becoming clear that anything that had to do with me was engineered by my father.

"I can't believe he went that far," I said, more to myself than to her. "I can't believe he was so scared of who I might really be that he turned the world upside down to make sure I stayed the obedient son." I pinched the bridge of my nose as hurt, disappointment, and anger fought for dominance. I'd been betrayed by the only blood tie I had left in this world, and for what?

"Fuck, dammit," I said, hitting the table with my fist and causing Sydney to jump.

"I'm sorry," she said. "Maybe I shouldn't have said anything——"

"No. Absolutely not. I was always too scared to tell anyone the truth, and look where it got me. I thought the worst thing that could happen was I would lose everything, and by that I meant my family, my job, the money." I let out a disgusted scoff. "Now I know that wasn't the case at all. The worst thing I could've lost was Lucas. And I did. But I'm not letting that happen again." All I knew, all I cared about now, was that Lucas was it for me, and always had been. He was my present and my future, and I'd deal with the rest of it soon enough. There was no amount of money in the world that would keep me tied to the man I called my father. In that moment, the ties that bound me to him were slashed, and I was no longer his son.

Sydney's eyes were watery. "I hate to tell you this, but knowing your father—"

"I couldn't give a fuck about him. Not anymore. This time I'll be gaining something even more important. Some*one* more important."

She hesitated. "And he's worth you, right, Jax? You promise?"

That was the only thing I knew beyond a shadow of a doubt. "I promise. He's worth everything."

"**E**XCUSE ME," CAME a syrupy-sweet male voice behind me as I stood in the middle of the Rosemont watching the revolving doors. Not that Jackson would be coming through them again anytime soon, but I couldn't bring myself to move. Had that really just happened? The woman Jackson was basically promised to had come crashing into Savannah with the grace of a wrecking ball, and he'd run along after her.

He had to, came the small voice of reason from somewhere in the far recesses of my brain. *He would've rather stayed with you, but he couldn't just leave her.* That was what the rational side of my brain said. The irrational side saw how devastated she'd been and remembered what that felt like, especially at the hands of Jackson. It was enough to send anyone into a straitjacket—or in my case, into a club full of willing cocks, and she didn't exactly look the type to relieve her sadness with a good fucking or thirty. Not that that had made me forget for long, but it at least took the edge off before the realization of what had been lost came crashing back in.

What would he tell her about us? That it was a mistake? That he hadn't meant it? Or would he tell her it was more…

"Oh honey, don't feel bad," came that voice again, and this time a blond with a lip ring came around to stand in front of me. "That happened to me once too, only he was married with two kids." He tsked. "Those straight guys. They never leave their wives. We're just their naughty little experiment before they go back to a life of monogamy and boring vanilla sex." His eyes trailed down to my hips, and he sucked the lip ring into his mouth. "But don't worry. I can make you forget aaall about ole whatshisname."

I stared at the stranger offering himself up for rebound sex. A week ago, I may have taken him up on his offer. But tonight? And sober? Fuck. That. I had to get out of there.

Ignoring him completely, I headed toward the exit, and he called after me, "If you change your mind, I'm in room seven fourteen!"

Yeah, and now all the straight married guys on vacation know, I thought, pulling my car keys out of my pocket. *Go grab yourself one of those.*

I jumped into my truck and slammed the door, but I had no idea where the fuck to go now. There was no telling how long he'd be, so it didn't make sense to stay, but did I really want to go somewhere else? Sighing, I leaned back in my seat and rubbed my face. This was not how tonight was supposed to go. I only had a handful of hours left with him, and Sydney was here to commandeer those? Like she wasn't the lucky one who got to see him every single day of her perfect existence.

Fuck. The green-eyed monster wasn't letting me off easy tonight, but I was feeling selfish, dammit, and didn't I deserve to?

Calm down, asshole. He won't be long. He'll just tell her he's crazy about you and then you'll go upstairs and he'll show you.

As I looked out at the people walking arm in arm down the street, ready for a fun night out, I felt the irrational jealousy unfurling. They were all exactly where they wanted to be, with people they—

Fuck, there Jackson was, crouching down to where Sydney was sitting—why sitting?—on the sidewalk. They were back-and-forthing it until finally Jackson swept her into his arms. Even from here I could see the look of adoration on her face as she put her arms around his neck. It made me queasy, but I couldn't stop watching, not until they disappeared into the Montview Hotel.

What the fuck? A hotel? Was he going up to her room now? Seriously? And carrying her up there, no less?

My heart battered my chest until I thought it would tear free, and as the blood pumped through my veins, rushing in my ears loud enough to drown out my common sense, I knew exactly what would happen next. I started up the truck and peeled out of the parking spot before I changed my mind.

I DIDN'T HAVE to push my way through the crowd at Argos, since my mood seemed to announce my presence to anyone within ten feet of me. Shaw stood at the bar, and it was obvious he was on the prowl by the bold look he gave to the man he was talking to, but if I wasn't getting who I wanted, no one else was either, so I inserted myself into their happy little personal space so that I was face to face with Shaw.

He was about to tell me off when I said, "Tequila shots. Five, and don't give me a hard time."

The annoyance on his face was replaced with confusion. "What's—"

"Five, Shaw."

He was quiet for a minute as he studied me, and then he apologized to the guy behind me and sent him on his way. After signaling over one of the bartenders, Shaw placed my order while I drummed my fingers on the bar and looked out at the crowd tonight. Lots of regulars, but several new faces. Decisions, decisions.

The tequila came out just the way I liked it, with no preamble of salt or lime, and I did the shots in quick succession.

"He left, didn't he."

I finished off the last of the tequila and wiped my mouth on the back of my hand. "Not exactly."

"You mean Jackson's still in town? Why the fuck are you here, then?"

"Not tonight, Shaw," I said, turning to leave, but he grabbed my arm.

"Don't do anything fucking stupid, Lucas."

"Sure, Dad."

His grip on me tightened. "I mean it. You'll hate yourself tomorrow. It's not worth it."

"Who gives a fuck about tomorrow, Shaw," I said, ripping my arm from his hold. I could feel the burn of the alcohol flaring down my chest, moving through my veins. Soon I wouldn't be able to feel, and that was just the way I wanted it. There, no one could touch me. They couldn't hurt me, couldn't leave. It was my wall of protection, the one I could retreat behind when I couldn't face things. It wasn't the healthiest coping method, but meditating or doing some stupid yoga shit wasn't gonna cut it—not tonight, not ever.

"Sorry to cut in, but…you're Lucas, right?" Lean and somewhat attractive in a quirky way, the guy looked nervously between me and Shaw, and then gave me a shy smile. "I'm—"

"I don't care," I said before the twink could give me his name. I didn't want names. I didn't want conversation.

Grabbing a fistful of his shirt, I dragged him onto the dance floor as the music changed and a grinding rhythm came over the loud speakers. Yeah. He'd do for tonight. I took him deeper into the depths of the club and I turned to face him, giving him a cocksure smile as I began to dance.

The guy's eyes were wide as he watched me, like he

couldn't believe I'd actually agreed to dance with him, but then he grinned back and stepped in closer, moving his hips and pulling me forward against him. I could feel how hard he was behind his jeans, and even through the fog of my brain, I knew this was wrong.

Come on, tequila, I thought, closing my eyes so I wouldn't have to look at someone who wasn't the man I wanted. *Don't let me down.*

"I thought you'd be home consoling your man tonight," Bash said in my ear, and my eyes flew open to see him standing beside me in a low-cut black jumpsuit, a scowl marking his pretty face.

"Nice of you to answer your phone earlier."

He ignored my jab. "What are you doing here, Lucas?"

"Dancing. Care to join?"

He shook his head as Shaw came up behind him. Great. A man couldn't just enjoy himself without those two playing the role of conscience.

"Ignore them and maybe they'll go away," I said to my dance partner in an exaggerated whisper, and then I rolled my hips against his in a way that made him groan.

"Listen," Shaw said, "it's obvious something's up. I'm the last person to tell you not to have a good time, but you're askin' for trouble, man."

"Since when is that anything new?"

Bash raised an eyebrow at Shaw. "Since last Friday, isn't that right?"

"Yeah, that's about right," Shaw replied.

I turned my back on the dirty grinder as he continued

to dance behind me. "Guys, I appreciate the gangbang approach that's happening right now, but I'd like it even more if you two would mind your own damn business."

"We're the ones your stupid ass is gonna be crying to," Shaw said, and then over my shoulder, he told the brunette, "Get lost, kid."

"Don't you go anywhere," I said, reaching back to stop him from trying.

Bash sighed and inspected his dark nails. "You know, I don't typically say this sort of thing, since it's more Shaw's brand of brashness, but you really are quite a dumb shit, Sully boy."

"You're finally getting that, are you? This is me," I said, spreading my hands wide. "This is what I do."

"It doesn't have to be. Go home to Jackson," Shaw said.

"Gee, what a great fucking idea," I said. "Oh, wait. Nope, can't do that. He's busy with his fiancée."

"His what?" they said at the same time, and the looks on their faces would've been comical under any other circumstance.

"Yeah, the woman he's supposed to marry just happened to come in town tonight and caught us on our way up to his room. Of course, he chased after her, so you'll have to excuse me if I didn't want to sit around waiting like the third fucking wheel."

Sympathy lit Shaw's eyes. "Lucas—"

"He's just gonna leave again. I've been here before. I

know how this works." I shoved Shaw back into the crowd. "Now kindly fuck off."

Bash moved in front of him and glared at me. "You're making a mistake."

"Mine to make."

"That's enough," Shaw said, taking a hold of Bash's wrist. "Just let him do what he's gonna do. We can't stop him."

"Glad you finally figured that out," I said, and then turned my back on my friends and let the music dictate my next moves.

CHAPTER 33
JACKSON

HEADING OUT INTO the street after making sure Sydney got to bed safely, I dialed Lucas's number. I hadn't meant to stay with her so late, but I needed to make sure she was okay, and I couldn't deny that I felt better after our talk. Still, I'd missed Lucas tonight.

When the call went to voicemail, I thought about going back to the hotel, but it had been hours, so there was no way he had stuck around. I should've given him my room key, but in my rush, it hadn't even crossed my mind.

I called again, and this time he picked up on the first ring, but it was so loud that I had to pull the phone away from my ear. "Lucas? Lucas, where are you? I can't hear you."

"…out… busy…" I thought I heard.

"What?"

"I said I'm out. I made other plans," he shouted over the music. "Since you were busy."

"Well, I'm done now, so can we meet up?"

There was a muffled response.

"Lucas, where are you? I'll come there."

"Don't bother. Have a good night, Jackson."

The connection went dead, and I stared at my phone in disbelief. What had gotten into him? He sounded pissed, but he was the one who'd told me to go after Sydney. Had something happened after? Where had he gone?

I had a sinking feeling of unease, and I hailed the next taxi I saw.

Shit. I knew exactly where he was.

IT FELT LIKE déjà vu to be back at Argos almost a week later, doing the exact same thing as I did last time. Looking for Lucas. One thing was for sure, though—his friend Shaw was never hard to find. The guy was huge, and with his ice-blond spikes, he stuck out of the crowd like there was a spotlight on him. I made my way over to where he was standing in front of the bar, drinking from a lowball and engaged in an animated conversation with a similarly built guy.

"Where is he?" I said, not bothering with formalities. Shaw knew exactly who I was now, even though we'd only met once, and if he'd seen Lucas tonight—and I would bet money he had—then he knew why I was there.

Shaw looked my way, ready to tell me off, but then he did a double take and froze.

"Jackson," he said, relaxing into an easy smirk. "No khakis tonight?"

"Cut the shit. I know he's here. Where?"

"Look, I don't know what happened between you two, but—"

"You can fucking show me where your buddy ran off to, or I'll have to shove that glass up your ass."

"I might like it," he said, sucking his bottom lip into his mouth and then releasing it with a pop. "But you know, I'm getting real damn tired of assholes interrupting me tonight. How about I just let you run around and find him yourself? There's a back room you might wanna check."

The thought of Lucas going into any kind of back room only made the pounding in my head worse, and I grabbed hold of the back of my neck in frustration. "Tell me. Please."

Shaw sighed, took a long gulp of the clear liquid in his glass, and set it on the bar. "If you two start a scene, I'll have to remove you. Both of you."

I moved so he could lead the way, and he grudgingly weaved through the crowd toward the back of the club, farther than I'd been the first time around.

Please don't be in a fucking back room. I didn't know what that was, but I could guess that it wasn't anything good.

Shaw came to an abrupt stop, and I almost ran right into him. "There," he said, pointing over to where Lucas was dancing way too close to some twat who had his hands on Lucas's waist.

God, this really is déjà fucking vu.

"Aaand this is where I leave you," Shaw said, bowing low like a smartass. "Try not to kill him."

With the way the guy's hands were roaming all over what was mine, it looked like Lucas wouldn't be the only one I'd have to kill. *What the fuck is he doing?* My confusion and frustration ramped up another notch as I stalked through the crowd toward the man who owed me a few answers.

"So," I said, coming up alongside him. His shirt was unbuttoned down to mid-chest, and a sheen of sweat glistened on his forehead, and even as pissed off as I was about being here, I couldn't deny the guy was stunning. The problem was, he knew it. "We're back here, huh? Back to the no-names and easy fucks?"

Lucas jerked his head toward me in surprise, but it was quickly replaced by anger. "Wow. She let you off early. For good behavior?"

"Excuse me?"

"You heard me."

"You mind explaining to me what the hell happened with you tonight? What you're doing here?"

"Not really."

"I wasn't asking, asshole."

Lucas stopped dancing and stepped toward me, standing toe to toe. "Fuck. You."

"No, fuck you, Lucas," I said, grabbing two fistfuls of

his shirt and jerking him forward. "You think this shit is easy for me? That I don't have everything on the line? I'm risking my entire life for you. I'm all in, jackass. And you're here feeding off attention from people whose names you won't even remember tomorrow."

"I don't remember their names now. Tomorrow won't make much of a difference."

I dropped my hold on him like he was on fire.

Lucas straightened his shirt and didn't look at me when he said, "You're leaving, remember? You came, you conquered nothing, and now you're leaving. You don't get to tell me how to live my life down here any more than I can tell you to give your old man the fucking finger."

I stared at him in disbelief. "You think that hasn't crossed my mind?"

"Thinking about it and doing something about it are two different things. And let's face it—you're never gonna give up your career or all that mo—"

"Don't you dare say the fucking money," I said, my voice sharp enough to cut through ice. "It's never been about the money."

Lucas cocked his head and met my gaze. "No? It's a pretty good incentive to keep your ass in line, right? After everything, I can't imagine it's your father's sparkling personality that keeps you around. Or the way he's micro-managed your life."

My fists clenched and I practically growled, scaring off a few of the eavesdroppers dancing nearby. I gave them a passing glance and uncurled my hands before shoving them into the pockets of my jeans. "Can we not do this here?"

Lucas lifted his chin toward his dance partner. "I'd rather not do this at all. If you can't tell, I'm busy."

"Is this about Sydney? Are you mad because I went to—"

"Can we not talk about your girlfriend? Jesus."

"For fuck's sake, Lucas. You're being ridiculous."

"*I'm* the one being ridiculous?"

"Yes. You act like we did something more than talk. About *you*, not that you deserve it right now, you selfish prick."

Lucas's dark eyes flashed. "Then maybe you should leave."

Maybe he was right. He hadn't stopped the guy behind him from grinding all over his ass while we'd been talking, and it was apparent he didn't plan to anytime soon. If he was trying to make a point, then he'd done a damn good job of it. But I couldn't just leave. Even fighting with him was better than not seeing him at all, even if he tried to tear my heart to pieces in the process.

"Lucas…this isn't how it's supposed to go."

He stopped. "Right. You thought you could just come back into town and I'd flip a switch and be at your beck and call for a few days. Surprise—it doesn't work like that."

"I don't want you at my beck and call. Aren't you listening to anything I have to say? I'm trying to tell you I want you—"

A heavy hand landed on my shoulder, and I looked up

—way up—at a guy in a fitted shirt with *Security* on the front. "Seen you boys making a scene. He bothering you, Lucas?"

Of course Lucas was tight with everyone in this place, and as the guard waited for an answer, Lucas narrowed his eyes at me.

"Yeah, he's a little mouthy. Nothin' I can't handle."

"Sorry, can't take that risk. He's gonna need to come with me," the guard said.

"We're just talking," I said, and when the guard looked at Lucas for confirmation, Lucas shrugged.

"Take him. I don't care." Then he looked me dead in the eye. "He's not wanted here anyway."

THE PAIN THAT had flickered on Jackson's face as I verbally slapped him and had him kicked out of the club had been almost enough to have me on my knees begging him for forgiveness. But then I remembered why I'd come out tonight, why there was no future between us, and Christ… I couldn't deal with that right now. It was easier this way. Easier if he hated me and left me alone. A few more hours or days or whatever it was he wanted to give would only make it harder when he walked away.

At least, that was what I kept telling myself even as my heart seized in my chest, threatening to stop beating entirely.

Fuck. It would've been easier, so much easier, to find a random stranger to fuck. One like this twink I was dancing with, where I didn't need his name. I didn't need conversation. All I needed was the tight fit of an ass around my cock and the high that came with it.

All of that would've been preferable to facing my feelings head-on, and that summed me up good and well right there, didn't it? That I was willing to risk the chance of a real *something* for a quick fuck to take my mind off my life for five minutes.

When had I become this man? That part was easy enough to answer. The transition into slut-who-didn't-give-more-than-a-fuck had started after losing my parents, had blasted into full gear when I'd left my heart in Connecticut on Jackson's doorstep, and had become complete with Gram's death. Like it was anyone else's fault but my own. I could blame every person who'd come and gone from my life all day long, but it didn't change the fact that I'd done it, fucked myself into this shithole, to myself. That I thought so little of my worth that I'd based my value around other's actions.

I pushed against the guy's chest as I stumbled back, feeling dazed all of a sudden. "Not tonight," I found myself saying, and he must've decided all the drama wasn't worth it, because he was gone before I had to ask again. I debated briefly whether I needed to puke my insides out in the bathroom before deciding fresh air and a slice of humble pie were the better options.

I passed Bash and Shaw as I staggered through the crowd, and they wisely didn't say a word, but I could feel their stares on my back as I headed toward the club's exit. There was no way I could drive tonight, so I'd have to grab a cab and figure out where Jackson had run off to so I could—

I pushed open the door, and sitting across the alley against the brick wall with his arms on his knees was Jackson. He looked like hell, like he'd aged ten years in the minutes since I'd seen him, worry and sadness etched in the lines of his face, and his tie haphazardly thrown over the collar of his shirt. His eyes met mine, and then drifted past me as if to see whom I'd chosen to spend the rest of the night with, but as the door slammed shut behind me, and only me, relief filled his face.

Now that I was out here, where I wanted to be, I didn't know what to say. An awkward silence filled the space between us, and Jackson got to his feet and brushed off his pants.

"I…thought you left," I finally said.

"No."

I looked down the alley to where a few small groups of people still lingered, far enough away to be out of earshot. "Out here hoping to get lucky, or—"

"Waiting for you." Jackson took a step toward me. "Just you." Another step. "Always you. Even when you're a fucking prick."

My eyes stung something fierce as he came even closer, and even harder when he reached out to cup the side of my face. I leaned into his touch and closed my eyes to keep the tears where they belonged. This, this right here, was what I'd been running from. The man comforting me now had the power to break me. How did I just drop all my defenses when he could change his mind any second? I took a deep, shuddering breath. "I don't know how to do this," I admitted.

"Me either. I don't even know where to start. But Lucas, look at me." I opened my eyes to see Jackson's filled with understanding, and he held my face with both of his hands. "I know it's stupid to keep pretending we don't matter to each other. You can tell me all day long to fuck off, to go away, but I'm not going anywhere. I know you don't mean any of those awful things you say, so stop fighting me. Please."

The shame I felt in that moment as he saw right through me was one I'd remember forever. With Jackson's hands holding me steady, forcing me to look him in the eyes, I had to face my demons, one by one, starting with my knee-jerk reactions, my viper tongue, my inability to let anyone in who had the power to hurt me... I didn't deserve Jackson's quick forgiveness or his compassion, but I needed it, just as much as I needed him.

"I'm sorry..." I said, trembling with the sincerity of my words, and clutched at his shirt, a silent begging. And then, to hell with being silent, because I needed his forgiveness more than I needed oxygen. "Jackson, I'm so sorry. You're right; I didn't mean any of those things I said. God, I'm so fucked up... Please...please forgive me. Tell me I didn't fuck this up completely before we've even had a chance. Tell me you want to try and that I can be fixed. Tell me, Jackson, please."

Jackson's thumb brushed my cheek, and I could feel his

eyes searching my face, even as I couldn't bear to look up at him. Then he lowered his forehead to mine and whispered, "I forgive you. But Lucas, you've got to stop pushing me away."

Hot tears trailed down my face as I stood there holding tightly to his waist, and Jackson's arms provided the solace I needed to let down my walls. If anyone walked by and could see me now, they wouldn't know who I was or what had gotten into me. But I knew. I'd always known.

Jackson Davenport had burrowed his way into my soul a long time ago, and damn if he hadn't ever let go.

I WOKE UP the next morning with my head throbbing something painful, but a mix of tequila and assholism could do that to a man. Turning my head on the pillow to where Jackson lay facing me, still fast asleep, though his forehead puckered like he was having a bad dream, I briefly thought about waking him. But if he was reliving the verbal assault I'd lashed out at him last night, then I was probably the last person he wanted to see.

Still, I was glad he was there. In my bed, a place no one else had woken up before him. After Jackson had driven my truck home last night, we'd showered separately, the wounds we'd inflicted on each other still tender, and I knew we'd wake up and deal with whatever happened next together, but for the night, it had been enough just to…be. I'd given Jackson a pair of boxers and a shirt to sleep in, and then turned down the sheets, and he'd climbed in my bed beside me, watching me until his lids grew heavy and sleep claimed him. I'd stayed up for a while after, taking in every moment in case I never got it again, and then finally, just as the sun peeked up over the horizon, I fell into a shallow sleep.

I threw on a pair of shorts and grabbed my toothbrush out of the bathroom to use in the one down the hall so I wouldn't wake him. After a quick brush, I slipped on a pair of flip-flops I'd left in the mud room and headed out into the yard.

Whenever I had a lot on my mind, there were two places I went—one of the private beaches or to get some advice from the person I'd always relied on to listen and tell me the truth.

Past the shop, toward the forest at the edge of the property I walked, taking in a deep lungful of the honeysuckle in the air and making a mental note to mow the grass this week. It'd shot up after all the rain, and with summer well on its way, so were the frequent showers.

Coming to a stop underneath the magnolia tree that had been Gram's favorite, I plucked a flower bloom from one of the limbs and then carefully laid it beneath the stone marker I'd erected after she passed. Then I wiped off the fallen leaves from the two-seater bench nearby, the one I'd built so I wouldn't have to sit in the dirt when I came to visit, and sat down, wondering where to begin today's conversation.

"Hey, Gram," I said. A brown thrasher flew over my head, chirping in response, and I smiled. "Care for a chat?"

CHAPTER 36
JACKSON

LUCAS'S SIDE OF the bed was empty when I woke up, but when I ran my hand over the sheets where he'd slept, they were still faintly warm. He hadn't been up long.

Rolling onto my back, I put an arm over my eyes and thought back to last night and how differently things could've turned out. I understood why Lucas had reacted like he did; I just hadn't expected Sydney to be the trigger, not after telling him how I felt—or didn't feel—about her.

The man was so scared of letting me in that he'd resorted to self-sabotage. Well, that shit wasn't gonna work with me. If I had to prove to him that this thing between us was real, then that was what I'd do.

A low vibration caught my attention, and I looked over to the nightstand to see my phone lit up with an incoming call. The time on the screen read after ten—damn, I'd slept in—but the person calling was listed under an unknown number. Many of my higher-profile clients preferred to keep their personal numbers private, so I hit accept and sat up.

"Jackson Davenport speaking."

"Good morning, Jackson. This is Sebastian Vogel."

"Sebastian," I said, raising my eyebrows. Now that was a surprise. Had he been there last night to witness the epic fight between Lucas and me? Or was this call of a business nature? I hadn't expected to hear from him again after leaving his office yesterday. "Reconsidering my offer?"

Sebastian chuckled. "I like a man who's persistent."

"So do I. Was that a yes?"

There was a bubbling sound coming through the line, like water boiling. "I've been thinking, and I'd like you to swing by my office later. You and I have a few things to discuss."

"So you *are* reconsidering the offer. A simple yes or no would've sufficed." The bubbling grew louder. "Are you in a hot tub?"

He ignored the comment and said, "This has nothing to do with your offer, and I have no intention of changing my mind about what we previously discussed."

"Then what is it you want, Sebastian?"

"To talk."

I frowned, wondering what he was up to. A sneaking suspicion told me this was a personal call. "If this is about me and Lucas—"

"I assure you, I have no interest in interfering with my

best friend's love life. Whatever happens between you two can stay between you two, though I hope you find yourselves in a better place than you were last night."

Ahh, so he *had* heard about our little row. "Then what is this?"

I could almost see the smile in his voice. "Maybe nothing. But I've got a proposition for you, if you're willing to hear me out..."

CHAPTER 37
LUCAS

I T WAS SILLY, perhaps, but talking to Gram always made me feel better, even if it was a one-sided conversation. When she was alive, she'd have made me sit at the kitchen table while she whipped up some of her famous red velvet crinkle cookies, and then she would insist that I tell her every little detail about what was going on so we could hash out the problem and fix it. She was amazing at that, and I'd felt lost without her.

Stretching my legs out, I ran my palms over my shorts. "I guess you know why I'm here." I could almost see the disapproving look on her face as she braced herself to hear about what mess I'd gotten into now.

"Yeah, I did something fuckin' stupid. As usual for me, I guess."

That mouth of yours, Lucas, she'd say. *Your mama should've washed your mouth out with soap more, you little heathen.* Then she'd tousle my hair and kiss me on top of the head, like I was eight, not eighteen. And I'd love her all the more for it.

"I know what you'd say. Nothing's permanent and can't be fixed, and I guess you're right about that." I looked down at my hands, marked with scars from my days in the shop, and ran my fingers over them. "Jackson's back, Gram," I said. "I guess this is the part where you say, 'I told you so,' because you always said he'd come back one day, and I never believed you. Because that's what I do, right? Always think the worst, 'cause it's easier than hoping and getting let down."

I chewed on my lip. "I've tried everything to get rid of him. I was mean. I pushed him away. I ignored him. I said horrible things. And the fucked-up thing is, I didn't mean any of it. So why try to hurt him, huh? I suppose it's because it's hurting me in the process too, and I feel like I deserve it."

The sun shimmered down through the trees, and I cracked the smallest of smiles. "You're biased and you'd have to tell me I deserve only happiness. But that's only because you love me and you have to see past my faults."

Scooting forward to the edge of the bench, I rested my elbows on my knees and rubbed the sleep from my face. "The truth is, I'm scared. I'm so fucking scared I'll put my heart out there and then I'll turn around and he'll be gone. That I'll have to push reset on my life, and I don't...think I can do it. Not again. Hell, you remember the last time. When I came back from Connecticut, I was a mess, so imagine that times ten. Yeah. It wouldn't be pretty. Your boy Lucas would self-destruct, and surely Jackson doesn't want that on his hands." *Way to turn it around and use a guilt trip to force things into going your way.*

My lips twitched at the edges as I imagined her lecture. "Yeah, yeah. You'd say that's just a risk I have to take, because that's what you do for people you care about. You put your whole heart out there without asking anything in return. But if you get something in return, well, that's just gravy." I chuckled. "I think you said it better. See, the problem is—and it's a problem, so don't try to tell me it's not—I...love him. Jackson. I told you that, but I never got the chance to tell him that, and Gram...I don't think I ever stopped. I mean, if you really love someone, that doesn't just go away because they decide they don't love you back, right? Or because they leave? It's not a switch you can flip off, because trust me, I've tried."

A couple of cardinals joined the one sitting on the limb watching me, and I shook my head. "Inviting my parents to join in our private conversation now?" I teased. The birds chirped at each other, back and forth, before the two newcomers flew away again.

"I understand now why you never married after Grandpa died. I get how you couldn't even look at anyone else because it couldn't begin to compare with what you had before, and then what's the point? I feel that way about Jackson. He's the only man I've met and just *known* he was supposed to be there, and everyone else falls short when I put them up against him. But I've gone through the motions for so long now that it's easier to stay closed off and be on my own. Why ask him to deal with my brand of crazy?" I snickered. "Right now, you'd be telling me I'm no good on my own, because how's the washin' gonna get done? I'll have you know I figured it out, and the only time my shirts come out pink now is if it's on purpose."

With a sigh, I said, "You'd tell me if I was making a mistake, wouldn't you? Maybe give me a sign somehow... send another tropical storm." I smiled. "That was a brilliant move right there, by the way. Thanks."

I fell silent, the question that had been at the forefront of my brain looming. "What if..." I closed my eyes. "What if I wanted him to stay? Asked him to stay here with me and give us a chance? He'd have to give up his life in Connecticut, and that seems so fucking selfish, but...I guess I am selfish. I can't imagine not having him in my life now that he's here. And I don't want to." Dropping my head into my hands, I said, "You'll have to help me out here. I don't...know how to tell him any of this. Or if I should."

"You just did," Jackson said from behind me.

My ass was off the bench and turned around in the span of a heartbeat. With his feet bare, and in the same clothes that he'd slept in, Jackson stood a few feet away.

"How much did you hear?" I asked.

"Enough."

My heart thumped erratically in my chest. This wasn't the way it was supposed to go. I wasn't ready for Jackson to know my deepest fear was that he'd push me aside like I meant nothing.

"Maybe you could turn around, go back in the house, and pretend you didn't," I said, half joking, half terrified.

"Now, why would I do that," he said, stepping forward, "when I've been waiting such a long time for you to finally open up to me?" Then he looked past me to Gram's grave. "Well, not intentionally to *me*, so it's a good thing I caught you."

"It's rude to eavesdrop."

"Don't. Care." He walked around the bench and came to a stop in front of me. "Tell me."

"Tell you…?"

"All the things you said to Gram that you were too afraid to say to me. I want you to look me in the eye when you do."

My throat closed up at the thought of having to look at Jackson while I spilled my guts. It was one thing to be honest with someone who couldn't talk back; it was quite another to have to face my fears head-on. God, when had I become someone who pussyfooted around the hard stuff? *Just fucking say it.*

"Lucas, I get being afraid to open up again," he said. "When you've been burned as many times as you have, you don't want to risk playing with fire. Trust me, I understand. But we're never gonna get anywhere if you don't talk to me."

"How are we supposed to get anywhere anyway? This thing, it's temporary. Fleeting. You'll go back to Connecticut any minute now, and I'll still be here, and we'll be worlds away. Again. So please tell me what good it'll do for you to know how I feel about you. It won't change anything."

"It changes everything." Jackson's stare penetrated right through me. "Isn't there something you need to ask me? Something you told your gram?"

"I'll tell you again: eavesdropping is rude."

"Maybe. But it's been the only way to get the truth out of you. I can't read your mind and you've sent some conflicting signals, so if you want something, then I need you to fess up, Lucas," he said, running his fingers lightly down my arm, leaving goosebumps in their wake. "Ask me."

As Jackson's hand reached mine, he threaded our fingers together, giving me the reassurance I needed. To trust. To let someone in. No, not just someone—*him.*

"Stay," I whispered. "Stay here. With me. Be with me…at least try."

"Why?"

"Because I'm a selfish bastard and I need you."

Jackson cracked a smile. "That's a good reason. Is there anything else?"

"Goddammit, Jackson, you know I'm fucking crazy over you, and the only reason I'd nut up and show my ass is because I love you. There. Okay? I love you. I loved you even in that ugly-ass school uniform, I loved you when I thought you hated me, and I still love you even though you've forced me to say it about twenty times now. Now will you stay?"

Jackson's eyes twinkled with amusement, and his smile,

that huge, brilliant white smile, lit up all for me. "Since you asked so nicely…"

"If you say no, I'll just have to force you at this point. Choose wisely."

"I love you, Lucas Sullivan. You know that?"

Those words coming from Jackson's lips made my heart swell in my chest, but along with it came the fear. I was still waiting for the "but" part of that sentence, waiting for the bomb to drop, and I squeezed my eyes shut so I wouldn't have to look him in the face when it came.

"What are you doing?" he asked.

"Please…don't say you love me if you're gonna walk away. If you mean it, then please love me enough not to say it if you're just leaving tomorrow anyway."

"Lucas. Lucas, open your eyes," he said, lifting my chin. "I do love you. And nothing could make me leave you again. Not this time."

My smile grew so big I could feel my face practically splitting in two. "In that case, I hope you know what you've gotten yourself into, Davenport. You're stuck with me now."

"Promise?"

"Promise."

"But Lucas." Jackson's face grew serious. "What happened last night? Don't ever do that again."

"Which part?"

"All of it. Running off, not talking to me, getting irrationally angry, letting some fuckhead touch you—"

"Okay, okay, I got it."

"You sure? I could go on."

"No need. I already know what a jerk I am."

"Maybe, but you're my jerk."

"I think I can live with that."

There was a loud squawk from up in the tree, and I pulled away from Jackson, laughing. "Gram approves."

"Does she?" Jackson looked over to the burial stone. "I should go say hi. And, you know"—he winked at me—"ask for permission to date her grandson."

AFTER CALLING OFF work and cashing in some long-overdue vacation time, the next few days passed in a blur of legs tangled in sheets, in the shower, claiming every part of Lucas's house…

It was fucking bliss.

That was not to say I wasn't more than aware that I'd have to face dealing with a few of my responsibilities—namely, my father, my job, and relocating—but for now, I needed Lucas to know I wasn't going anywhere. We needed this time to reconnect, and it also gave me the chance to scope out a few apartments on the island until I was ready for something more permanent. Of course, Lucas brooded any time I brought up the subject.

"I don't see why you won't just move in," he said the following week, as we lounged on his bed before having to get up and get ready for the day. As I circled a few listings the realtor had sent my way, Lucas stared disapprovingly from where he was leaned against the padded headboard.

"Lucas, we've been over this."

"Just think how inconvenient it'll be if you're not here. We'll have to trade off where to sleep every night. Go buy two sets of everything to keep at your place and mine."

"As inconvenient as, say, Connecticut?" That shut him right up, and I smirked. "Didn't think so."

He uncrossed his arms and scooted up next to me, putting his chin on my shoulder. "You're not gonna decide you like sleeping better alone, right? I'd hate to have to tie you to my bed so you can't leave."

"You'd hate it, huh?" I said, grinning, and then I gave him a quick kiss, which only made him groan when I pulled away.

"You can't just kiss me and mention getting tied up when I know you're naked under these sheets…" His hand roamed up my thigh, and my cock jumped to attention at his touch. "See, I think you want me to interrupt. You don't *really* want to look at those boring apartments."

"You're trouble," I said, my head rolling back as Lucas gave my dick a couple of slow strokes, bringing me from semi-interested to fuck-I'm-never-leaving-this-bed.

"I'm an insatiable bastard, what can I say?"

"And this is exactly why I need my own place. We'd never get any work done otherwise."

"I disagree. I think *Jackson: professional bed warmer and sex slave* is a perfectly respectable job."

Laughing, I got to my knees and pinned him to the

mattress with one hand while the other followed the curves and patterns of the dragon tattoo that curved over his shoulder and onto his chest. "I wouldn't brag too much about that or someone might offer me a better rate," I teased, lowering down to capture his mouth.

Lucas wrapped his legs around my waist, and just like that, the listings were forgotten and everything went on pause, like it did whenever we came together like this. I rocked my hips over his, joining our cocks together in a delicious slide, and as I took his mouth with mine again, my cell went off.

"Ugh. Don't answer it," Lucas said against my mouth, and I gave him one last lingering kiss.

"Can't." I moved up to my knees and rolled off him before he could convince me otherwise. "You know I'm expecting a call."

"Ah, yes, the 'surprise.' And just when do you think you'll let me in on whatever it is you have planned?"

"When the paperwork's dry." I winked and hit accept on my cell without looking at the caller ID. "This is Jackson."

"Jax, I'm so glad you answered," Sydney said, sounding relieved.

"Oh, hey, Syd," I said, and Lucas shook his head as if to say, *If it's not the surprise, hang up and get underneath me.* "I meant to touch base with you to thank you for covering things while I took some time off. I—"

Lucas bit into the cheek of my ass, and I sucked in a breath and nearly dropped the phone.

"Dammit, Lucas," I whispered, as he muffled his laughter into a pillow, and I tried not to smile and encourage him. Putting the phone back up to my ear, I said, "Sorry about that. How are you? Everything going okay up there?"

"Actually, that's what I was calling about. Your father's..." She kept talking, but I couldn't make out what she said because Lucas slid his hand up my thigh, and I slapped him away before holding up my finger to shush him.

"I'm sorry, Syd, could you repeat that? We must have a bad connection."

Lucas grinned and propped himself up on his elbow as he lay across the bed, fully on display. *Fucking tease.*

When she repeated the words, I thought my brain was making shit up. "It sounded like you said my father's on the way to South Haven," I told her.

"Uh, Jax? I did say that."

In that instant, my smile dropped, and Lucas noticed the change in mood and had to know what I'd just said was happening, because he sat up with a wary look on his face.

"When?" I asked.

"He should arrive within the hour, if he hasn't already. His secretary said he was heading straight to AnaVoge."

I held the phone away from my face as I cursed so loudly it echoed off the walls. Then, to Lucas, I said, "Get Sebastian on the phone. Now."

My father coming to South Haven meant two things: first, he was coming to nail down what I hadn't, and second, the fact that he hadn't alerted me to his arrival meant he was hoping to catch me off guard.

CHAPTER 39

LUCAS

J UST LIKE THE darkening sky indicated, a storm was brewing, and it seemed like it was doing so directly over AnaVoge as Jackson and I made our way up to the main doors a half-hour later. We hadn't spoken much since he'd gotten the heads-up from Sydney about his father's arrival, quickly getting ready and rushing out the door in an attempt to get there before the senior Davenport did.

Today, Jackson looked every bit the headstrong businessman in his tailored blue suit and silver tie, and if we'd been under any other circumstances, I would've taken a moment to enjoy the view from the front *and* from behind.

Jackson's jaw was set as he opened the door for me, and he radiated a mix of calm and nervous energy, as well as something else I couldn't put my finger on...anticipation, almost?

When we stepped inside the lobby, he grabbed my hand again, and the way he laced our fingers and pulled me close to his side as we walked over to where Astrid was already waiting for us by her desk screamed of possession. He moved with purpose, and I couldn't help but notice that everything about Jackson was making it abundantly clear that he was not fucking around today.

And damn. I was *not* complaining.

As we greeted Astrid, she quickly opened the door.

"Mr. Davenport Sr. got here about five minutes ago," she said, keeping her voice low as she led us through the back office area. "He didn't even ask to be seen; he just went on through."

Wow, what an aggressive dick. Not that I didn't already know that much from my own experience with him, but for him to show up unannounced and expect to be seen? That was ballsy.

Through the glass walls of Bash's office, it was easy to see them both now: Bash sat casually behind his desk, and I could see the profile of a man the spitting image of Jackson but with lighter, greyer hair in the chair opposite. As we approached the office, I tugged on Jackson's arm, and he stopped to look at me.

"You go. I'll wait out here," I said.

"I'm not going in there without you."

"But—"

"No."

I knew better than to argue. If he wanted me in there,

then that was where I'd be. I glanced back at Bash's office. Freakin' nowhere to hide. *Great.*

"Fine," I said. "But you go in first. I'll be behind you, but don't let me distract from what needs to happen in there."

Jackson considered it for a moment and then nodded. His shoulders lifted as he took in a deep breath. I couldn't even imagine what was about to happen when he came face to face with his father after everything we'd learned since he'd been here. If I wanted to punch the guy and dig him an early grave, there was no telling what Jackson would do.

"You got this," I said, squeezing his hand briefly before letting go. Jackson's mouth turned up at the edges at my encouragement, and then he opened the office door and walked inside.

"Jackson," Bash said, standing up and greeting him with a smile and a handshake as I hovered near the door, trying to remain unseen. Bash's eyes briefly flickered to mine, and when I shook my head, he got the picture and looked back between the men standing at an awkward angle to each other.

"Well, would you look what the cat dragged in," Davenport Sr. said, as he plastered the fakest smile I'd ever seen in my life on his face. He stood tall in a black suit, though Jackson had him by an inch or so, and he was still in great shape. I'd even call him attractive if I didn't know what a complete fuckhole he was. "I was under the impression you were on vacation."

"Sir." Jackson gave a curt nod to his father, but didn't say anything else.

Davenport Sr. appeared baffled. "Is that any way to greet your father after the disappearing stunt you pulled this week? Avoiding my calls. Leaving messages with my secretary. Gotta say, I'm not sure what to think, Jax."

"I'm sure Sebastian doesn't want to hear about any family disagreements," Jackson said calmly.

"I wasn't aware we were having a disagreement, but by all means." His father gestured toward the seat beside him as he sat back down. "Let's get on with it, shall we?"

Bash looked between the two men and smiled. "Well, well, well. Two Davenports in my office. Jackson, your father was just telling me he'd like to renegotiate."

"Yes, well, I understand the meeting with my son did not go advantageously, so I'd like the chance to make things right. Open up the lines of communication and see if we can come to an agreement."

"Then I suppose I should take another look," Bash said.

"I thought you might like to," Davenport Sr. said, throwing a smug look in Jackson's direction as he handed Sebastian a folder. "As you can see, I'm willing to offer you considerably more than the original proposal. I'm confident that you'll see how enthusiastic we are about your company and what we can offer you."

Bash, never easily surprised, lifted his eyebrows and stared down at the figure in the packet, and he didn't move again for a good two minutes. Then he closed the folder, and when he looked up again, his face was unreadable.

"Mr. Davenport, like I told Jackson last week, my company's not on the market."

The self-satisfied smile dropped from Davenport Sr.'s face.

"I appreciate that you say you value my company and are willing to part with such a sizable amount, but I'm afraid there's no amount of money to make me sell. And I'm sure Jackson told you a couple of the reasons why."

"Ah yes." His father sniffed and lifted his chin. "Close, personal relationships and well-being of your staff, is that right?" He leaned forward. "You do know I have close, personal relationships with many of the investors you seek."

"Meaning?"

"I'd hate to see such a promising young company flounder under its growing pains."

Sebastian's face remained a mask of impassivity. "Is that a threat, *sir?*"

Davenport Sr. tugged at his sleeves, making sure the diamond cufflinks he wore caught the light. "Of course not. I'd just highly suggest considering what would be in your best interest moving forward."

Oh hell. That wasn't a thinly veiled threat, and even Jackson side-eyed his father in shock.

Bash, to his credit, didn't blink. "I see. And I'd like to take this moment to discuss the reasons why I don't think we're a good fit."

"Excuse me?"

Bash held up his hand. "First, I don't appreciate you marching in here without permission or an appointment. You disregarded my staff and disrespected my time by assuming I would drop everything for you. I find it rude. Second, I'm appalled that you would come here after I turned down Jackson's offer. That tells me you don't trust him to do his job. And if you don't trust him to do his job on behalf of Davenport Worldwide, then I also question why you didn't come down here in the first place if my company was so 'important' to you."

Davenport Sr. sat in stunned silence, but Bash wasn't finished.

"And third, that offer is an exorbitant sum of money that would be better served handling your own company affairs or donating it to charity instead of using it to flex your muscles at me."

Holy shit. Bash was a fucking badass.

While Davenport Sr. looked ready to blow, an easy smile crossed Bash's lips, and then his attention turned to Jackson. "Was there anything you wanted to add to that?"

Jackson nodded at Bash and said, "I think now's as good a time as any."

Sebastian stood and opened a side drawer, and after pulling out a folder, he tapped it against his hand and said to Jackson, his brow arched, "Should I do the honors, or…?"

"Let me," Jackson said, smiling as he took the folder from Bash. "You see, I've had some time to think about things, and—" He stopped and looked over at where I was still standing by the door. "Actually, come on in, Lucas— this pertains to you, too."

His father whipped his head around to look in my direction, and when recognition lit his features, he growled. "What the fuck is that pervert doing here?"

"Hello, Mr. Davenport," I said, strolling forward. "I'd say it's good to see you again, but it was a nightmare the first time around. Now's not any better."

"You have no business being here—"

"Actually," Bash spoke up, "seeing as Mr. Sullivan, the pervert, here was one of AnaVoge's first investors and owns a stake in the company, I'd say he's more than welcome to be here for discussions pertaining to any business decisions we make. I'd also say he has a somewhat...*private* interest as well."

"Yeah, I'm sure he does. I know all about his private interests. He tried to corrupt my son in school, and now he's got his hooks in you." Davenport Sr. shook his head in disgust.

"You've got that part all wrong," Jackson said, coming to stand beside me. As he reached for my hand, a small smile played on his lips. "I was the one who corrupted him. And he's mine, not Bash's. Not anyone else's."

Jackson's father reared back like he'd been slapped, and as he looked between the two of us, his lip curled. "What is this?"

"I've been offered a job here at AnaVoge and I've accepted. Consider this my notice," Jackson said, and then he squeezed my hand and looked at me, a question in his eyes. *Is this okay?*

Was this okay? He had to be fucking kidding if he thought I'd be anything other than ecstatic about something that would anchor him here. Besides me, of course.

"But Sebastian's offer isn't the only thing keeping me in South Haven," Jackson continued, and the way his hand had a death grip on mine told me the *oh shit* moment was about to hit. "I found out a few things while I was here. Important things. Life-altering things. And do you know what they all had in common? You. Your interference."

Jackson took a step toward his father, but didn't let go of my hand. "You had me followed. Watched. You pulled me away from the only man I ever loved—this man," he said, looking back at me. "And it's only now, years later, that I realize what you did. How could you? How could you mess with my life, take away all my decisions? I was so fucking blind, because it's the same thing you do to these companies—you force them into submission, into doing things your way, and then you break them apart. And for what? Money and an ego trip? To be in control? Please tell me what I ever did that was so wrong you couldn't love me the way I was."

"The way you were?" he sneered. "You mean the way you *are?*"

If that reaction surprised Jackson, he didn't let on. "I trusted you, and you lied to me. About everything. I don't even know who you are."

"That makes two of us," Davenport Sr. snarled. "You think I wanted a fucking faggot for a son?"

The room went dead quiet, and I wasn't sure who would be the one to hit him first. Bash, ever the voice of reason, made the first move, coming out from around his desk.

"I think it's time for you to leave," Bash said.

Davenport Sr. went to respond, but the red heels Bash wore must've caught his eye, because he looked down at them and then back up at Bash, with a baffled expression on his face. "What the... What kind of place are you running here? Queers 'R' Us?"

Bash's patience was wearing thin, but he still had more than I did, because he managed a tight smile. "The *place I'm running*, as you so eloquently put it, is a multimillion-dollar business that's the envy of every startup in the country, and it's one you've been salivating over. But my company, *sir*, will remain just that—mine. And there's no amount of money or threats that would make me sell it to a man like you. Now get the hell out."

Jackson's father stared Bash down, but then must've decided it wasn't worth it to stay, and turned back to Jackson. "You can't possibly be serious about this. I'll give you one last chance. Come back with me now, and I'll forget this ever happened."

"Sorry, Mr. Davenport," Jackson said. "I got a better offer."

A flush creeped up Davenport Sr.'s neck. "You're making a mistake."

"You're wrong," Jackson said. "For the first time in my life, I know I'm on the right path. And it's not yours. It's no one else's but mine, and you know what? It feels damn good."

"Jax. You're all I have left. For God's sake, think about that. Think about the family name. If you choose to be with this...*man*, then how can you possibly carry that on? It's selfish."

"Selfish?" Jackson shook his head sadly. "I can't believe you just said that to me. Is that all you care about? Is that all I am to you? A *name*?"

"A good name's the only thing a man has. I've told you that."

Jackson gripped my hand to the point of pain, but I held him back just as tightly, giving him the support he needed.

"You know, I used to look up to you. I thought because you dressed nice and made a lot of money at your job that it meant you were successful, that you were a good person who deserved it. But all you do is climb on top of the crushed bones of everyone you've beaten down to get to where you are. One day you're gonna look around you and see there's no one there, and that's because you're nothing but a miserable, scheming bastard. And if I didn't hate you so much, I'd feel sorry for you."

At Jackson's words, Davenport Sr.'s face had turned an angry red, and his chest heaved like he was going to tackle Jackson any second, but then he uncurled his fist from his side and pointed a finger right in his son's face. "You're not getting another goddamn penny from me."

"I don't want one."

"I mean it. You don't come back. You're not welcome. You're nothing to me. Nothing."

Jackson's jaw clenched. "I was never anything to you anyway but a disappointment. Consider this my parting gift."

As two huge security officers entered the room, Bash said, "If you'll please escort Mr. Davenport—Senior— from the building—"

"That won't be fucking necessary," Davenport Sr. spat, but they grabbed hold of his arms as he struggled to get free. "Get off me. I said I'm leaving."

Bash nodded at the guards to let go, and Davenport Sr. straightened his jacket. Then, like the bastard he was, he kicked his chin up and didn't look Jackson's way, much less mine, as he made his way out of the room and toward the lobby, the guards trailing him the whole way.

The anger and tension that had been in the room evaporated, and as Jackson's shoulders visibly sagged with relief, I wrapped my arms around him, vowing I'd never let go.

"I'm so proud of you," I said against his neck so only he could hear me. "I would've killed him."

"I almost did. If it hadn't been for you holding my hand..." Then Jackson lifted his head, and I was relieved to find only steely determination there instead of any sadness over what had just happened. He leaned in, and the rough kiss he planted on my lips promised many more of those to come.

"Well, I don't know about you two," Bash said, strutting over to the window to look outside, his cheeky self reemerging. "But I'm a little disappointed. I always thought *I* was the tightest ass of the bunch."

We laughed and rolled our eyes, and then we watched as Davenport Sr. exited the building—and Jackson's life.

CHAPTER 40

THREE MONTHS LATER

Lucas

THREE MONTHS, SEVEN days, and twelve hours, to be exact, and every damn day I had to pinch myself that Jackson and I had been lucky enough to get a second chance, something I'd never expected in a million fucking years, but was grateful for, even if I hadn't yet stopped reaching out in the mornings to make sure Jackson was still there. I knew this time he wasn't going anywhere, but old fears died hard.

Tonight, after much pressure from Shaw and Bash, I'd invited over a few dozen friends to knock out two birds with one stone—celebrating Jackson's twenty-seventh birthday and introducing him at our official housewarming party.

Yep, I'd suckered Jackson into moving in with me a

couple of months after he'd relocated to South Haven, but, admittedly, that was because another tropical storm came through and flooded his apartment.

Thanks, Gram.

"Quick, hide—I think there's about to be a toast," Jackson said, coming up behind me. His hand went to the small of my back to push me toward the stairs, but he was a little too late, because Bash had discovered the microphone, and he pointed us out before calling everyone to attention.

"All right, all right," Bash said, standing up on one of the two chairs Shaw had commandeered. As he snapped his fingers at the ones still talking in the corner, his tank rose up to expose a thin strip of his taut stomach. "Hush, you hookers, we'd like to make a toast."

As the room fell silent, I glanced at Jackson, and he had a *told you so* expression.

"On behalf of Lucas and Jackson, we'd like to apologize to you all. I'm so sorry, fellas, but our longtime resident sex god is officially off the market." As groans mixed with a few cheers, Bash put his hand over his heart. "I know. It's almost a shame. But not to worry—Shaw and I will more than happily make up for any sadness or sexual frustration you may be feeling."

Raucous whoops broke out as Bash and Shaw both lifted their drinks, and I wrapped my arm around Jackson's waist, pulling him close. "You hear that? All mine," I whispered, and he turned his head to kiss me.

Then Shaw took the mic, and someone in the crowd

whistled. "And on a serious note, because you know there has to be one and we should really get that shit outta the way before we all get naked and do body shots, we'd like to say happy birthday to the guy who's made our friend less of a dick than usual. Jackson, we didn't think it was possible, but we've seen Lucas smile more in the last few months since you've been here than we have since we met the guy. Granted, it makes him look a little deranged when he's not scowling, but whatevs, you're the one who has to wake up to him."

"Fuck your face," I shouted, lifting a finger to go with my well wishes.

Shaw blew a kiss back and continued. "We know you guys have been to hell and back, so the fact that you're here, together, and you choose each other…well, I guess that's pretty fucking beautiful. What do you say, Bash?"

Bash leaned in toward the microphone. "I say make sure to use a condom. We know Jackson's pretty, but we don't need any mini Sullies crashing our orgies."

"And on that note…" Shaw held up his drink. "Congratulations, you two. We love you." As a chorus of *awws* swept through the crowd, Shaw added, "And those down for body shots, you can meet me in the kitchen." Then he hopped off the chair as a group of eager participants followed him toward the back, and they all stopped on the way to say congrats and clink their glasses with ours.

"Okay, so that could've been worse," I said.

"How so?"

"There could've been sing—" As soon as the word was

out of my mouth, someone turned the music up, and—
God help us all—Bash began to sing. Badly.

"Shots?" I said, raising a brow at Jackson.

"Shots," he agreed.

Jackson

"I SUPPOSE YOUR friends aren't half bad. Most of
them," I teased Lucas a couple of hours later when I
finally escaped from one of the guys who had wanted to
tell me every hilarious story about his Chihuahua. I'd
finally had to tell him I hated dogs just to get away. He was
probably running home to call PETA now.

"I was wondering where you'd run off to. A party for
us and I haven't even seen you. I'm not fucking okay with
that," he said, drawing me to him.

There was a crash, and then Bash's voice rang out from
across the room. "Oh, I'm so terribly clumsy. Please forgive
me for falling into your"—Bash ran his hands up and
down the guy's bicep—"thick, muscular arms."

"Oh for fuck's sake," Lucas muttered, as Bash gave the
guy one last pat-down and then sauntered over to us.
"Think you can go one night without molesting our
guests?"

With his hand on one hip and reaching for a glass of
champagne on one of the platters in the corner with the
other, Bash feigned shock. "Are you implying that I fell into
that gorgeous specimen's big, brawny arms on purpose?"

"It does seem like a rather *Bash* thing to do."

"Well, la di da, all in the company of friends. Frankly, I'm surprised everyone is still clothed. Well, except for Shaw's myriad of conquests." As he took a dainty sip of his champagne, he stumbled a bit, and I grabbed his elbow to hold him steady.

"You okay tonight?" I chuckled as Bash righted himself.

"Oh dear. I suppose eating a cube of cheese today *does* have me a little lightheaded, but how else was I supposed to fit into these pants?" he replied, skimming his hand over the tight leather that looked like it'd been painted on his slim frame.

"Bash—kitchen. Food. Now," Lucas said.

"Mmm, he's so bossy," Bash said, and then leaned over to stage-whisper to me, "I hope he's that way in bed too."

"Go eat, fucker," Lucas said, rolling his eyes and steering me away. "Why did we agree to have a party here again?"

"Because you wanted to introduce me to all of your friends and show off all the hard work we've done on the house." As much as we'd loved nostalgia and the way Gram had things set up when she'd been alive, it had been time to overhaul the inside with paint and furniture Lucas and I could agree on. The result was a cozy mix of soft brown leather and shades of blue that he claimed matched my eyes—both of them.

Cheesy, lovesick bastard.

"This is where you should've told me no. We could be

in bed right now." As Lucas pressed his lips beneath my ear, I playfully pushed him away.

"But I'm not even tired."

"I wasn't talking about sleeping," he said, coming back to lightly nip at my earlobe. "Come on. No one'll miss us if we head upstairs."

"And miss your own party?"

"For once, I'm not in the mood."

Those words from Lucas Sullivan's mouth would've caused anyone to do a double take, so my reaction couldn't be helped. "What's this? South Haven's former sex god is bored two hours in? Is he turning over a new leaf? Say it ain't so."

"Not *completely...*" Lucas slipped his hands into the back of my pants to grab my ass and use it as leverage while he rubbed himself against me.

God, those hands of his. There was something to be said for dating someone who worked with their hands for a living, because fuckin' hell. He could incite my cock to action without a touch, sure, but with those magic hands? He could bring shit to a full throttle in two seconds flat.

Then there were his lips...those full, bitable lips were equally as tempting, especially when they were trailing down my neck, and I grabbed a handful of Lucas's hair and pulled his head back so I could suck his bottom one into my mouth.

"Mmm," he said. "See? This is why we should—"

There was a crash from the kitchen, and Lucas sighed. "Stay here. Don't move."

I laughed at his put-out tone as he went to check on whatever shenanigans had caused the breakage, and as I watched him disappear around the corner, it amazed me yet again that this was my life now.

The past three months had flown by so fast: starting a prominent position at AnaVoge, moving three times, renovating our place...it had been a whirlwind, the best time of my life, even when combined with the bad. I hadn't spoken to my father since that day in Bash's office, and there was no doubt in my mind that the ties between us had been completely severed. Part of me thought I should feel sad about that, because he was, after all, still my father, but I felt nothing but repulsed by even his name. Disowning my father had completely changed the direction of my life, and if I had to do it all over again, I wouldn't think twice.

Sydney still called on occasion. After hearing what had happened with my father, she'd left Davenport Worldwide not long after me, and she was currently taking some time off to travel. In my attempt to help her bring her dream of being a mom to fruition, and to resolve some of the guilt I still carried from leading her on for so long, I'd had Bash get in touch about solo destinations for singles, and from what he said, she'd made plans to meet up with several of his acquaintances while overseas also.

That just left...Lucas. My Lucas.

As he stalked back toward me, the expression on his face changed from one of annoyance to one of pure love, with a healthy dose of lust for good measure.

"I shot them all with NyQuil darts. We should be alone soon," he said. "Now, where were we?"

I hooked a finger under the corded necklace he wore, the one he'd made an exact replica of recently and given it to me when I'd moved the last of my things into his house —now *our* house. "What am I gonna do with you, Lucas Sullivan?"

His brown eyes sparkled. "I can think of a few things."

"Does one of them involve that candle you just bought that turns into massage oil?"

"God, it's like you know me so well. Yes. Yes, it does."

"You get the lighter; I'll get Shaw to distract everyone so they don't know we're missing."

Lucas jerked me forward and kissed me until we were both breathless. "Fuck," he said, holding my face between his hands. "Have I mentioned I love you?"

I grinned. "Not in the last hour. You're slacking."

Lucas brought his lips to mine again, and this time, the urgency gave way to passion, the kiss that always told me just how much he loved me.

"Lucas?" I said against his mouth. "I don't think the darts are working."

"Shit. Think we can make a run for it?"

"That depends."

"On what?"

I gave him a smile full of mischief as I fondled the button of my shorts to distract him and said, "How fast you catch me."

"I caught you the first time we met, Davenport. Have you already forgotten?"

"No," I said, and unzipped my pants. "But I had no idea what I was getting into back then."

"Oh yeah? And now you do?"

I took the one step I needed to close the gap between us and kissed his lips, and God, he tasted like everything I wanted, everything I needed. "Yeah. And it's something a little bit like love."

THANK YOU

Thank you for reading **A Little Bit Like Love**! I hope you enjoyed Jackson & Lucas as much as I do.

Want more of the South Haven men?

A LITTLE BIT LIKE DESIRE
Book Two in the South Haven Series
Shaw's Story

Coming Fall 2017

If you enjoyed A Little Bit Like Love, please consider leaving a review on the site you purchased the book from. Jackson & Lucas will send kisses your way!

Want more from Brooke Blaine? Check out her books at www.BrookeBlaine.com.

ACKNOWLEDGMENTS

To my other (deviant) half, Ella Frank: You keep me on task when it's difficult, you hold my hand when it's impossible, and you're my biggest cheerleader when it's sunshine and rainbows. There are not enough thank you's in the world, and I wouldn't even know where to start. I adore you, my FLF, and there's no one else I'd rather be on this insane (seriously—are we crazy?) journey with.

Brellas! Thank you for making our Naughty Umbrella group such a happy place for both me and Ella, and I hope for all of you too. You share your lives with us and we truly think of you as our little book family. Love all of your (hooker) faces, and I can't wait to see many of you on the road! Oh…and you know I grab many of my character names from you guys, so thanks for letting me steal your first or last names. I hope that when you see it, it makes you smile. (Most of my Faaabulous Hooker Team is a Brella, but just figured I'd shout you guys out too. Thank you for being my "firsts" for every book. MUAH!)

Hang Le - This cover is beyond anything I could've imagined. THANK YOU. You know how much your favorite emailer loves you. Your talent is beyond.

Eric Battershell - To say we sat on this one for a while is an understatement, but it was worth it. Thank you for the unbelievably gorgeous photo you took that helped to inspire this novel. What a killer first collab for us—and many more to come!

David Wills - I had an idea of what I wanted for the cover of this book, but when I saw your photo, it wiped everything away. It may be the most perfect photo that ever existed, and I'm so grateful to have it on my cover. Thank you.

Jenn Watson, Sarah Ferguson, & the asskickers of Social Butterfly PR - you ladies are at the top of your game, and

I'm thrilled to be able to work with you and call you friends. I appreciate all you do for me, and I can't wait to see you soon for some big ole bear hugs!

Shannon/Shanoff Formats - Woman! You are a rock star for these beautiful teasers. Thank you for doing those in, oh, two seconds. I swear I won't send them to you so late next time. Err...maybe. Don't hold me to that.

For making my bookie book the prettiest it can be, so many thanks to my 'eyes,' my editor, Arran McNicol, & my proofreader, Judy Zweifel of Judy's Proofreading. Unless my novels go through you guys, it won't see the light of day. And since that can't happen, I suppose you're both stuck with me. Muahaha.

I'd like to thank (or spank) Devon McCormack, but please don't tell him this is in here or his ego will expand to ludicrous proportions. Seriously, though, for reasons he knows, this book may not have ever been completed (this year, anyway) without his brand of crazy to help. Now go back to your corner.

The authors of the M/M Daily Grind - you welcomed me

(and loserface) with open arms, and I think the world of you all. Thank you so much for allowing me to be a part of your fabulous group.

If you're reading this, I want to thank YOU, amazing reader/blogger, for taking the time to read A Little Bit Like Love. I truly appreciate you choosing my book out of the thousands you could spend your time enjoying. I do not take that for granted, and I'm grateful to have you join me on Jackson & Lucas's journey. I hope it was time well spent. For your enthusiasm, patience, and support, I thank you from the bottom of my heart. And, of course, I'm virtually tackle hugging every one of you.

The initial concept of this book was born out of heartbreak, as many novels are, and though it's taken quite a few turns to get it exactly where it needed to be and no longer resembles much of the original, I'd be remiss if I didn't thank SM for not choosing me.

I hope you'll stick around, because there's so much more to come! Shaw's story is just itching to be told, so I think I should get back to it...

Until next time,

<3 Brooke

ABOUT THE AUTHOR

About Brooke

Brooke Blaine is a *USA Today* Bestselling Author of contemporary romance that ranges from comedy to suspense to erotic. The latter has scarred her conservative Southern family for life, bless their hearts.

If you'd like to get in touch with her, she's easy to find - just keep an ear out for the Rick Astley ringtone that's dominated her cell phone for years. Or you can reach her at www.BrookeBlaine.com.

CPSIA information can be obtained
at www.ICGtesting.com
Printed in the USA
LVOW12s1304070917
547887LV00001B/46/P

9 781973 836230